EMBERS

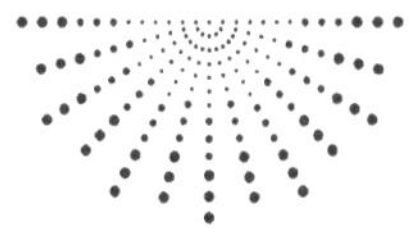

A.H. CUNNINGHAM

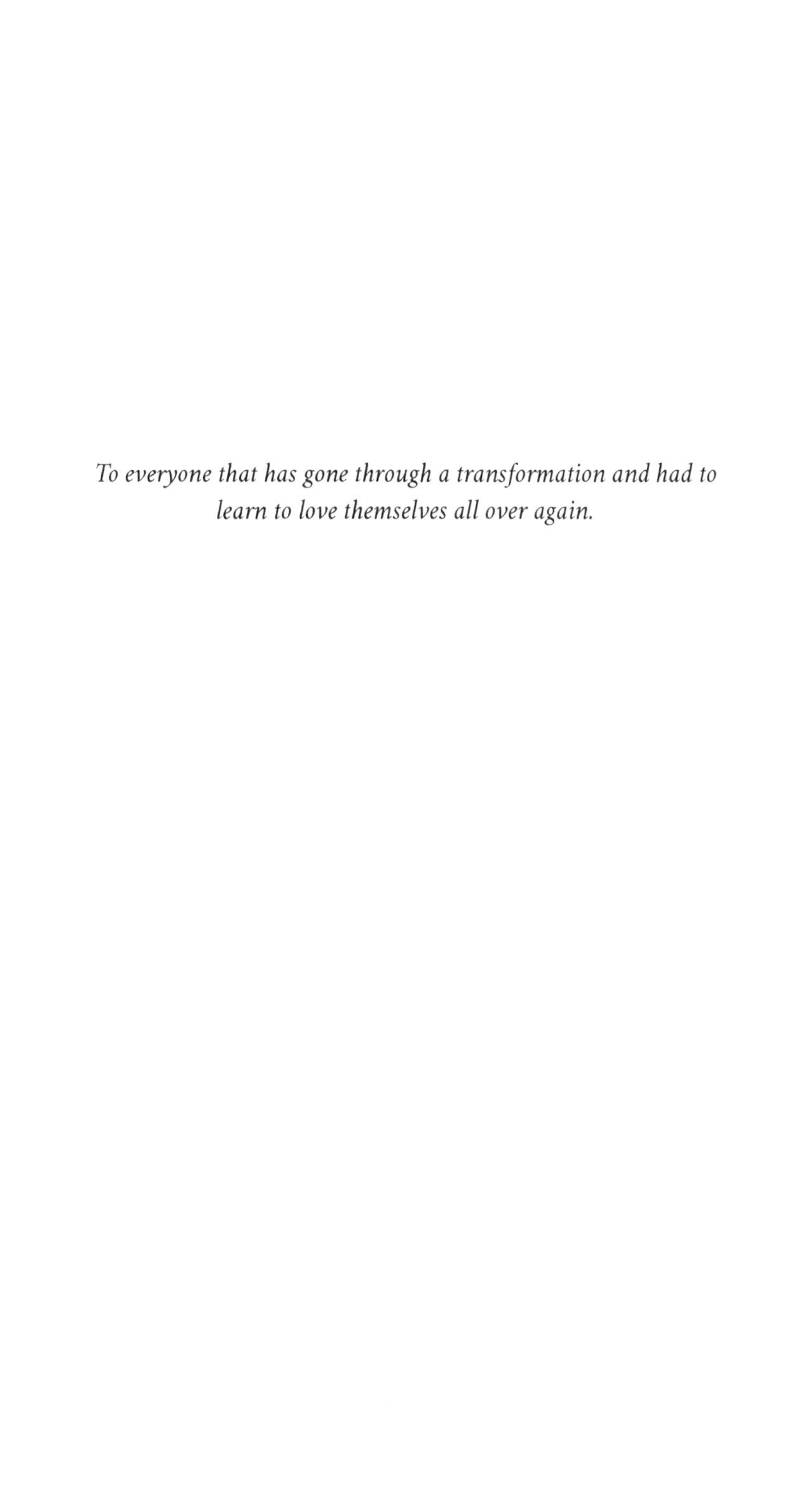

To everyone that has gone through a transformation and had to learn to love themselves all over again.

CONTENT WARNING

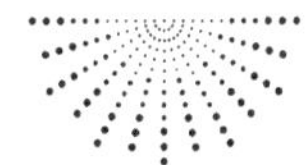

- Difficult parental relationship
- Recount of emergency preeclampsia birth/no details.
- Postpartum depression/ potential body dysmorphia
- Mention of breastfeeding/over production.
- Power dynamic/Daddy Kink

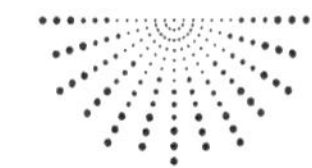

CHAPTER ONE

"Right…there—oh, oh, oh!"

That was the last coherent phrase to leave Aayala Campbell's mouth because she'd just been awarded the best dick she'd ever had in her thirty-seven years on this earth. Aayala had enjoyed some good dick in her formative years, but nothing like this. Nothing that made her levitate with only a few strokes.

The whole day and night, they circled each other, pretending around their friends, denying the energy they were creating as their hips whined together to soca. This new dynamic wasn't the normal flow of their friendship.

What was it about this night that had changed things?

By the time they reached her car in the darkened parking lot, they were wrestling each other with tongues and caresses. He couldn't get enough of her, and Aayala wanted to climb his tall frame and get acquainted with his unleashed power. When he spun her around and ripped a hole in her tights around her ass and pussy, she whimpered in surrender.

Whatever he wanted, he could take. Tonight, she was all his.

"Are you ok? Does this feel good?" He thrust inside her wet sex with a move that made her eyes cross and had her holding onto the car for dear life.

Does this feel good?

Didn't he know how good he was? Maybe his other partners hadn't told him. That little swirl he did at the end of each thrust was going to ruin her. His hand snaked over her torso toward her breast, and he managed to reach her nub around the costume cups. He squeezed her nipple, her legs shook in response, and everything inside tightened.

"Oh, yes… it's goo—!" Aayala threw her ass back at him, lest he thought she couldn't keep up with him. She gripped him tight, squeezing him, and felt vindicated when he grunted, his body faltering on top of hers. She held the bottom of her costume to the side so that he could have easy access. They were so far gone someone could walk over to her car, and they would have kept going. They were acting like eighteen-year-olds who had to bust a nut before going home.

The rushed, illicit feel to the night added to the eroticism of the moment, and she wondered what that said of the two of them.

"Do that again! Squeeze my dick like that again," he pleaded, and she complied. After that, he lost it in her. His wasn't a fast stroke. His was a methodical, soul-sucking, Shalala-inducing, forget your name and where you came from, make you believe in Santa and vaginal orgasms type of stroke. Before she knew it, Aayala was speaking in tongues.

"Lawd! Lawd!" She did not recognize her own voice. The noise of the band truck carried over in the distance. The smells of roti and grilled meat wafted toward her, reminding them how exposed they were to anyone around. His hand flew from her breast to her neck, and he squeezed. Her heart fluttered in recognition of a kindred spirit, and she pressed her entire body back against him in response, wanting more of him.

"I need you to come, Aayala, I'm—yo! Your pussy is… fuck!" He reached around with his other hand to touch her clit as he bent his tall frame around her, not quite resting his weight on her but imposing his presence more fully. His breath tickled her ear, his teakwood scent mixing with the little rum he drank tonight greeting her nose as he whispered, "Say my name, baby."

She shook her head, wanting to pretend for a while longer that they hadn't crossed this line she'd never pictured crossing with him. But he knew, and he didn't want her to pretend anymore. He wanted to remind them both what this meant.

"Say. My. Name," he growled, and she felt that growl in the depths of her stomach. It traveled all over her body, raising the hairs of her arms until her fingers tingled against the car hood, and her tongue only existed to say his name…

"Yes! M—"

Aayala woke up with a cry as her legs shook from the almost-orgasm her dream had produced.

"Oh no, no, don't leave me now," she whispered, begged, hoping against hope that this would be the time she could get hers. That this would be the first time she'd come after her life turned a full 180 in the past months. She needed an orgasm so badly, and her body had become a complete stranger to her, requiring a completely new manual that came in hieroglyphics and refused to work for her anymore.

Why? Why was this happening to her? She'd never had any issues with her body, enjoying her sensuality, her partnered time, and her alone time with toys. But ever since that day…everything had changed.

She ran her hands slowly down her belly. The belly that now had more flesh than ever before, down to that hump adorned by silver stretch marks—the living proof of that night, the scar barely noticeable but ever-present.

Her hand kept traveling down to coarse, curly hairs, which she parted to find her swollen nub and stroke it. The tingling sensation returned, and hope sprang into her heart. Maybe this would be the time.

She circled her clit in slow motion first, the tension in her spine gathering, the finish line visible to her when it usually wasn't even present. She could do this!

She looked down at her tank top and dared use her other hand to slowly caress the outside of her breast. Her breasts, which had betrayed her the most, changing day by day and becoming tools instead of one of her most erogenous areas. She ran her hand lightly on the fleshy part that spilled over the side of her top and felt…a frisson down between her legs. Not sure, she let things be and focused on her clit.

Little by little, pressure built, showing her that maybe, maybe, things were possible. But as she was about to ride the crest, Aayala lost something. Some of that sweet urgency right before her orgasm transformed into anxiety, and her motions became mechanical instead of pleasurable.

She cried out again in frustration, trying to relax her mind, bring back that tingle that the dream had conjured, but it was elusive, that spark fully dampened by her worries and lack of confidence.

A wail blasted from the baby monitor on the corner of her nightstand, and Aayala knew her orgasm would not visit her tonight.

Another wail, a shuffling sound, then a full-blown cry set off the speakers of the monitor, the sound more effective than any wake-up alarm she'd ever had.

Aayala tossed the covers away from her and darted to the

bathroom, heart hammering in her chest, hands tingling as she tossed her wet underwear in the hamper and hastily changed into a clean pair with new sleep shorts. She washed her hands while cooing at the baby monitor, "I'm coming, baby! I'm coming!" —the only coming that would happen tonight.

* * *

AAYALA'S EYES FELT DRY AND GRITTY AS SHE SAT IN FRONT OF her desktop computer, looking at her three screens. One screen had the list of ten jobs she had yet to process, all boudoir couple photo shoots. She had no idea how to even begin to tackle them with her lack of inspiration.

She picked up the phone to accomplish the first task waiting for her.

"Hi, Joanna, I got your email about the boudoir shoot with Lindsay."

"So good of you to call! I was about to reach out to you again. I know you're still on maternity leave! So sorry to bother you, but we wanted to lock down our shoot so that it's right before our anniversary."

The sound of Joanna's voice on the other line and the knowledge she wanted to book a session made Aayala's hand sweat uncomfortably. What if she'd lost her passion for photography, too?

"Oh, ok. I wasn't putting anything on the books yet, but you both are some of my favorite clients… Let's do this. I'm planning to open my books in the next month." *Lies.* She wasn't ready to open them, not one bit, but maybe if she said it out loud, then it would happen.

"As soon as I open them, I'll call you and get you in. That work?"

"Ok, thanks, girl! Take your time! I'm just being a nervous

Nellie, not wanting to lose my spot, but you deserve all the rest! I look forward to your call. And give that cutie baby of yours hugs and kisses! I can't get over those cute cheeks of his every time you post a picture of him on IG!"

"Oh, thanks!" Aayala responded, uncomfortable with the grace Joanna had given her about resting and taking her time when she gave herself none.

Ok, one thing down. On to the next.

She looked at the next screen, where it showed an email from a prospective client. They were looking for a commercial photographer to do a complete overhaul of their lifestyle photography over fifteen hotel properties in South and Central Florida. The start date of the project loomed close, and she had to decide soon.

Aayala knew she had to take this job. Even though her boudoir shoots had been expanding in the past few years, her steady work had always been commercial photography. Having a son now meant she had to take a step back from taking too many risks in her career. Another change…

The last screen had *his* most recent email, letting her know when he would be back in town. Her hands grew damp as she reread the words. She hadn't responded to that one either. Malik had sent his regular messages all these past six months to utter silence from her, except for her email letting him know Andre had come early.

In the past, they'd always exchanged correspondence back and forth: her keeping him up to date with things at home and their circle of friends, him sharing pictures of the places he visited and his new experiences. They could email about everything and nothing. After eighteen years of what she could only describe as penpal behavior, Aayala knew her sudden silence must bother him. But she had no way of communicating with him when everything had changed in her life. She couldn't pretend their friendship was the same.

Her calendar for the year was behind the screens, reminding her of her priorities. Her mum had promised her six months. Six months for Aayala to get used to being a mom, learn the ropes, and get her shit together with her career. That time was golden—for all her cousins helped her out, they didn't know much about parenting. Even though her mom had been absent during her teenage years, she had nothing but the best memories of when she was a little kid. So, she had marked a calendar with the days she had left while her mum was there to remember not to fuck around and forget. Her time was limited. Post-it notes were stuck all over the calendar with her list of goals. *Be the best mom. Get back to boudoir photography. Learn how to be a single working mom...*whatever that meant.

At the end of those six months, Aayala planned to have her entire shit together.

"The prince is up and hungry!" Aayala's mum breezed into her office, holding her squirming baby, who made squawking sounds that warned he was about to lose his ever-loving shit if someone didn't feed him right now.

Her mom deposited Andre in Aayala's waiting hands, pushing back to lean against the door while she adjusted her nursing top and bra to feed him.

Andre, at his two months, had enough time on this earth to recognize the person who could feed him by scent and feel and immediately quieted when he felt Aayala's arms surround him. The same sense of peace swelled inside of her as he started nursing, knowing this was something she had done well in a sea of things she seemed to fumble.

"So the fada arrives today, huh?" Linda said, looking at her short nails, then back at Aayala with an eyebrow hooked high.

"Yes, ma, you know he does." Aayala sighed, settling herself for at least a half-hour of feeding. She had followed

Andre's cues and overall schedule since he was born and had been blessed by a steady, mostly predictable pattern of feeding and sleeping. She knew she was lucky in that regard, no matter how grueling the schedule could be sometimes.

Aayala looked at her mom, wondering when the time had passed and the tender, caring woman had transformed into the tired warrior that stood in front of her. Lines creased her face as she stood in what Aayala could only describe as a caftan.

"Ma, for real, you are wearing a caftan? I mean, you know I don't think you should get back with dad, but resigning yourself to muumuu-wearing now? You're young!"

Linda sucked her teeth and dismissed her only child with a wave of her hand.

"Don't talk nonsense, child, your fada and I are still together no matter where in the world he is right now. He always comes back to me. There is no 'getting back' because we're not separated. You understand? And who says muumuus are for old ladies? You be showing your ass sometimes, so judgmental. Now, you finish feeding my baby boy so I can get him ready to meet his fada. And you, go get yourself ready before your cousin comes to pick you up. You need to look good for him, nuh?" Linda said with a smirk on her face, hands planted on her ample hips.

"No, mama. Andre's father is just that—Andre's father. Him and I will co-parent. We're friends, that's it." Aayala repeated the same sentence she had said to her mother at least a thousand times since she got pregnant.

"Well, if you say so, child. All I know is that once you have a baby with a man, your lives are forever entangled, so..." Her mom shrugged and walked off to find something else to bother.

There would be no entanglement between her and Malik. No matter how much she was tempted by everything that happened between them in October, he wasn't the person she needed. He spent more time away than at home, and she had grown up in a household just like that. She knew what that could do to a partner. She knew what that could do to a child…

No, thank you.

Aayala sighed and looked down at her baby. He looked peaceful, eyes closed, his face still mostly all cheeks and soft lines, but the promise of his father's features threatened to burst through soon. For all the months she carried him, he came out looking just like his father.

Oh, well. She couldn't complain. His father was handsome, after all.

She nuzzled Andre's cheek and inhaled the scent distinct of newborns, that mix of diaper cream, milk, and sweet baby. "Are you ready to meet him, Andre? I must confess I don't know how to feel about him being back, but we'll manage, ok, buddy? Him and I will be the best parents ever to you, I promise."

***

"Girl! You ready?" Mariana's voice boomed in her living room as Aayala rushed down the stairs to greet her and Daniel. Mariana, though not her cousin by blood, was her cousin by heart and one of her best friends, and she had been a rock during her pregnancy and these two months as she navigated life as a new mother. She and her men, Daniel and Mason, were always close by, making sure she had what she needed and lending a hand whenever she or her mom needed a break.

The decision to move permanently to South Florida had hinged on the support system she had with the three of them, as well as her cousin Alicia and her husband Gabo.

Even though Malik technically was also in South Florida, his career as a merchant marine meant he spent more time away from home—not someone she could rely on day-to-day.

But their circle of friends had grown tighter during the past couple of years as relationships evolved and solidified in the group, which was why everyone had high expectations for her and Malik now. Expectations she continued to deflate every time they came up.

"What are you wearing?" Mariana asked, looking her up and down.

"Told you…" said Aayala's mother, coming out of the kitchen carrying Andre in her arms.

"What did you tell me, Ma? You were just wearing a muumuu earlier on." Aayala scoffed.

"Yeah, but it was for home wear. I changed to meet my son-in-law."

"He ain't your son-in-law, Mada!" Aayala said through gritted teeth.

Mariana's eyebrows went comically high, and she looked back at Daniel with a face that said, "I ain't touching that." Daniel walked in behind Mariana, closed the front door, and shook his head, his equanimity a balm she sorely needed right now.

"There is nothing wrong with what I'm wearing. I'm not looking to impress anyone." Aayala shrugged in her loose beige dress that had cool secret access for her to nurse. It was practical and easy to slip on and off. She put on her brown sandals, and she was ready to go.

"Aayala, baby girl…"

"Nope. I just had that nine-pound baby inside of me for eight months. So what if I wear big easy-to-wear dresses, huh? I have zero time for pants right now. Let's go," Aayala said, deploying one of the tried-and-true sentences that shut everyone up who had something to say about how unlike herself she'd been since Andre was born.

She didn't need the reminder. She knew it herself.

They got in the car, nervous energy coursing through Aayala. Thank God Mariana and Daniel stayed quiet, allowing her some space while they cruised the streets heading to the port in Fort Lauderdale.

"It's going to be good to see him again," Daniel said as he maneuvered his car into a parking lot. Mariana, who was sitting in the front, glanced at Daniel, then turned her eyes with a secret smile. Daniel's excitement was palpable, a counterpart to Aayala's nervous anticipation.

"Daniel, you're so cute. Ever since you started dating me, you've had a bro-crush on Malik. So wholesome. I agree, it's gonna be good for you to have Andre's dad here to help and shoulder that responsibility," Mariana said, uncharacteristically soft-spoken. Even Mari could tell Aayala didn't need and wouldn't respond well to too much pushing right now. She appreciated her cousin's gentleness.

"Mmmm, I'm not looking to get too used to this. After all, he'll only be here for six months," Aayala said, getting out of the car. The sultry August air crowded around her, and she was glad she wore such a loose dress. It would keep any sweat marks from her nervousness from showing.

She stood behind Daniel as they approached the deck, and there he was, standing on the deck in front of the luxury yacht he'd been on board for the past two months.

Malik stood tall, all lean strength with dark ebony skin smooth in the afternoon sun. Shades prevented her from seeing his expression.

The father of her child, the best dick she'd ever had, and the friend she'd never thought of sleeping with before that fateful night. The nervous current she felt at seeing him washed through her, leaving a sense of completion.

Now that he was here, she could stop fretting about his arrival and get on with the next steps to getting her life together. Hopefully, all her concerns about him being a good parent to Andre would fade away with his actions, but if not, that was alright. She could be mother and father to Andre.

After all, Aayala had a plan for the six months while her mother was here to help her. The plan was simple: get the hotel lifestyle job, figure out how to be the best mom and the best co-parent, get back her inspiration for her boudoir photos, and get the old Aayala back.

Easy.

CHAPTER TWO

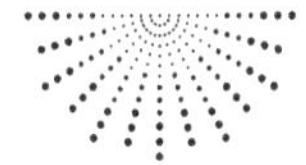

Back ashore.

Six months away from home. Malik took in the scents of salt and sea mixed with the heavy heat and humidity of his hometown and exhaled the anticipation coursing through him.

Back home…if he could call this joint home. Every six months, he left this place to go travel the world, doing back-busting work as a mariner every day of the week. His days comprised of methodical work when at sea, interspersed with unforgettable experiences every time he visited a new city or town. Apprehension flooded through him, the same apprehension that visited him each time he returned. What would be different this time?

Malik glanced around, trying to see if he could spot Aayala or any of his friends. He'd emailed Aayala on his last stop, asking her to pick him up. Usually, his brother did the pickup, but this homecoming was different. This homecoming meant he finally got to meet his son, Andre.

Regret flooded him to think he hadn't been there for Aayala, for her emergency birth. In all their plans and conversations, she had assured him it would be ok for him to arrive a month after Andre's birth, claiming her mother would be more than enough help until he arrived. After all, the plan was for them to co-parent, and a month's difference wouldn't invalidate his commitment to his son. But when he received that one email, the only email she sent over these past six months since he'd been away, he realized he had miscalculated. He should have been there for her.

All that changed today.

"Son, you have someone picking you up?" Captain Peter Joseph, an old sea head and captain of the yacht, asked him.

"Yeah, Cap. They should be on their way." *Hopefully.* Aayala hadn't actually answered his last email, but he knew she was no flake. She'd either be there herself or have one of their friends pick him up.

"Are you nervous?" Cap asked with a kind smile. He stood next to Malik on the deck, his rugged mahogany hands holding his bag. Malik could see that today was a good day for Cap, his hands relaxed and not twisted in pain. Rheumatism had been plaguing Cap for the past two years, making the man consider early retirement.

Malik had known him since his first years as a merchant marine. Cap had been the first officer on deck during his intern years on a large oil tanker that became Malik's home away from home for six months of the year. Cap, seeing Malik as the only other Black merchant mariner on board, had taken him under his wing, showing him all the ropes and becoming his mentor.

Eight years ago, Cap had finally left the deep sea voyages behind him and joined the crew of this family-owned luxury yacht, moving his way up to Captain. For the six years that Cap had been at the helm of this mega-yacht, he had Malik as his second-in-command whenever Malik was available.

Workaholic that he was, Malik would do up to two

months with Cap after his six months in the tanker. Good money in the bank ain't hurt nobody, especially not his family. The dedication and isolation at sea all had their benefits, which he'd learned to reap at eighteen, when he had to step up as the breadwinner for his family.

Through the years, he dreamed bigger, past just helping his parents maintain. He wanted to build enough wealth for them to retire comfortably and for his brother to start adulthood with no obstacles—not like the ones that were in front of Malik at eighteen.

All his work ethic he had learned from his father. Every year, his dad would be gone six months at a time, providing for his mother, Malik, and his little brother. It had allowed his mother to be home with them for most of his childhood until things had irrevocably changed.

"Alright, son. I'll wait with you if you don't mind. The missus is probably eager to see me, but I can tell you need the company." Cap patted him on the back, and Malik felt some of his tension release at the support. He could wait on his own, but he welcomed the company.

"While we wait, what about the proposition I made to you? I'm not getting any younger, and it would be a good change of pace for you…"

"I'm not sure, Cap. Listen, I've been making six figures for the past ten years since I became a chief officer, except for the past two years that I actually took six months of leave. I have to run the numbers. You know my parents need the bread, and my brother gotta go to college."

"Yeah, but your father's settlement finally came through, thanks to your insistence and support. So, he has enough money now for him and your mother to retire in peace," Cap said, knowing the whole story about his dad's accident right before Malik graduated high school.

"I know, I hear you. Look, I know they're good, but I want

to make sure they don't want for anything, you know? The money they got is alright, but not the life I envision for them after retirement. Taking a step back, even if it means being ashore way more feels..." Malik trailed off when a frisson of awareness had him looking up. That was when he saw her.

Aayala stood at the far end of the deck, looking around for him. She had changed. Before, she could be described as borderline thin. Lean with all the right curves, especially the curve behind her—the woman had an ass on her that defied explanation. Now, her face and overall body had filled out to fit thick, and he liked it. No lie. He liked everything about her. Having these feelings for his best friend was overwhelming. To be aware now of all those thoughts he'd kept at bay for years, never allowing them to materialize as more than a mere whisper in his mind...to have them now be loud and insistent in his brain was a new adjustment he'd had to undergo these past six months.

Her extravagant curls were put up in a bun, and her eyes were as determined as ever. Aayala had the kind of eyes that made you stand at attention, that made you wonder what she'd glean from you without even talking. She had the type of arresting presence that spoke of discernment, of strength, of knowledge of herself and everyone surrounding her.

Some men might be intimidated by a woman like her, but that quiet resoluteness had always drawn him.

Aayala was his homegirl, the only one that kept up with him religiously during his travels. Not even Mason could compare to the level of dedication she'd put into corresponding with him through the years. He could thank her for always keeping home close to him, no matter the miles between him and Florida.

On that fateful night last October, he saw a side of her that had him wishing he could explore more. He had no shortage of women during his travels, but he kept all his situationships casual. Being at sea most of the year meant he couldn't give a woman any stability.

Aayala made him dream for a minute.

When she had made it clear she wanted nothing beyond their friendship and a chill co-parenting situation, he'd agreed readily, knowing that was the smartest thing to do for both of them—no matter how loud the feelings were inside of him.

Aayala had ambitions, and she kept her eye on the ball, same as he did. There was no space for any romantic feelings that could jeopardize his parenthood to Andre or his career.

At the thought of Andre, he smiled in anticipation, and that's when Aayala saw him. She stopped walking for a second. He saw her take a deep breath before she marched her way to where he stood. He felt that deep breath all the way through his body and had to convince himself all over again that co-parenting was the only thing that made sense between them. Because if he ever went with his instinct…

"My boy, are you sure this is just a co-parenting situation, as you call it? Because I…" Cap said, trailing off when Aayala reached them.

"Wa gwaan, baby daddy?" Aayala said with a smirk.

"Nah, Aayala, we ain't gonna call each other that," he said, shaking his head. He would let her set the pace of their parenting, but he wasn't about to call this woman a baby momma. She was in another category in his eyes. He waited to see what she'd do, but his arms wanted to wrap around her and feel her strength surround and surrender to him. She smiled at him, and he took the hint with disappointment.

"Alright, I hear that. Hello, you must be Cap?" Aayala said to Peter, extending her hand in greeting.

"Yes, my darlin'. I've heard great things about you through the years, but this boy here clearly lacks imagination or good vocabulary because he did you no justice," Cap said, deploying his old man charm. Aayala giggled, and damn if he wasn't impressed that shit worked for Cap even after all these years.

"Aht-aht, old man, stop hittin' on the mother of my son. You have a wife waiting for you at home," Malik said with a mock frown.

"It's true, the love of my life is waiting for me, but if you ever want to know what it is to be with an old man, you call old Cap, ya here? I have what you young people call a hall pass. She has one too. She says she's using hers if she ever meets Denzel Washington," Cap said, and Aayala busted out in laughter.

"Well, I'm honored I'm being placed in the same category as Denzel. I'll keep your offer in mind." Aayala winked. She probably realized that Cap was all bark and no bite.

"Oh, child, I'm sure I wouldn't know what to do with all of you. Let me go home before I get myself in trouble. Take care of that boy, ya hear?" Cap said, hobbling his way down the deck.

The second Cap walked away, Daniel and Mariana approached.

"Maliiiik!" Mari shrieked before she tackled him with the force of her enthusiasm.

"Welcome home, man," Daniel said and dapped him up, bumping shoulders with him. This was as effusive as Daniel could get, and Malik was glad to see him, too. Their friendship had grown during his last leave when Daniel had just started dating Mason and Mariana. Kindred spirits and shit.

"Good to see you, bruh. Thanks for picking me up," he said to all of them.

"Alright, let's go to my house so that you can meet Andre. Are you ready?" Aayala asked him. A frisson of nervousness ran through him at her words.

"I'm ready."

HIS SON.

He looks just like me, was the first thing Malik thought when he saw the wide eyes blinking up at him. The little man was chilling, wearing a onesie that said 'Yardie' and laying on top of a blanket spread on the large couch. Andre's chubby cheeks and pouty lips opened and closed, and he made squawking noises. Malik for sure soon would learn what they meant. Andre's little fists were squeezed tight, and when Malik gave him his finger, Andre opened his hand and wrapped his little fingers around his large one.

"Y'all already claiming him as full Jamaican. I'm gonna have to buy him some 305 fits, stat." His throat felt like sand had taken residence in his airways, and he had to collect himself before he embarrassed himself in front of the mother of his child.

Malik's chest felt full to the brim with so many emotions —awe, love, and trepidation among many. This boy, this baby, was his. His responsibility. His to teach and show him the way. Malik glanced up, looking for the only other person in this room that would understand how he was feeling, but she wasn't there.

They were in Aayala's living area, which was set up with a playpen and changing table and had everything she could need to watch Andre. The entire space screamed Aayala, and he could see she'd used the same decor as her old apartment in New York, with earth-toned furniture, plants in each corner, and dark pillows and rugs. The centerpiece of the room was a large five-panel canvas with a map of Jamaica shaded with the flag colors, in case one forgot where her family was from.

He stood up, placed a burp cloth on his shirt, and held

Andre to his chest, the solid weight of the baby's body providing the balance Malik needed to stand strong.

He heard Linda, Aayala's mom, whom he'd just met, sigh in contentment and made eye contact with her. Linda smiled and winked at Malik, staring at him and Andre unabashedly. That he'd known Aayala since high school and had never met her moms until now was wild. Aayala loved her mother but was usually cagey about their relationship, so meeting Linda was a pleasure and an enigma all wrapped up in one.

He approached Linda, Mariana, and Daniel, who sat on the other couch watching TV, giving him time to meet his son at his own pace.

"Where is Aayala?" he asked Linda.

"The gyal is probably inna there in the kitchen," Linda pointed, excitement shining through her eyes.

He strolled into the kitchen, the warm weight of Andre bolstering him.

"Are you alright?" he asked as Aayala stood, arms braced on the sink.

"Yeah, I'm straight," she said, her voice muffled.

She turned around, and he could see her dabbing her face dry with a paper towel. Had she been crying? Tough-as-nails Aayala? It couldn't be. She probably was washing her face, most likely. Yeah, that made more sense.

"You sure?"

"Yes, I'm good. So, you've met Andre," she said, and her voice softened around their son's name.

"I did. I'm…" He cleared his throat, fighting against the multitude of emotions churning inside him. "You did good. He's beautiful, and I can tell he's gonna be smart—"

"How can you tell he's gonna be smart? He's two months old." She laughed and shook her head, and the knot that had lived in his stomach since he saw her loosened up. He'd been worried things would be weird between them, and her laughter was a balm.

"I just know. The way he grabbed my finger right away, I just know. He's gonna be smarter than his pops, and thank God for that."

Her beauty was ever-present in the slope of her eyebrows, in her brown eyes, on the high cheekbones and full lips that matched each other in lushness. But there were bags under those eyes, her cheekbones appeared sallow, and the lips? Well, let's just say they'd been turned down more than up since he saw her at the port.

None of that sat well with him. The mantle of responsibility he felt for her had intensified from that best friend love to so much more. All that she was going through, she'd had to do it without him, the person who should be the main partner in this new adventure with baby Andre. And he hadn't been there.

"Hey, I know I keep asking, but you my co-parent, and I need to make sure you good. You look…" He hesitated, not wanting to make her feel like she wasn't looking fine as hell because she was. If anything, she looked more beautiful to him than ever. Maybe it was that connection, the fact that she was the mother of his child, but she took his breath away. Still, she didn't look herself.

"I'm just tired, that's all. Having a newborn is no walk in the park," she said, and he detected a bite to her words.

"I hear you, but I'm here now. I've been reading. I know you told me you're breastfeeding, but maybe I can take him a few nights so you can rest—"

"No!" she blurted out, not letting him finish. Her eyes widened, and she pushed toward him, holding her arms out. For a second, he hesitated to give Andre to her, but he knew it was an irrational impulse. But he would not pretend that it didn't hurt to find her closed off to even the idea of him helping. That smile from before had been a decoy to make him believe things were alright. He should have known better. She was masterful at keeping herself aloof when working through potent emotions. She took Andre from him, cooing as the baby settled into the crook of her arm.

"Well, I know we haven't talked about how we'll divide time now that I'm here, but I want to spend time with him, and I want to ease some of the load for you." He finished his thought, feeling bereft of Andre's weight against his chest. Just a few minutes and already, the little man had him wrapped around his little fist.

That's why he'd planned everything in his mind, reading a bunch of books about solo parenting and breastfeeding and all the ways they could manage this. He was ready. But then he saw Aayala's frown, and he knew whatever she was planning to say wasn't going to be something he wanted to hear.

"I…yeah, we do. But I don't want to get used to a schedule that won't make sense come six months. Maybe it's best if you just come and visit him here? I mean, that way he's used to seeing you here, but it won't be a big difference once you are gone?" Aayala said, her tentative tone a concession to him because he knew her enough to know she had already decided in her head.

He crossed his arms and leaned against the kitchen counter, hoping the tightness of his jaw didn't betray his thoughts.

"I want to be a permanent part of Andre's life. I thought we agreed upon that?"

"We did, and you will. All I'm saying is having you take him to your Mom and Pops to have him stay with you… All of that might be a bit too much, at least now. He is a newborn and barely has a set schedule, there are a lot of moving pieces, and…" She shifted Andre to her shoulder, soothing him even though he was clearly chillin'. The one that needed soothing was Aayala. Because of that knowledge, he decided not to push.

"Alright. Let's keep talking about this. In the meantime, I'll be here daily to see Andre," he conceded, knowing it was going to take more than today to convince her to let go a bit. But that was ok. He was nothing if not persuasive.

For all that his plan was to be a good father to Andre, he was now more than ever convinced that having equal time with his baby was the right thing, not only for Andre and himself but for Aayala as well.

CHAPTER THREE

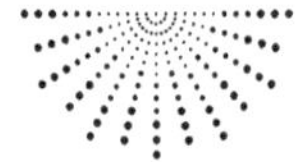

Life may have flung some curves at Aayala, but it certainly had bestowed her with plenty of gifts as well. She peered around her cousin's guest room, which Alicia had essentially transformed into a baby's room the instant Aayala had told them she was moving to South Florida.

She remembered that day—four months pregnant, sitting in her New York apartment, figuring out how her future would pan out and realizing that her core support system was actually a thousand miles away. She had always had one foot in Broward and the other in Brooklyn, but in Brooklyn, she had young cousins that still were partying the night away and older aunties and uncles who would have gladly helped but had their share of grandkids of their own to look after.

The fact that Malik had insisted to her he planned to be an active parent might have been in the back of her mind, but in the end, it was her cousins that propelled her to make the moves she needed.

Alicia and her husband Gabo didn't plan to have kids. They instead had plans to be the most amazing auntie and uncle possible and had decked out their third bedroom with a pack and play, changing area, and toys that Andre probably wouldn't be able to use until he was at least a year old.

To have people in her corner who cared so much for her son was all wonderful, but it came with a price Aayala hadn't expected.

Every time she came to their home, it was the same song and dance.

"Where is my baybeeeee?" Alicia whispered as a greeting and gently took the sleeping Andre from her arms.

Sigh.

Aayala felt Gabo's eyes on her, and she turned to find him smiling widely at her.

"How are you, cuz? You good?" Gabo asked, actually making eye contact.

How refreshing. She smiled back at him, and he took the baby bag away from her.

"Aayala, I already told you, you don't need to bring a baby bag here. We got this. We have all the things you have at home. I can't wait to have my nephew stay with me. Once you are ready, of course." Alicia turned, whispering nonsense to the baby. "I'll go ahead and put him down, and I'll be right back, ok?"

Aayala stood, immobile. *Was this how it was going to be forever?*

"Never mind her. You want something to drink? I keep asking her if she's sure she's good with not having kids, and she keeps telling me yes. She says she loves all the cuddles and can do it for a few days, but that it takes a brave woman like you to do it every day," Gabo said, a gentle tone to his voice while he searched her face.

Aayala only nodded, acknowledging the words for what they were. In the back of her mind, she shared Gabo's same concerns. Old Aayala would have sat Licy down for a talk and made sure she was good, but this new Aayala…she had no bandwidth.

"Thanks, Gabo, I'll grab something from the fridge. Don't sweat it. And thanks." She smiled, returning the olive branch.

"Where's my other cousin?"

"She's outside by the pool with Migue. I'm heading out to the Center to play ball with the crew and some students. We'll see y'all later for dinner?" he said, grabbing his keys and sports bag.

"You know it."

"Bet. Later." And Gabo walked out of the house. She stood there for a while, listening to Alicia sing some lullaby to Andre, shaking her head as she walked toward the guest room to check on her son.

"So I've taken the lifestyle shoot. It's steady money for six months, and it allows me to take things easy with the boudoir shoots until I'm in a better place with…everything," Aayala said, reclined against one of the lounge chairs on Alicia's patio.

Licy had finally come out after twenty more minutes of fussing. Aayala had tried to convince her to leave Andre to sleep, but no, Licy needed to make extra sure he was good. Aayala prayed all the fussing wouldn't wake Andre up before his time, but he'd settled in well in the bassinet, and they had the camera monitor in case he woke up.

"Ok, ok. So, who's gonna watch little man while you're going to each of the shoots? Aren't those long days?" Mari asked.

"Not all the hotels will have long shoot days. The beauty of it is I get to create the schedules with the other photographer. But it's fine. I mean—"

"Who's the other photographer?" Licy asked as she watched her across the rim of her cup.

"Oh shit! Come on now, Aayala, you're the smart one among us!" Migue chimed in from the chair next to Mari.

Of course, they'd pick up on her vagueness. Great. She loved her friend group, she really did, but the way they were all on top of each other's business… Doling out advice when the person asked for it was one thing. Giving it unsolicited was another. She had no problem talking about anything if her cousins came to her, but she tried not to prod and push too much—unlike them.

"Hold up…not him…" Mari said.

"Yes, yes, him. Sergio is the other photographer. They want two opposing styles for this rebranding. The edgy industrial feel will be his, and the more sensual, luxurious approach will be mine. It suits our styles perfectly," Aayala said, shrugging. Maybe she did want Andre to wake up. That would be a great distraction.

"Well…" Mari said, shaking her head but holding back her comment. Mari knew her well, and she wasn't in the headspace to debate the merits of working with her ex-lover.

"So many old penises coming back to your life, Aayala," Migue said.

Laughter spilled from all of them at the same time. Fucking Migue with the one-liners.

"Excuse me, but neither penis is old, and both are excellent," she corrected as tears ran down her face.

"Girl, you never dished how Malik was! I remember the whispers from the girls back in high school and college, and if those stories were true… I mean, they were lining up every time that man was back inland," Migue said, reminiscing.

"That's the father of my child. I won't speak of his stroke skills."

"Excuse me, no one said anything about strokes, so that's his superpower?" Mari said.

"Don't start with me. Did I ask you about Mason or Daniel, lady?"

"Listen, I have no problem telling you that Mason is a Pussy Pro, and Daniel is Mr. Dexterous Dick."

"Not Dexterous Dick, Mari, I can't with you!" Licy cackled.

"Well, I still didn't ask. You offered all that info without prompting, girl. I have nothing to say."

"So you won't call him Thrust Titan?" Migue asked.

"Dick Dynamo?" Mari added.

Silence.

"Stroke Seducer?" Licy said, barely able to get the last word out before she dissolved into a fit of laughter.

"Licy, et tu, Brute? I can't believe this!" Aayala said, laughing, thankful the topic had deviated to this and no one was focusing on Sergio's involvement in the photo shoot.

Sergio, her ex-lover of five years, was more a casual fling that had survived the span of many years because of her level-headed approach to relationships where she didn't give any energy she didn't receive.

Aayala liked steady dick from someone who could take her out for a few dinners here and there and was discrete and sincere. Delightful conversation was a plus.

That was exactly what Sergio had provided.

Their on-and-off arrangement was convenient...until it was not. She'd found herself restless, wanting a deeper connection that Sergio didn't seem inclined to give, so about two years ago, they parted ways. It was amicable, clean, and easy. No hard feelings.

"Look, I know you're super level-headed and have the zen thing going on where you know how to fuck and vibe with dudes, and that's what you had with Sergio. But don't you feel it could get messy working together? Especially with Malik back?" Mari asked.

"And Aayala, why not let Malik help you with Andre if you are going to go back to the workforce so soon, and he is on his extended leave? I mean, the job is for what, six months? The exact time he'll be home. You know Gabo and I will support you in any way we can, but we work too. Malik will legit be home every day, just chillin' and volunteerin' at the Center and helping his parents. Seems like a win-win to me," Licy added.

"But hold on, why not just get it in with Malik? I mean, he's yo' baby daddy. That seems to be the answer to all your problems. You need to let some things go, girl, you don't need the entire world on your shoulders," Migue said on top of Licy's words.

Argh. All this information thrown at her at the same time. This was nothing unusual to their hangouts, but with the way she had been feeling lately—overwhelmed seemed to be an understatement—the number of questions they were slinging at her was draining her faster than her favorite battery-sucking camera.

"Look. Let me make this easy. A: Sergio and I are professionals and ended on the best terms. We'll be fine. Two and three: I'm not looking to catch feelings for the father of my child. He and I fucked once, on what I can only describe as a night where we both lost our damn minds, and now we gotta live with the consequences. We're both old and wise enough to realize we are just friends, and if we were meant to be anything else, that would have happened way back when. Malik is my homeboy. That's it. Not spit-swapping homies like you and Mason…nor you and Gabo.

"And I'm not looking to get used to having him taking care of Andre for days at a time just for him to leave in six months. I don't operate that way. You know me, I have my habits, and I need to create new ones as a mom. Having him in the middle of that process would only set me back six months, and I don't have the time for that." Her friend and cousins' reluctant agreement allowed the topic to change to her extreme relief.

Hopefully, that would rest this case, and she could chill in peace with them.

CHAPTER FOUR

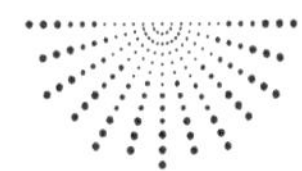

The smell of eggs, sizzling bacon, and what could only be his mother's famous cinnamon rolls woke Malik from his deep slumber. His stomach rumbled at the welcome aroma. During these few weeks back home, his mom had vowed to 'bring some meat to his bones' and had prepared all of his favorite dishes. Who was he to get in the way of a woman with a mission?

He rolled over and looked at his phone. 6:30 in the morning. For many, that might be an early rising on a vacation day, but for him, it was taking it easy. Usually, he woke up at 3:30 when at sea. The first few weeks back home were a period of change for him, finding his land legs, and even though he'd been home for more than a month now, he was still a bit wobbly.

He stood up and stretched, then did thirty fast pushups to awaken his body. Once his blood was pumping, he went into the restroom to wash his face and brush his teeth. After putting on a shirt so he wouldn't scandalize his momma, he headed to the kitchen.

Many mornings, he felt as if he was looking at himself

from outside of his body. Out-of-body Malik was still on the vessel, looking at vacation Malik and dreaming of his next leave.

Vessel Malik had a purpose and a value. Vacation Malik usually second-guessed his entire existence.

At this point in his leave, he still missed the vessel, the day-to-day tasks, the reliability of every minute of his day. He mostly was a creature of habit until he craved adventure, which he got plenty of at the stops along the way.

Four months used to be enough for him—enough difference in his regular monotony to bask in the presence of his parents and brother, hang out with his friends, date a few women, and not have every minute of the day dedicated to a chore. But these past couple of years, the months at sea on the oil tanker he worked for had started feeling like years instead. By the time he embarked on the yacht with Cap, he felt himself craving land. Craving familiar faces and the comforts of home. Once he arrived home, though, shit started to get muddy in his mind.

Malik stopped by his brother's room, hoping his younger brother would be up already so that they could work together on some house improvements he'd noticed as soon as he walked in upon his return. After five knocks and silence, he knew Damian wouldn't answer, so he let him be.

He'd mentioned to Cap his restlessness, surprised that after eighteen years, he seemed to struggle with his current setup. Cap hadn't been surprised at his words, though. He swore up and down that Malik needed a better anchor and less time at sea.

"You need a woman, boy. Not one of those ladies who you barely dine and then give them the business. I'm talking about a genuine connection, like my Bonnie. That's what you need. That way, you wouldn't be second-guessing that it's time to make a change."

Malik knew Cap might be right, but he was content with his voyages and especially with the salary he was making, which held things down back at home for his parents and his brother. It also gave him more time to work on a nest egg for himself.

He had a plan, and to fulfill the financial goals he had, he needed to work until he was forty-five. That was the magic number. Then he could retire in peace, buy himself the house of his dreams, chill, and still travel.

That he now had a son weighed heavy on his mind. He'd wondered more than once these past months if he should change his plans so he could be more present and watch his son grow. Or should he persevere and attain his financial goals so that he could give his son everything he needed?

"Malik!" his momma hollered from the kitchen.

"I'm right here, woman," Malik said, rounding the corner to find his mother at the stove.

Cecily Johnson was the CEO of the Johnson family. She was a small woman with ample hips and thick arms that she used to her advantage to pull down her two tall sons when she needed to cut them to size.

Her ebony cherub face made you think she was a docile, sweet woman until you realized she swore like a sailor with the purest heart. She gave all of herself to her family, to her Oldies, as she called them at the senior center where she worked, and to her community. Everyone loved Mrs. Cecily.

"Don't you fucking talk to me like that, boy. I'm your Momma."

"Isn't it too early for cussin'?"

"Ain't never too early to remind you I'm the boss here, boy. Start the coffee. Don't stand there looking like you got no sense. I ain't raise no lazy chump."

"Hmph," he mumbled under his breath, not wanting to point out that Damian was still in bed.

"Excuse me. You have something to say?" she asked him, raising one of her delicate eyebrows.

"Momma, Damian…"

"Alright, Malik, I know Damian is still sleeping, but he was at work late last night."

"But he shouldn't be working. He should be starting college, why did y'all let him skip another year?" He was frustrated to find out his brother had again decided not to start his studies this next semester. Nah, he wasn't frustrated. Malik was pissed the hell off.

The moment Malik started making some decent bread, he'd wanted to make sure his brother would be set for college. Having to bust his ass playing basketball, while enjoyable, had been an added pressure on Malik's years at school. The money his dad made was enough to keep his household and for his mom to be home, but it didn't come with any surplus, like fancy college money, because his dad had tried his best to be home at least six months a year. Cap had guided him, explaining to him the moves to make to ensure he wouldn't spend all his money on frivolous shit.

"Your brother is a fucking adult now. When you were eighteen, you came to me and told me you were gonna be a merchant marine. Didn't ask me for my thoughts or my advice." She pointed at him with a wooden spoon splattered with egg. "So now you wanna ask me that frustrating ass question about 'why y'all let him?' Child, please." She turned around and placed a plate heaping with eggs, bacon, and two cinnamon rolls in front of him.

"Come on, stop fussing and sit down and eat. It's gonna get cold, then I'm really gonna be annoyed with you. I didn't wake up at the asscrack of dawn to make you this…"

"You know you didn't wake up this early to make me breakfast. Pops probably woke you up when he got up."

"Fine, you got me there. He woke me up at 5:00 a.m.

today! I worked 10-7 last night. He must be out of his damned mind, talking about *'let's wake up early and go take a walk.'* Shiiit. He's still out there walking. He'll probably be in soon."

"Ma, why you cuss so much?" he jokingly asked, knowing exactly what she would answer.

"Because it's the authentic manifestation of my personality," he sing-songed at the same time she said, "Because it's the authentic manifestation of my personality, that's why."

"Boy, stop now!" She sat down across from him and took a bacon strip from his plate.

Malik shook his head and immediately stood up and fixed her a plate. He knew she was waiting for his dad to come back, but if his Pops had gone out to walk early, that meant he was having one of his mornings.

Same way Malik was restless about his current situation, his Pops sometimes grew restless about missing the sea. On those days, he would need to clear his head, so who knew when he'd return from his walk? And Cecily here would wait for him, even though she was dying to eat now.

Love. Makes you do some ridiculous shit.

"So, what you doing today?" she asked, giving him time to savor the bite of cinnamon roll he had just taken. Damn, his momma could cook. The way that buttery sweetness dissolved in his mouth and the cinnamon that came in to enhance it all? Nothing could top that flavor.

"I'm gonna holla at Mason and Gabo at the Center, then I'll go to see Andre since your secondborn there still sleepin'."

"Oh, my sweet baby, I'm so fucking in love with his cute face! When you gonna bring him to see his Nana again?"

"I think Aayala has a meeting tomorrow with a client, so I'll give Linda a break and bring him over with me."

I'm so glad you here. Aayala is sweet, but she be overpro-tecting that baby. He's our family too, you know. I'm glad you're bringing him around, even if it's for a couple of hours. Before I felt I had to make an appointment with royalty just to see my baby Andre."

He paused, knowing for all his mother could be sweet, she had her edge, but he didn't find any shade in her words. She honestly thought Aayala was just being overprotective, just like he was feeling overprotective of her.

He saw how much Aayala was trying to be the best of everything. In these past weeks, he'd seen how much she tried to give him space to spend with Andre and, on top of that, listen to his thoughts on how they should do certain things. She might not agree with it all and often still did things her way, but he knew it took her a while to get used to new ideas. It was alright. He knew how to slog his way until he changed her mind.

He'd done it with movie and music recommendations in the past, with some of his thoughts about religion and spirituality—shit, you name it, and Aayala had a set opinion on something. But he always finessed his way to having her see another point of view.

"I know. Her and I are working out some details of how we'll move forward with our co-parenting even when I'm not around. She knows it's important for Andre to spend time with y'all, and she agrees it needs to happen more often. You gotta give her some grace, though, Momma. This is new for both of us."

"I know, baby. I remember having you. It ain't easy, and that was me and your Pops being in love and shit. I don't know how you two doin' it. You sure you don't have any feelings for that girl? Sure would make things easier for you."

"Nah, Ma. I mean, you know I don't lie to you. She is fine as hell—she ended up having my baby, so clearly, you see what I think about that, but that's my friend, that's all. I wish there was something there, but truly, it's just friendship."

Never mind the voice that kept telling him he would be open to exploring more with her. That voice kept sounding thirstier and thirstier anytime he was at Aayala's and he saw her in her shorts, golden brown plump booty winking at him from the bottom of the fabric. In those moments, he got the urge to wrap his arms around her, lift her up, take her to her room, and…yeah, never mind that voice. He was afraid one day he was just going to burst out and say the wrong thing to Aayala. Or was it the right thing?

"If you say so, Malik. I mean, I'm just sayin', would make things easier."

But the reality was it would make it way more complicated because Malik was leaving after six months, and he didn't know if he could walk away from Aayala and his son if he got another taste of her. And no matter what anyone thought, Malik only had a very specific set of skills, and those skills were only executable in the sea.

So, better to leave things as they were.

Friendship only.

Less mess, less stress.

***

His second-favorite thing about visiting Andre was watching his mom move around the house. It reminded him of how focused he could get on the horizon while standing on deck, looking out at the sea in awe of something larger, indescribable in its magnificence. He'd always walk away humbled but with renewed purpose after those instances of standing eye-to-eye with the vastness of the world around him.

Each time he stood in this kitchen while Aayala moved around picking up bottles, cleaning up, tinkering, he was in awe of the brave way she had embraced her new place in life.

He'd known her since they were young teenagers when the most stressful thing about their lives was what party to attend each weekend. Now here he stood in her presence, watching her manage so much in her life, which had expanded and intensified since their last time together. He wanted to reach out and grip her hand, hold onto his best friend, hold still enough to find their center again.

He knew he had a ways to go. His every day barely changed except for his visits to his son. But for her, it meant a complete transformation, not only of her habits but her body, her soul. He could feel it when he was around her and tried to grasp with both hands the sensation that not all was well with her.

But then she moved, as she was doing just now, reaching over to get some bottles for her pump, and her ass showed underneath her shorts, and his mind short-circuited any deeper thoughts to sinking into her again.

She turned around with the bottles in hand and caught him staring.

"Can you please stop gawking at me like that? Every day, you sit there, and I just feel those bedroom eyes… Just…" she said, her cheeks reddening under his gaze.

Fuck. Was she really just blushing around him? His Aayala?

Malik was trying to act like everything was normal between them. He'd spent the last few weeks convincing himself they were just best friends, convincing himself he could leave all the simmering want inside him untouched.

This vulnerable side of Aayala which she only trusted very few to see…it was his kryptonite. It made him want more. He couldn't help but push a little, see where her mind was because if it was even a few miles away from the need that he felt for her, it would be enough…

"Just what, Aayala? Finish that sentence."

"No, I won't. You and I agreed to be friends only."

"Oh, I know, and we cool. But I'm not gonna stand here and pretend I don't find you sexy as fuck, and if you'd let me, I'd have you bent over that counter, taking my dick to heaven as you took it that night." Well, that just escaped him. At this point, it was inevitable, but he felt like an ass for pushing her now.

He had to fight for his life every day, being around her and not pulling her into a corner and showing her how good it could be between them…again.

"Oh, boy, you ain't gon' tempt a gyal like dat," she said, letting her Jamaican accent flourish, something she did when her emotions ran high.

He noticed.

He'd noticed a lot about her all these years, and the proximity of these past weeks had only confirmed to him that Aayala was the type of woman one couldn't let go. But he wasn't in the position to hold onto her, and he needed to be fair to her and to himself.

"Nah, I'm not looking to tempt you. That comment was out of line. But you can't fault me for admiring the view. What's with the business on top, party at the bottom look you got going on?" he said, and she nodded, accepting his weak ass apology.

"I have a meeting in…" She checked her phone. "Shit, I gotta go to my office and set up. My meeting starts in twenty. I thought I'd have time to pump one more time. But there is some fresh milk in the fridge, and the freezer stash is good, too."

"No, I'll use the freezer stash. Follow the rotation you have going on. You think I don't pay attention, Aayala? If you have your system going on, I won't mess it up, ok?"

She stood there, a mix of expressions crossing her face.

The one he caught the most was surprise, then she took a deep breath.

"Alright, I appreciate that. Mum keeps doing her own thing with the bottles, and I don't have it in me to argue with her no more." She shook her head. "She's been on the phone and her computer the whole day, so she's probably not paying attention to the monitor. Can you—"

"Are you about to ask me to watch my own son? Go. Go to your Zoom meeting."

Aayala walked away toward the stairs, and his eyes lingered all the way up with her.

He had to breathe because the less stress, less mess mantra was sounding weak as hell in his head.

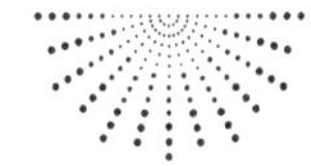

CHAPTER FIVE

The treachery of her pum pum, the audacity. Every night, she tried for an orgasm. Every night, it denied her. Her pum pum acted like they were strangers, and she didn't know what to do about it. No amount of sweet words, caresses, or vibrators—not even that rose toy—worked on her.

The promise of release mocked her, made a fool of her. It seemed that motherhood had brought an unexpected consequence Aayala was not ready to accept.

She'd attempted all her tried-and-true methods, but her orgasm kept answering back, "Who dat?" She'd been worried something had gone wrong down there and went to her doctor, but after checking her top to bottom, her doctor shrugged and explained that physiologically, all was well with her.

At first, she'd been pissed, but now she knew her doctor was right because that treacherous ho woke right up for Malik. Any time she was in the room with him doing chores or chilling, and she sensed those bedroom 'come fuck me' eyes on her, her punnani remembered. Oh, she remembered, and it went from the Sahara to Dunns River Falls in a second.

Treachery.

She couldn't even try to go to her room and attempt something because her meeting with the hospitality company for the lifestyle shoot started in less than fifteen minutes. Aayala rubbed her legs back and forth, causing friction and making her pussy throb. She had no time for this horniness.

Thoughts of the cloth diapers waiting for her in the laundry room did the trick to calm her down enough to focus on this meeting, but she'd soon have to succumb and test this theory that Malik might be the code to crack her problem. A little fantasizing might be all she needed.

"OK, FANTASTIC! AAYALA, SERGIO, WE CAN'T WAIT TO SEE THE magic you both produce with this concept. This dual perspective of looking at our properties through two different lenses will be the main catapult to our rebranding. Once you confirm the schedule that I'll send you today, we'll be good to start. Two weeks," Michelle said with a bright smile.

Michelle was the main marketing executive in charge of the rebranding of the hotel company and had worked with Aayala in the past when she was part of a social media agency. Michelle was an advocate of her work and a Brooklyn native like her, also from Jamaican parents, so when this opportunity sprung, she had immediately called Aayala.

"I'm excited to be working with Aayala again. It's been a minute," Sergio's smooth ass said from his screen. That smile had once done things to her, but with everything else that had changed, she wasn't susceptible to his charm anymore. He affected Michelle, though. With his deep brown skin, trimmed beard, wavy hair, and dazzling smile, Sergio was irresistible to many.

"I'm excited to work with you too, Sergio." Aayala smiled back, unfazed by his attempt to make her panties drop. He knew that smile used to do it for her.

"Oh, before we end the call, Aayala, do you need any accommodations?" Michelle asked.

Aayala paused for a moment, wondering what Michelle meant by accommodations, and she could see Sergio's puzzled look as well. Then the light turned on in her sluggish brain, and Aayala realized Michelle probably wanted to know if she needed any time and space for pumping.

"Actually, yes. Can we sidebar on that offline?" Aayala answered. Just then, Andre's wails came through the office, clearly audible through the call. Her body tensed to go to him, attuned to his every need.

"Oh, is that the little man? He is adorable. Thank you for the pictures you sent me last week," Michelle said.

Sergio's face went from puzzled to enlightened to perplexed.

"You have a baby?" he asked.

"I do. Andre, my son. He is three months old." She smiled, unbothered by Sergio's face transforming once more to amazement.

"Oh. Wow, I… Congrats, Aayala."

Michelle's eyes went wide, and Aayala could have laughed at the awkwardness of the situation. This was certainly not the way for your ex of five years to find out you had a kid two years after your breakup, but she couldn't find the energy to care too much. She needed to go.

"Thanks! Ok, you two, talk to you next week. Duty calls."

Then she disconnected the call, leaving an uncomfortable Michelle and a stunned Sergio behind.

Aayala's breasts started tingling, the letdown immediate when she opened the door and heard Andre's wails. He wasn't usually this loud. She'd been blessed with a mellow baby that knew what he wanted and kept a tight schedule. She wondered what was bothering him and wished she could teleport downstairs to get him.

She ran down the stairs to find Andre sucking on his bottle like it was the first meal he'd ever had. Malik, in turn, looked relieved as he sat down with Andre. Malik was doing the paced feeding she'd taught him when he first started coming to hang out, and the sight did something to her chest that she didn't want to examine too much.

"What happened?" she asked.

"Little man was pissed at me because the nipple in the bottle wasn't workin' as fast as he wanted. So, I switched to that three-month one we got the other day, and..." He gestured at Andre.

"Oh, right. I guess that makes sense," she said, a pang hitting her stomach at the fact she'd missed updating the nipples of the bottles. She should have known to do that.

"It's alright, Aayala. He cried for a second while I switched them, and we good now. Right, man?" Malik asked Andre, while Andre kept eating with the concentration of a neurosurgeon. Her baby did not play with his meals. Sigh. If he was eating, that meant she had to pump. Great.

"Whappin' to ma baby?" her mom asked, popping up like a jack in the box.

"Where did you come from?" Aayala asked, startled.

"I was in the living room, child, calm down. Good, you are down here. I need to talk to you two."

A chill traveled through her shoulders and down her arms at her mother's words.

"I'm leaving. This afternoon. Ya fada back," her mom said. The words came out of her mom's mouth fast, but for some reason, they traveled slowly to Aayala's ears—as if both the words and her ears were reluctant to ever connect.

"But I thought you'd stay for the six months… I took that job because you and I talked and…" Aayala struggled to find the words to say to her mother right now. Her calendar flashed large in her mind. An image of herself at fifteen years old holding back tears while saying goodbye to her mother yet again crystalized, making her gaze blurry. Her bubbling frustration threatened to overtake her.

Of course, her mum was running back home to her father. He just had to ask, and she dropped everything for him. Aayala wondered how long he'd stick around this time. A headache gathered at the back of her head, and no amount of positive affirmations would get her through the frustration coursing through her.

"That's why I wanted to talk to you both. I got a solution."

Aayala stared at her mum, waiting for the grand solution.

"Malik should move in while he is here."

Oh no. No. No. No.

The face of that fifteen-year-old girl morphed into her baby boy, and she shuddered.

"That's not a bad—" Malik started.

"No. That doesn't work. You and I…" Again she struggled with words when she usually was smooth with them. This day truly could go straight into the trash. "You, in my space. I mean, you're my friend and everything, but…" She flinched at Malik's look of prideful hurt, which quickly changed to a mask of nonchalance.

"You need help. Andre is my son. I'm used to deck watch late at night. Feeding Andre at night and being here during the day so that you can schedule your shoots with no worries makes sense," he said, but again, her son's face flashed in the back of her mind, reminding her what it would mean if desire made her make the wrong decision regarding Malik. He was temptation personified, but temptation she knew she had to ignore.

"No, it doesn't! I'll get a babysitter. We aren't together, we just co-parenting, that just sounds messy," Aayala said, shaking her head. That bubbling feeling took over, and a strong sense of anticipation and dread mixed deep in her belly, to the point she had to hold herself.

Aayala couldn't have him that close. That would be too much temptation. She didn't need any complications, and she didn't want to get used to him being there. How hard would it be when he left? No. She had to be smart, needed to remember she was an expert in self-perseverance.

Malik stayed quiet, face impassive, while he burped Andre, patting his little back with his large hands. Those hands…pat, pat, pat. *Lawd, could he be...less? Could he stop doing all these nice sexy baby father things?*

She accepted his examination, his bedroom eyes searching, his face pensive. Let him realize how sure she was about this.

"Alright. When you need me, you let me know. I'll still be here every day to see Andre, but I'm not looking to push." He said it with such calm confidence, she worried she'd fold. Both of them had thrown a silent gauntlet. Where was their easy friendship, and how could she get it back?

One week after her mom left, and she was at her wit's end. Aayala had underestimated how much the night help from her mother allowed her to rest, even on the nights insomnia visited her. She'd still fed Andre once in the middle of the night to keep up her production, but besides that,

Aayala would pump right after his last feeding at eight, then go into her room for much-needed peace and quiet. Now, she was feeding him every three hours, and that was on a good night. Last night, he'd hit her with a one-hour, two-hour combo, then promptly woke up at seven in the morning like he hadn't just had a party that night.

He was lucky he was so cute.

"Yikes, you look discombobulated," Alicia said as she breezed into her house with breakfast in hand. Thank God for her cousins. They'd managed to either cook or bring her food most of the week. At first, she'd refused, but after the third day, she realized she needed all the help she could get. Between work ramping up now that she was accepting bookings again and Andre, the hours in her days rushed away from her faster than water in a river.

"I'm sure you're not using that word correctly," she said, rolling her eyes at her cousin.

"Whatever you look, you wouldn't if you'd let Malik stay here." Alicia set up the table and opened the insulated bag she'd brought, and the most delicious aroma wafted toward her.

"Mrs. M's arepas?" Aayala asked.

"Yes, she made them special just for you." Alicia pulled her gently toward the table.

She plunked down on the chair and held her head with her hands.

"I'm so hungry, but I think I'm more tired than hungry. Do I really have to chew? Because I don't know if I can do that at all."

Alicia claimed the chair next to her and gazed at her with concern in her eyes. That concern activated the steel in her back, and Aayala sat up and took a bite of the arepa.

"You know, Mrs. M stays outdoing herself, lawd," Aayala said after the bite.

Her cousin stared at her for a second longer, the two of them waiting for the other to buckle. Of all her family, she was probably the most like Aayala in personality.

Alicia broke the staring contest first, shaking her head slowly. "Eat, go upstairs, and lay down. Even if you don't sleep, you need to rest. I'll take care of Andre when he wakes up. And after you're done resting, call your baby father."

As Aayala walked up the stairs to her room, the weight of the night still heavy on her shoulders, she realized she was going to fold and couldn't believe it took so little.

Aayala: Hey baby father... about that offer of you staying here to help...

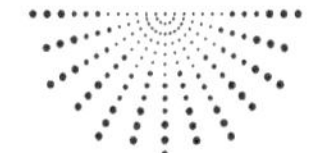

CHAPTER SIX

The Olds versus The Students.

The basketball court outside of the Center for Gifted Athletes of Broward had never seen such a heated battle. It also hadn't seen a man so ready to be on his way, that man being Malik. Today, he was moving in with Aayala. But first, a quick game of pickup with the crew because if he flaked, he'd never hear the end of it, and he needed to temper his eagerness to see her. Man, their friendship had gone from easy and breezy to charged with so much tension.

Malik didn't mind being called old by seventeen-year-old students, but Mason and Gabo seemed to have caught some feelings when the students had suggested the team name.

"Come on now, Jay, we ain't old. Have you ever seen an old man move like this?" Mason said while doing some intricate footwork he'd learned from Malik back in the day.

"Y'all don't know what old looks like, but that's alright. When we beat yo' asses, then you'll learn," Gabo added, running over to Mason to get the ball.

"We gonna change the name of the team. How about The

Crew? What you think about that, babe?" Mason asked while dribbling the ball away from Jay, one of the new seniors, toward the hoop.

Daniel stared at Mason and shook his head, then shared a look with Malik, who stood on the side, fists on hips, watching the foolishness. Malik kept his face straight, but he really wanted to burst out laughing. Gabo and Mason were doing the most, and the game hadn't technically started. By the time their four-on-four game began, they'd be winded, proving the teens right.

"Babe, we can name the team whatever we want," Daniel finally responded. For all he had his thoughts, Daniel wouldn't leave his man hanging. One reason he liked Daniel so much was that he treated Mason right with all the care he deserved. Mason, for all he was a showoff, had this soft, unprotected center that only his friends truly understood. Daniel got it too.

The game finally started, and the teens gave them a run for their money, as he'd expected. The saving grace was Mason, Gabo, and Malik had been playing together for twenty-six years, so the synchronicity was unmatched. Add tall ass Daniel, who killed the two-point shot, and they were holding their own.

"Y'all sure you're almost forty? Y'all lied," Jay panted while trying to swipe the ball away from Malik.

"What's the matter? Can't keep up, young blood?" Malik taunted, pivoting to the left and leaving Jay behind to get two points for his team.

"Told y'all you couldn't hang, but did you hear me? Nah," Mason said from the other side of the court, whooping after Malik's shot.

Jay got possession of the ball, flew past Mason, and dunked on his ass.

Daniel scratched his neck. "He just can't stay quiet."

In the end, Daniel pulled through, and they won the game.

They sat down on the benches beside the court and got their water bottles.

"Y'all want to go another round?" Jay asked, breathing hard but clearly still energized. His friends all stood waiting for the answer.

"Y'all, I gave it my all on that court. I don't have it in me again," Gabo whispered while Mason chugged water to cover his groans.

"Nah, we'll get a rain check. Malik gotta go to his son's house," Daniel said.

"Yo! Fucking brilliant excuse, babe," Mason muttered under his breath, then said in his regular ass loud voice, "Y'all can't handle any more of this smoke. So you got saved, really."

"Says the man that got dunked on five times," Malik said.

"For real, Malik? You gon' do me like that?" Mason asked him while Daniel and Gabo howled. Gabo couldn't breathe, he was laughing so hard.

"No support, this one, the weakest link," Mason said, offended.

"I call it like I see it, but I always got your back," Malik replied.

"You ready, Malik?" Daniel asked him.

"Yeah, now I'm thinking I should go to my Mom's first to shower. Don't want to roll up all sweaty to Aayala's spot."

"But you just going there to move in, right? Why do you need to shower first? Want to see if you can find that tux you wore for prom, so you can look good for her?" Gabo asked, his voice muffled by the towel he used to wipe his face.

"Negro, it's common courtesy. That's not my house, so I gotta show some respect."

"Ooooor you want to impress Aayala, smelling all good

and shit, and make your dreams come true. Don't think we don't see what this is..." Mason said, giving his bottle to Daniel.

The fact that they were hitting the real reason he wanted to go home didn't bother him, but he'd be damned if he let them know they were right. He'd never hear the end of it.

"No, I'm not moving in for that. I'm moving in to help Aayala. Truth is, she spreading herself too thin. It worries me. And Andre is mine too. It shouldn't just be her responsibility." For all they might be right, that was truly the real reason for his move. He wanted to be a true father to Andre and pull his weight.

"Yeah, I hear that...but you also want to see if things could work out, don't lie," Gabo said.

"Honestly, I think that's what y'all want because it worked out for the two of you and Licy and Mariana. But Aayala and I are different. You best get used to it." He wouldn't examine the lazy flip his stomach did at the possibility of making things work out with Aayala because he knew he wouldn't be here for long, and he needed to be responsible with her and his feelings too.

"These two have no sense. Like they wouldn't do the same as you are doing. Come on, let's go so you can get freshened up." Daniel nodded toward the front of the Center.

"Later," he said to his friends, secure in the knowledge he was moving in with Aayala for all the right reasons.

AAYALA STARED AROUND HER LIVING ROOM, AND SHE SAW chaos. Chaos wouldn't do. The bottles in the corner connected to the pump machine were the first to go.

Why did she have four different packs of wipes in the same space? Who did that? She picked up two and took them from the living area, resetting the changing stations she'd created in each room after Andre was born.

The flutters in her stomach kept her moving fast around her house while Andre cooed from his pack and play, for the moment content to entertain himself with the toys dangling from the contraption.

Would she have time for a quick shower? Andre was calm right now, so she took the risk. Mari had made fun of the little bassinet in her bathroom, but this proved Aayala was a low-key genius. The clock in the living room blinked 1:00 p.m. Malik had texted her about an hour ago, telling her he was stopping by his house to get some additional things, then coming over. Maybe she still had a few minutes for a quick rinse.

She turned around in a circle and still felt the space appeared messy, so she rearranged some of the things she'd just moved around.

Ok. That wasn't great, but it was an improvement. She surveyed the room, then picked up Andre and hurried upstairs.

A few minutes later and she was in the shower, letting the steam loosen her tense muscles to mediocre results. *Why was she feeling so jittery?*

There was no reason for her jitters. Since his return, she had seen him every day. She should be unfazed by living under the same roof with him. She clearly wasn't flustered by being close to him at all hours. Aayala certainly didn't want to know what he wore to sleep or what type of mood he woke up in or how his voice sounded first thing in the morning…

Aayala was so glad she was on her own because her cousins would have called her on her bullshit right now. She rubbed her skin vigorously until her loofah scratched more than soothed.

Ding-dong.

The bell startled her out of her thoughts, and she rushed out of the shower. At the same moment, Andre decided he had given her enough arms-free time and started fussing. The fussing would go on for a couple of minutes as he ramped up his complaints until he received the attention he deserved.

She dried herself in record time and hopped into her bedroom, trying to pull up her underwear and pants in a hurry. She gathered her curls in a bun and pulled on her nursing bra and a large tank top, put on one of her baby carriers, and gathered Andre.

The bell stopped ringing, then her cellphone began. Lawd! Could the man wait?

"I'm coming!" She bounded down the stairs, holding onto the rail with one hand while the other rested on Andre's bottom, his warm weight settling her nerves. His little heart beat so fast, it convinced hers to slow down a bit.

She yanked the door open, and there he was with Daniel.

"What's up, are you alright? You seem a little winded," Malik said.

Understatement of the day. She took him in, the air of relaxation oozing from him forcing her to get her head straight. He was so fine with his tall frame, smooth dark skin, and those bedroom eyes that made it seem nothing fazed him. How could she have missed how those eyes could make her feel before? She'd taken her comfort with him for granted, and boy, did she miss it now.

If he wasn't affected by this arrangement, then neither was she. She had always planned to be a levelheaded co-parent—this circumstance didn't need to change that.

"Hey, I'm alright, thanks. I need to get you a key so you don't have to wait," she said and patted herself on the back for sounding so calm compared to the rocky ride she'd been through these past minutes. See, she could do this.

"OK, SO WE DOING THIS," SHE SAID, SITTING DOWN ON HER large recliner while Malik sprawled on the couch with Andre dozing off on his chest.

"Yeah, we are. I mean, you know I told you I wouldn't push, but I kinda knew we'd end up here." He chuckled, the conceited man.

"Don't be so smug. I had no other choice."

"Alright, Aayala, tell yourself that. So, you sure you good with me sleeping in your office? I can just sleep down here. I have no problem with that."

"No, that daybed upstairs is way more comfortable than the couch down here, trust me. And if you're going to be waking up with Andre, you wanna be close to him."

"That's true…and that sofa is for real horrible to sleep on. I hadn't wanted to tell you before, but…"

"What? Every time you visited me in New York, you were low-key thinking my sofa was uncomfortable? Damn. You could have said something!" She shook her head in laughter.

"Nah, you clearly love that sofa. It made the trip from New York to here. I want no problems," he said, laughing. "So, tell me what I need to know for tonight."

"Well, I was thinking of waking up with you at least—" She paused when she noticed him shaking his head.

"Nah. No offense because no matter what, you're beautiful, but you got bags underneath your eyes. You need rest."

She licked her bottom lip as she received his words, sure and gentle. She found no offense in them. That he wanted to take care of her made her feel conflicted, wanting to lower her guard enough for him to see how truly not put-together she was. But she couldn't; that way led to trouble.

"Up to you." She shrugged. "I've been doing it, so one more night won't break me."

"I know, Superwoman, but let me figure it out on my own. I know his schedule varies a bit, but he sticks to similar windows each night, and from what you've told me, it's just a matter of having the milk warmed up and changing him before he feeds. I got this."

"Ok, I hear you. I'll take my rest after I feed him tonight at eight."

"Good. So, you ready for next week to start the shoot?"

"Yeah, I'm actually excited to get out there and shoot again, even if it's lifestyle." She stood up, went to the kitchen, and rinsed the few cups that were in the sink, then started on her pump parts. Her mouth dried to think of what would happen if she didn't get her passion back.

"I know your boudoir shoots were what you wanted to focus on more this year. How come you took this gig?" Malik asked, knowing all about her master plan from their many emails exchanged through his last two voyages.

"Yeah, well, I still haven't finished editing the last shoots I took before I had Andre, and I want to make sure I catch up before I start back up." She turned around and leaned back on the counter.

"Mmmm." He scrutinized her for a minute, and she took it with equanimity.

"But what's the real reason, though?" he asked.

"The real reason for what?"

"For why you aren't doing your boudoir shots? Why not pursue your true passion?"

She could tell him. Aayala knew he would listen without judgment or predisposition and give her his true thoughts.

But whatever was happening to her drive and eye didn't make sense to her, so she couldn't say. Not now.

"No other reason. You are overthinking it, sailor."

"Oh, so you're gonna distract me with that nickname of yours, which I've told you is wrong."

"But you like it, don't you, when I call you sailor?" She walked over to him and collected Andre from his chest, resting him slowly down in his pack and play insert.

"I like that you have a nickname for me. I don't know about the sailor part."

"But that's what you do. You know how Jamaicans do."

He chuckled, stretching his arms above his head. The sliver of belly that peeked at his movement got tucked into her personal spank bank to be used later to stimulate that perfidious ho down there.

"Yeah, I know, y'all Jamaicans ruthless, just finding a person's trait or work and using that as a nickname."

"Nah, we nah ruthless, we factual, that's all." She turned around to avoid ogling her baby father.

Because that was what she was dying to do.

"Listen, are you staying down here? I'm gonna take advantage and work a bit," she asked, tinkering with the left-over pump parts in the sink that were already clean. But he didn't know that.

"Yeah, that's alright. Will the TV bother little man?"

"Only if you play it too loud. He's a sound sleeper."

"Alright. And Aayala…you've washed those pump parts three times since I've been here."

Oh, shit.

"Right. I'm going upstairs now before you roast me." She avoided eye contact while passing by him, pretending to be immersed in her phone calendar.

Aayala bounded up the stairs two steps at a time, his words

chasing her all the way up. Malik had just been his regular self, demonstrating an ease in being a father that captivated her. If this was what he did to her during a normal day, how would it be if he decided to make a move on her? She didn't need to get caught up with him just for him to leave, and she didn't need to complicate their currently uncomplicated co-parenting.

Lawd, let this man not make a move.

AAYALA'S BED HAD NEVER FELT MORE INVITING. SHE LAID down, and her bones melted into the mattress, the past week flashing before her eyes and leaving her behind, exhausted.

Her phone rang, and she saw it was Alicia.

"So, how goes it with your baby father in the house?"

"It goes well. He took over thirty minutes ago, and I'm in my room ready to sleep."

"Good! Well, I was just checking in, making sure you good."

"Hmmm, you were callin' to get some tea, and I've none to give."

"Who, me?"

"Yeah, you, cousin. There is nothing to tell because nothing is gonna happen," Aayala said while sinking further into her pillows.

"Mmhmm." Now it was Alicia's turn to be skeptical.

"Listen, I know what I'm telling you, ok? Nothing goin' happen here, you understand?"

"If you say so. Alright, I won't bother you no more. Go to sleep."

Aayala hung up and settled in her bed, knowing sleep would overtake her with a quickness.

· · ·

TWO HOURS LATER, AAYALA'S TOSSING AND TURNING HAD intensified, and her mind refused to shut down. Her body screamed in annoyance, wanting to relax, but her brain assumed command, deciding to gift her with a collage of images of Malik and his bedroom eyes.

"Arrghh!" She ripped the sheets off her body and made a beeline to her toy chest. Whenever she felt wired like this, there was only one way she could reconcile sleep.

"Alright, pum pum, you backstabbing ho. We gon' make this work, you hear me? I'll think of him, and you'll cooperate and free the O."

This was what it came to. She was negotiating with her vagina. But desperate measures and all.

She pulled out her new Sonic Lora—which she'd read in the blogs apparently only had to wink at your clit and you orgasmed right away—and laid back down in her bed.

Ok. Aayala closed her eyes and let the memories of that day take over. Her breath calmed down, her muscles relaxing with each exhalation she made.

Images of Malik's capable hands popped up, large and long. They mesmerized her with their utilitarian, confident moves. She remembered how those hands felt on her hips when Malik held onto her while he slid in and out of her, so responsive to her every moan, every clench. She remembered how his deep rumble caressed her ears, telling her how wet and tight she was and how he wanted to stay in her the whole night. And she remembered how her pussy enveloped his dick, her contours gripping him, welcoming him home.

Her body remembered, and it responded to her subtle coaxing, her hands gliding down her stomach and nestling between her thighs. Aayala didn't touch her sex yet, building that sweet anticipation with every memory she invoked from that night. Images tantalized her. She could almost smell the scents from that night, the outdoors mixed with the cooking of the stands and that woodsy smell. He'd smelled like that today when he strode into her house, freshly showered and looking at her with those eyes and that smile that said he knew all kinds of wicked, dirty things, and if she only dared, he could show them all to her.

Her breath quickened at the same time moisture gathered between her legs, her touch languid against hot skin. Timidly she touched her clit, a silent prayer that tonight would be the night she could unlock whatever was not working inside her.

She dragged her legs up until she lay wide open with her knees in the air, her hand emboldened by the progress her body made with each thought and touch.

The back of her spine tightened when she remembered Malik's words right before he came, and she grabbed the toy and turned it on.

She didn't know what to expect, but the instant the toy approached her clit, she knew this was the night. Aayala was going to break the orgasm strike today. Her legs shook as pleasure ricocheted around her body, starting deep within her and expanding and contracting.

Her moans grew louder, but she tried her best to be quiet, knowing Malik was two doors down from her room and could still be awake.

Did she care if he heard her? At this point, she was so close to her goal, so close to releasing every single pent-up muscle in her body that she could care less. The waves of pleasure intensified under the support of the toy, and her feet curled up on the sheets, holding on just a little longer…

The pleasure slowly morphed into something else, something that had the same texture and feel in her body but with an edge that made her shy away from fully letting herself go. Aayala wanted to come so bad, but the longer she went, the farther the end loomed.

"Come on now, toy, do your thing!" She begged the toy,

begged her clitoris, begged her damn vagina to comply. But that intense need decreased with each passing second until she felt that lock click shut completely.

"Arghhh!!" she wailed, the sound coming from deep within, and threw the toy against the wall of her bedroom.

The thump against the wall reminded her she currently wasn't the only adult in the house, and Aayala cringed at the thought of Malik hearing her.

Forlorn, she padded to her bathroom to take a cold shower. Another failed attempt, and worse, the death of the theory that memories of Malik would break her orgasm strike.

What would it take?

CHAPTER SEVEN

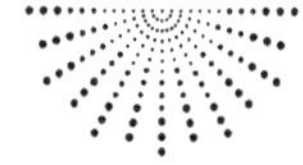

A *few hours earlier...*

"So, I wasn't looking to pile on with Gabo and Mason, but are you good with moving in with Aayala? You sure that's a good move?" Daniel asked him.

Daniel had this way of touching base with him that amused but humbled Malik. He had taken it upon himself to check in with Malik periodically during his months at sea, deepening the friendship that began the year prior when Daniel had just started dating Mason and Mariana, so Malik knew the question was coming from the right place.

"Yeah, it's a good move if it means she gets some rest, and I get to see Andre more consistently. I see no losing in that scenario."

"I hear you. So, what's bothering you?"

Malik laughed. "You know, being with Mason is rubbing off on you, the whole being in every people's business and shit."

"You're not lying. My entire life, I thought I was selfish and self-centered, but a year with Mason and Mariana and I find myself evolving more than I did my first thirty-six years of life. It's a good feeling. I finally gave myself space to be more than what other people expected me to be."

"That's what's up," Malik responded, attempting to keep his teeth from grinding and imagining the ways he could have woken up his brother from the deep slumber he'd found him in. Daniel was right; something was bothering him.

All those hours, and Damian was still in bed. His twenty-year-old brother needed to grow the fuck up and fast. Their father needed help in the house doing small repairs and upkeep, and it always waited for Malik's return to land, even though Damian lived under the same roof and had the same eyes everyone else had.

When Malik had suggested waking his brother up by force, his momma had stopped him and cursed his head off, talking about "the baby needed to sleep longer." Hearing that was Malik's cue to leave, and the knowledge he wasn't coming back that night was a welcome thought.

Malik needed to find a way to speak with Damian, if he ever found him awake, to talk about the things that should happen in Damian's life. Damian didn't remember how it was before when dad was still working and moms had been able to stay home, but things had been tight.

The money Malik made being an officer compared to his father's lower rank had allowed for his parents and his brother to have an overall better life, and his savvy investments through the years had helped as well. So, Damian just didn't know, but Malik would make sure he laid it out in detail next time they spoke.

"You know I don't mind the silence," Daniel said as he turned into Aayala's development. "But if you need to talk, you know I'm here. And you know Mason always wants to solve everyone's life, so you know he'll listen too."

"It's alright, man, nothin' to worry about. I just need to have a man-to-man talk with my little brother. He's not taking advantage of the opportunities he has in front of him," Malik said.

"How old is Damian again?" Daniel asked.

"He turned twenty a few months ago."

Daniel kept his eyes on the road, but Malik could see the wheels turning.

"I know you were already on the sea, being a sailor and shit, but at that age, I still was figuring out a lot about myself. Maybe Damian is in a different stage than you were at that age. You gotta remember that. Not everyone grows at the same pace."

Malik took in Daniel's words, processing it all, letting a new perspective in, but was still not convinced that was the case with Damian.

"You know I hear you, man. I appreciate the perspective," Malik said, staring out of the car at the duplex house where Aayala stayed. This was it. "Ok, let's go. You gonna say hello?"

"You're kidding? If Mariana finds out I came and didn't check on Aayala, I'd never hear the end of it."

ALL THOUGHTS OF DAMIAN DISSIPATED WHEN HE WALKED INTO Aayala's home. The mere act of spending time with her and being close to his son had been soothing in a way that surprised him. Now, hours later, he sat on the daybed of Aayala's office, still too wired to go to sleep.

Malik contemplated going downstairs and seeing what Aayala was working with in the late-night snack department, but he worried the moment he went downstairs, Andre would wake up again.

Aayala had assured him Andre only woke up every three hours, but he knew from all his extensive reading on parenthood and new babies that there could be some disruptors to a baby's schedule, and him putting Andre to bed, instead of his mom, probably made the baby's day irregular. He welcomed the time he had to spend with Andre, cultivating their own routines and memories together, valuable time he intended to cherish and hold onto when he was away from home.

His stomach grumbled loudly in the room, making him reconsider going downstairs to rummage in Aayala's kitchen. As he opened the door to the hallway, a faint noise made him pause. Shit, was that Andre? No, he went to Andre's door and pressed his ear to it and heard nothing, and the intercom back in the room hadn't picked up any noise either. Again, the same noise came through. It sounded like a meow but much deeper—not a cat, really, more like a…

"Mmmmm. Ahhhh."

Malik froze in place. His entire body vibrated, and all of him coiled to full attention. He recognized that sound now—how he thought it was a cat he never could imagine. It was Aayala, and if memory served him right, a very aroused Aayala.

He willed himself to walk down the stairs, but his body had other plans for him. The reality was he wanted to hear her, wanted to connect with her even if it was across the hallway from her door.

What is she doing?

His imagination supplied him with an image of Aayala's golden brown skin glowing in candlelight. Her on all fours, her thick, sturdy legs opened, ass up, glistening pussy greeting him while her fingers rammed into her. Face pressed on her mattress while the melodic sounds of her moans lured him closer to her.

"Mmh, right there…"

He heard her faintly through the walls of the apartment,

and warmth flooded him from the top of his head to the bottom of his feet, all created by the mere sound of her voice.

Now a hum accompanied her moans, and he added a vibrator to his fantasy, pressed right next to her pussy, making that big ass booty of hers shake as the vibrations made her pussy quiver. How could the woman manage an ass that size with a frame like hers? That's why he knew there was some spirit out there watching over him because…damn.

His hand, which had been frozen for a few seconds, gravitated toward his hard-as-wood dick. His hand glided inside his basketball shorts, causing his brain to short-circuit when the movement coincided with a loud moan from Aayala.

He couldn't believe he was about to beat one out standing in the hallway of the mother of his son's house while he eavesdropped on her feeling herself.

Then Aayala's deepest moan yet reverberated through his entire body.

Fuck it, dick out, consequences later.

Warm steel met his hand, the pleasure of his proximity to Aayala so potent that precum already escaped the tip of his head. He used that to quickly match the intensity of her moans. He had to bite his bottom lip to keep himself from saying something reckless, something like "let me in" or her name.

The force of his need propelled his hand to move with a grace and dexterity that impressed even him, his dick heavy in his hand jerking every time he heard her voice.

Seconds away from coming, he attempted to pace himself when he realized they no longer were racing at the same speed. Her moans had decreased in strength, but like a jockey that had lost control of his racehorse, he was too far gone.

"Come on now, toy, do your thing!" He heard the frustration in her voice, but his dick lacked his perceptiveness, and the sound of her voice activated one of the most forceful nuts of his life. He pulled his shorts up to catch his cum as he spurted for long seconds, still biting his lip to keep himself from hollering in ecstasy.

"Arghhh!!" Then a loud thump, followed by his dick jerking one more time in his hand.

The last noise finally seeped into his consciousness enough to realize Aayala hadn't been able to orgasm.

Fuck. Now he had to go to bed with the knowledge he couldn't make her come as she deserved. That thought had him fucked up.

ANDRE TREATED HIM WELL THROUGH THE NIGHT. HE KEPT TO his three-hour wake-ups and barely fussed when he realized he was back to that bottle life at night. He didn't blame the little man. It must be different to go from the comfort of his mom's arms to Malik giving him the bottle. But one of the times he changed his baby's diaper, he could swear he saw a little smile bloom on Andre's face when he recognized his pops, and Malik stored that image to keep with him in the months when he would be away from his son.

Because he'd gotten some good shut-eye in between wake-ups, he felt energized. That, and the nut he busted last night had him determined to start the morning right. The way he kept replaying what happened tormented him, knowing he could have made her orgasm… He'd promised himself he wouldn't push her, wouldn't seek what wasn't freely offered, but now he found himself exploring possibilities in his head he knew were not feasible. But maybe, just maybe, he could be of service to her in more ways than one. Maybe Malik could offer to ease more than one tension, one stressor in Aayala's life. But he didn't want to make any assumptions.

What he could control right now was breakfast.

He stood by the stove finishing an omelet when he felt the air shift. Seconds later, he heard slow footsteps coming down the stairs.

She rounded the corner, dressed in a tank top and those damned shorts she wore at home with her hair in a silk wrap, holding four full baby bottles in her hands. She opened the fridge and placed them gently as if they were precious cargo.

"Morning," she said.

Uh-oh, she's in a mood.

"No grand rising?" he said.

"Nah, not really. You know I'm spiritual and intentional with my speech, but I'm also practical and Jamaican." She shrugged.

"I've always loved how you link your Jamaicaness with practicality."

"My Jamaicaness?" She chuckled.

The sound of her laughter calmed something inside of him that had been agitated since he woke up. The way he kept being soothed by her presence and Andre's flitted in the corners of his mind, inviting him to explore the phenomenon further, but just as it flitted through, it dissipated as he focused on the task in front of him. The toaster finished then, and he snapped to attention.

Content with the omelet and his perfect timing with the toast, he turned around and placed the plate in front of Aayala. A cup of the Blue Mountain coffee he'd found in the pantry accompanied the breakfast.

"Do you still take it black? So I know for tomorrow," he asked her. She gazed at him with an expression of suspicion mixed with something else he couldn't quite pinpoint. Whatever it was made him want to smirk, to rile her up more, but he wanted to start the day at peace with her.

"Yeah, still black, haven't changed since the last time you had coffee in my New York apartment. On the weekends, though—"

"Sweet condensed milk, which I already added to my grocery list." He nodded.

"Oh, you think you know me so well. But really, you don't need to do alla dis. You here to take care of our lickle youth, not me."

Mmmm, patois again. He wondered what bothered her more, the fact that he greeted her with breakfast or the fact that he implied he would do it every day.

"We're not gonna argue this early. Eat," he said, grabbing his plate and sitting down across from her. He really just wanted to enjoy her presence. After last night, he wanted to do significantly more than just enjoy her presence, but he'd take anything he could get from her right now.

"Nah. You don't need to do all of this, really. Maybe we need some ground rules."

"No ground rules. We just had a baby…you had a baby four months ago. You got a lot on your plate. I'm currently on leave. I'll do what I can to make your days as smooth as possible." His words made Aayala pause mid-forkful, her face expressing all that she didn't want to convey: shock, hesitation, concern, and dare he hope, a sliver of interest. He would hold onto that hope, however ephemeral. It sparked something warm deep inside that had been growing since last October. He suspected it had always been there.

Her poker face was usually better than this. He'd been the recipient of it in many instances throughout the years, and he chalked the slip up to her being tired. He could see the same brown shadows under her eyes from the past week. Damn it. She hadn't slept well.

"No. I don't need to get used to a routine that will disappear when you leave," she said, and his stomach dropped like it always did when she mentioned him leaving. But there was nothing to it. They both knew what his work was. He never promised anything that involved him essentially leaving the only career he knew.

Just the thought of starting over made his muscles tighten and his stomach decide to stay way down there. Better to focus on what he was good at, and hopefully, Aayala would grant him the gift of acquiescence. That gift would be everything to him. That gift made him worry he'd brick up, and then what would he do?

"I understand your hesitation, but I'm really not looking to negotiate this with you. You can be stubborn, but you know how persuasive I can be. So, if you don't want to deal with my campaign, you might as well fold already."

Aayala bit the corner of her bottom lip, making the other side of the plump curve push out, reminding him of the soft sensuality of her kisses. She closed her eyes, deep in thought, the conflict and need to be hyper-independent fighting within her.

Her long lashes greeted her cheeks, her eyebrows drawn up in concentration, and again that fleeting thought, that soothing sensation, washed over him.

Her eyelashes fluttered open, and her cheeks flushed at whatever expression she found on his face. A pull made him gaze further down, and he found her nipples were attempting to puncture holes through her tank top, begging to be caressed. He remembered yet again how she reacted to his touches on her breasts that fateful night. How responsive she became at any little caress to her nipples. How much he'd wanted to be around her, hear her voice, bask in her company, be more to her than just her best friend since that balmy night. Everything about her was essential now.

"Alright," she murmured.

Words weren't computing, the air in the dining room thick with the smoke of everything unsaid and unexplored between them. The smoke swirled around them, lured them to drop their guards, to tell the truths they dared not say to each other. He was shocked and thrilled she'd accepted, and his stomach decided to return and flip lazily at her low, husky answer.

"Did you hear me?" she asked.

"I did, and if giving me an answer makes you feel better, alright. But trust me when I say in this, you had no choice. I'll take care of mines."

When he saw her eyes flash in warning, his heart raced faster in response. His hands itched to hold her, and if Aayala was his, he wasn't sure if he would have spanked her or rewarded her right now. She had him in knots, and it was taking all of him to portray the calm and stability he knew she needed.

The adrenaline of the challenge that she posed in his life had him pushing his chair back, the scratching noise cutting through the smoke and cleansing the air. He cleared the table, staring at her all the while as she reciprocated with an intensity that threatened to make him forget himself. Forget that she had asked for them to keep things simple. Forget that he had agreed on that as well.

He tossed the plates into the sink, damn the noise and mess, and braced his hands against it, needing a minute to compose himself, the feelings inside threatening to take over. He needed to gather the usual relaxed demeanor that was his constant companion.

The air changed quality again, and he knew without turning around that she'd gone up the stairs. He heard Andre too and said a silent thank you to the little man for saving his old man from risking it all.

CHAPTER EIGHT

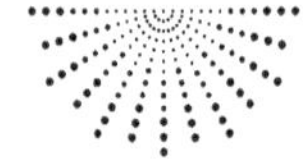

One day and one night, and Malik had already altered the fabric of her days, transformed the composition of her routines. He played havoc with her peace of mind, all with a few pointed words and a promise to take care of her.

Aayala took a deep breath while she finished changing Andre's diaper. Her baby boy cooed and smiled, oblivious to the tension that simmered in their home.

"How are you, baby boy? How's my Andre? Did you have a good night? Did you have a good time with Dad?" she asked Andre while he smiled and kicked his legs up. His soft little belly contracted with joy as she rubbed it and smiled at him. Her heart filled to the brim, the tension from just minutes ago flowing away to be a concern later.

"He had a good night. Woke up every three hours, ate, had his diaper change, and he was ready to go down right after each time." Malik's voice filled the nursery as he leaned against the doorframe, fully in control again. The deep breaths he took downstairs when she'd escaped to get Andre were no longer needed, she guessed, and her full heart skipped a beat. She gathered the baby, hoping his presence would aid her in maintaining the peace that had already escaped her.

"Oh, you were a good boy for Dad?" she asked Andre, who squealed. She envied Andre the time he'd had with Malik, but she knew she couldn't stay too long around him. She was liable to make a mistake and show him how much he was affecting her.

"Can I ask you a favor?" Malik said, compelling her to look at him.

"Yes?" she said, raising her eyebrow, refusing to let him make her more nervous.

"I need a ride to a car dealership."

"Oh? You getting a car?"

"Yes, I need one."

She hesitated, afraid that more time with him spelled trouble, but she never ran away from her challenges, and today wouldn't be the first day.

"Alright, get ready."

***

When Malik asked to go to a car dealership, he didn't elaborate that he wanted a luxury vehicle. The elegant showroom boasted top-of-the-line cars, all with the latest technology and features. Aayala knew Malik did well with his salary, but this told her he made even more than she expected.

"So, you looking for a fast car, something small and lethal?" she asked, bending to wipe Andre's face while Malik pushed his stroller. She detected the warmth of his gaze but decided she didn't want another staring contest with him yet. Her heart couldn't take all the rapid racing it had done just today.

"No, actually, I'm—"

"Hello and welcome to Blue Motors, your neighborhood car dealer. What can I help you with? My name is Chantal." A tall brown-skinned woman with long braids approached them, a wide, gorgeous smile on her face. Chantal's eyes sparkled with interest when she took in Malik, and Aayala caught the quick surveillance of his ring finger and watched her smile grow wider. If it wasn't petty, Aayala would roll her eyes, but it was, and she couldn't fault Chantal's good taste, so her eyes stayed firmly in place.

"Hey, Chantal. I saw online you have a top-of-the-line X5. I wanted to give it a ride, see if it's a good fit," Malik said with a polite smile on his face.

"Alright, alright, an X5, you say? I would have pegged you for an M4 type of guy," Chantal replied and winked at him. Her eyes disobeyed her command and rolled a little, and Malik caught the whole thing, smirking at Aayala before answering.

"Nah, I need to ensure I have a spacious car. That makes sense for my current circumstances."

"Oh, I see. Well, follow me. I have a couple of X5s in the lot that you might be interested in, any color that you like in particular?"

"I'm not picky. As long as it's a dark color, I'm good." Malik said, following Chantal and her swaying hips, which Aayala was certain hadn't been that mobile when she originally approached them.

Aayala kept pace with them but distanced herself from Malik slightly in case he was interested in Chantal and she ruined his flow. The fact that doing that made her stomach flip-flop and her hands curl around the straps of the baby bag was something to relegate to the back of her mind, where she kept all the things she was committed to ignoring regarding Malik.

"Oh, so what are these new circumstances? Are you a new uncle, perhaps?" Chantal asked with curiosity as she stopped by a stunning black SUV.

"Nah, not my nephew. This here is my little man Andre, and…" Malik turned and took Aayala's hand and pulled her closer to him. "This is Andre's mom. I need a car that's comfortable for the three of us to ride around town," he finished, squeezing her hand. She could feel his minty breath on her cheek and that heated gaze on her, and her heart somersaulted inside her chest.

Outwardly, she kept her shit together, knowing all her desire for him had become suddenly attainable and utterly confusing. She had a plan, and Malik kept throwing her signals that made her want to do the unthinkable: toss the plan away.

***

"Congrats, you got your first car," Aayala said as they walked upstairs to the nursery. After some savvy haggling, Malik had paid half in cash and financed the rest, so he could keep good liquidity, he explained to her.

"Thanks. I had avoided getting one all these years because I would just come home for four months. Why bother when I'm rarely here?" he said, walking behind her with a sleeping Andre in his arms.

There.

There was the reminder not to read too much into whatever signals Malik sent her. She knew better. She recognized what it would mean to get used to any of this and then have it snatched away. Every time he mentioned leaving, a flashback of her thirteen-year-old self deciding to move to Florida instead of gallivanting the world with her parents came through. She knew what it meant to love someone that didn't stay in one place. She knew what it was to be the child of someone so gone, so committed to love that they became myopic. Andre deserved better.

But why did he have to be so tempting? She stared at him as he held Andre with so much tenderness, his coiled strength contained for his son as he laid him down in the crib. She kept staring as his arms flexed underneath the short sleeves of his patterned shirt. When Malik kissed his hand, then pressed it to Andre's soft cheek, her underwear underwent a trial by liquid.

Why did he have to tempt her so?

They slipped out of the bedroom in tacit silence and went down the stairs together.

"So why get one now?" she asked him when they rounded the corner to the family room.

"As I said in the dealership, my circumstances have changed. I can't be relying on other people to move around if I need to take Andre to a doctor's appointment or if the three of us need to go to the store or something. I needed to be ready, and I wasn't. Now I am. Next step is getting a place of my own, but I want to buy, so that will take longer. Probably after my next tour."

A swig from her water bottle calmed her dry throat and calmed the tense knot in her stomach. All Malik's words sounded right and not right at the same time. Aayala wanted him to be responsible, and he was. She also didn't want him to be too involved because that threatened her status quo.

"Want a bottle?" she asked him, bypassing the images of them going on different outings together like a happy family.

"Yeah, thanks." Again, that intense gaze burned the back of her neck, but when she turned around from the fridge to give him the water, his face was the picture of relaxation.

"An X5, though?" Aayala asked. She, too, could pretend.

"Yeah, well, you know that has been my dream for years."

"Right, I remember the list you made the second year after you left, once you did the math on how much you'd make your first five years." She chuckled.

"Yeah, I thought I was gonna live a baller life," he said while he took down his water bottle in less than a minute. She stared at his Adam's apple as it bobbed and almost dropped her own bottle, so mesmerized she was with him. She always knew her friend was fine, but damn. Now all of his features were in 4D surround sound. Might as well be a virtual experience, she was so immersed in him.

"Yeah, me too. I mean, you had big plans. By now you should have a mansion, three cars, and if my memory doesn't fail me, a tiger too," she said, attempting to come out of her trance. Was that drool? She took another sip of her water bottle and wiped her mouth just in case.

"You got jokes! You know the tiger was for shits and giggles," he retorted, leaning back and spreading his legs, the solid strength of him showing even while he was in a relaxed state.

"Nah, I remember you being very serious about the tiger."

"Yeah, and I remember you scolding me for such a childish wish, completely missing my great humor."

"I don't know what you consider great humor, but that ain't it." They both laughed, her belly warm at seeing the crinkles in the corners of his eyes full of mirth.

God, she'd missed doing this with him.

For all she was close with her cousins, Malik had threaded his way into her inner circle for years, their correspondence back and forth becoming a touchstone of her days.

Their hangouts when he was inland further helped strengthen the knots of their friendship. It had always been an easy one, full of camaraderie and banter interspersed with deep conversations, the two sharing things with each other that were deeply private because they trusted each other's lack of judgment, connecting because of the similar ways their brains worked.

That's why this past year had been hard. Losing her friend to this new tentative temptation-fueled magnetism, weighted by the shared responsibility of a child, didn't leave much room for their friendship of old.

"I missed this," he said, his tone shifting to one of reflection.

He'd always been a mind reader.

"I missed this too," she said, sitting down across from him on the table.

"Did you? Because you kind of froze me out there these past months."

The regret that overcame her at his words tasted sour and foul in her mouth. She truly had frozen him out. She'd stopped answering emails but for the most essential communication, refusing his entreaties to go back to normal.

Any other person would have been mad, but he kept on writing, telling her about his days and sharing tidbits of the things he was learning from pregnancy and baby help books. He'd reassured her in deed and word that he wasn't taking her silence personally, that he understood their friendship had taken a turn, and he'd invested time in uplifting her and keeping up with her even when she had no words to return.

"I was wrong about that, and I'm sorry. It was all so much… You were here for part of the pregnancy, and we had our plan, and then you were gone, and it was something I no longer had anyone to go through with. Licy and Mari did their best to be there for me, but it's different, you understand? It was our child growing inside of me, and we had made a commitment to our baby, and suddenly I was on my own. It brought to light what it was gonna be like to parent with you…"

Malik nodded pensively, taking his time to receive her words. She knew this side of him well for all she pushed back at him when they had different points of view. He, in turn, took the time to see her side. That didn't mean he wouldn't still try to persuade her to agree with him in the end, though.

"I hear you, this is all new for you and me. This next trip…this next one we'll figure out better ways to communicate, for me to be more present, ok?" Malik said, and the plea in his eyes made the steel inside of her bend to his will. If he only knew how soft he made her…

"Of course, I'm better now. That's why I need to get used to my own flow…"

"No, nah, that's no excuse to not let me take care of y'all while I'm here. Let me cut that thought real quick."

"You can take care of Andre any time. I realize that's important for him and you," she said, sitting back in the chair, mimicking his earlier relaxation. Best she set boundaries now before they were completely obliterated. She'd found her strength in the reminder he would leave them eventually.

All thoughts of strength flew out of her head when she heard the scratch of the chair on the tiled floor.

Malik braced his hands on the table, all coiled force as he leaned toward her. His scent reached her, and his magnetism made her sit at attention. Everything inside her wanted to soften to his show of power.

"It's equally important for me to take care of you and make sure you recharge for the months I'm here. That's not up for negotiation," he said, his voice deep and calm, making every rebellious bone in her body react.

"Who are you, my daddy?"

"I'll be your daddy if that's what you need me to be. And Aayala…" he murmured, his eyes zeroing in on her mouth, which she realized she'd failed to completely close.

"Yes?" *Was that a moan? Fuck.*

"I will spank you if you don't behave."

"You'll what?" she spluttered. *Did he just...*

"Too much?" Malik's eyebrow quirked up in amusement.

Aayala shook her head and turned around, throwing her words over her shoulder. "Too much."

Now she just needed to ignore the way her entire lower body clenched after his words. She needed to work on her defenses and fast.

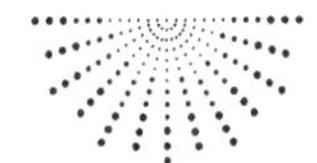

CHAPTER NINE

The sea breeze greeted her, heavy with last night's humidity. Meanwhile, the sun valiantly fought to dry the land, which refused to let go of the shallow water that pooled around most of the streets. The view from the rooftop of the boutique hotel proclaimed its superiority with the crystalline waterline and the familiar white sand off the eastern coast of South Florida.

Her eye attempted its own valiant battle to wake her curiosity up enough to create today.

Aayala's photography chops were unparalleled. Modesty had a time and place, and she wasn't a boastful person, but her quiet pride didn't allow her to fuck about with her gift.

She was an excellent photographer.

On the worst day, with the lowest motivation, Aayala could capture any subject and elevate its appeal to its maximum. She knew this.

But when her eye was awake?

She didn't capture, *she created.*

Aayala created magic in stolen moments. She evoked sensations by translating what her subjects rarely knew...but she did. She knew they were intrinsically beautiful. Beauty surrounded them everywhere, and when she saw the world through that lens, it all brightened behind the camera.

Today she settled for capturing. It would be great work that would elevate the hotel and the models. Michelle would be pleased. But it wouldn't be her best work, and that bothered her.

Aayala sat on one of the lounge chairs in her most comfortable black work dress, awaiting the two models as they finished with Sergio.

The plan was for her to take her photos first, then peruse the next location while Sergio took shots with his own perspective.

They had discussed what angles and close-ups they were going to do before the start of the shoot to ensure they told the story from different standpoints, their previous years together lending to a shorthand that allowed them to quickly map out the day.

"So…a baby." Sergio slid next to her, his breath hot on her ear.

"Could you not?" she said, recoiling away from him. A flash of hurt materialized on his face, his handsome features the picture of injured pride.

"Sorry, I…forget."

"That you're no longer invited into my personal bubble? Yeah," she said, scowling at him.

"Sorry."

"It's alright. What do you want to know?" She folded her arms underneath her chest, and immediately, Sergio's eyes flickered to her breasts and back to her face. The whole thing was barely perceptible, but she caught on. She knew that was one of his favorite physical parts of her… Once upon a time, she wouldn't have begrudged him the stolen glance, but things had changed with them. With her.

"Nothing, I just… Damn, preciosa. We'd been together for years, and you just up and have a kid the moment we break up?" Sergio said, his Puerto Rican accent deepening with each syllable and at the same time increasing in speed.

"The breaking up implies we had this whole relationship, but you and I were a casual thing at best," she said, shrugging at his outrage.

"No, we were not. You and I were together. Fine, we didn't live in the same state half the time, but we made it work. We're both wanderers. I thought that worked for both of us. I don't know what changed?" Sergio was a prideful man. This entire conversation was bizarre to her.

Half the time they were together—if you could call it that—the connection was physical. They spoke at the same level regarding their art. They had fun with friends and went out, but it never went deeper than that. She didn't share her private thoughts with him as she did with…well, her other friends and cousins. So, after five years of a casual arrangement that had been past due its consumption date, she'd called that shit off.

One day he was in New York talking about going to dinner with some friends and then stopping by her apartment, and an eerie certainty descended on her. She ended their arrangement that same day.

Now, standing with him, that same sense of certainty invaded her again, reminding her of all the reasons they were better off apart.

"What changed was I wasn't good with casual anymore, and I wasn't looking for anything serious either. Better alone than dealing with some of the drama that started between us. You always reminded me we weren't exclusive, and while you fucked other women and men, it was ok. But when I started fucking other men, it was a problem. I just couldn't deal with the hypocrisy of it all," she said, confused as to why she was explaining this to Sergio so long after the fact. She'd never pictured him as pining for what they had, but here he was, scowling at her words.

"You just never saw it, did you?" he asked her incredulously. Was this the Twilight Zone, and she'd taken the wrong turn?

"Serg, this is not the right place…" She noticed the models exiting the poolside suite the hotel had provided as a dressing room.

"It never is with you," he said, and she heard a pain that implied Sergio was the wounded party in their story, though she didn't understand what could possibly allow him to think that.

"Are you serious right now? Listen." She grasped his arm and felt the way his body jerked in response. He lowered his eyes, and she used the unguarded reaction to push him as far away as she could from everyone else involved in the shoot.

"I don't know what this is, but I need you to focus on your job, on what we are here to do. These are gonna be some long months if we can't get our act together."

Sergio's face was scrunched up in thought, a trait she'd once found endearing and now considered unattractive. Damn, she truly had moved on from him.

"Fine…because I'm a professional, and I know you are, too. But we need to talk at some point. I mean, you had a baby!" His voice rose in volume with each word he expressed at the same pace her sighs increased in length. She gave him a second to get himself back to the task at hand, rubbing her temple to calm the pressure gathering there.

"Shh, stop with the drama. Let's get to work," Aayala said, spinning on her feet in the direction of the models.

It seemed that work would not be the refuge she'd been looking for…

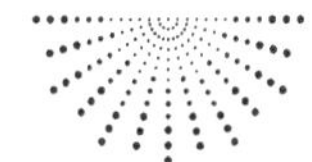

CHAPTER TEN

Peace. Cotton soft and tender, small, tiny buttons that defied every attempt to be hooked into the equally small holes they belonged to. Perfectly folded arms, brightly white with light blue clouds, and long-sleeved footies.

Malik watched raindrops against the window of Aayala's office, aka his room, as soft reggae played. The routine of washing and folding had become one of his favorite habits.

He thrived in following steps that together formed tasks that filled his days with expected seconds. There was security in routine. His friends and family might think he was adventurous spending his days at sea, but stability was what Malik had always craved.

His dad had provided that stability with the sacrifices he made with his job. He'd known early on that compared to many of the kids on the block, he was lucky. They might not be flush in the pockets, but his family was good. His dad held it down for them.

He'd been able to fully focus on his basketball scholarship because of his dad. Back in the day when he played ball, he'd loved the drills his coach would give him. He'd been the only one on the court with a smile on his face while running 17s. The same stability he felt at home he had felt on the basketball court.

The knowledge that he was creating habits that made his and Aayala's lives easier filled him with a deep satisfaction. That made him take a beat. Malik hadn't felt this fulfilled in a long, long time.

Every time Aayala protested after he cooked, cleaned, or got the groceries, he felt a warm glow deep in his belly that no cold looks could smoke away. Every frown Malik watched transform into a hidden smile on Aayala's face turned the dark coals inside his chest into brightly lit sparks.

The dictionary said the definition of obstinate was refusing to change your ways or ideas, but they hadn't met Aayala when they wrote that entry. She'd wake up before him and Andre, getting up as early as five a.m. to beat him downstairs to make breakfast, claiming she had to work early or start on a project. Or if he went out with Andre to his parents, she would manage to clean up the house by the time they had returned.

But what Aayala kept forgetting was that if she was the definition of obstinate, he was the definition of persuasion. He would find a way for her to lower her guard enough and let herself be taken care of for once. She was already relenting in small ways. Her new habit of sending him a text asking what was for dinner was evidence his campaign was effective.

Shuffling sounds from the baby monitor announced the end of Andre's nap time, pulling him from his strategic planning and into the present.

"Ok, little man, what do we have— Oh damn, Andre, this is a serious diaper you got for me." The distinctive smell of breastfed poop hit his nose, a combination of spoiled sweet milk and baby powder overpowering him for a moment. He held his breath before going in.

"Yo! How can so much shit come from someone so little?" he asked, and Andre kicked his legs up, making Malik move fast to secure the little chunky extremities.

"Alright, boss, let's get you cleaned up, so we can go downstairs and finish dinner for your mama, alright?" With deft precision, Malik had Andre dry and smelling right in no time.

He patted himself on the back and went on to his next task with Andre in hand, the two perfect mates navigating the house as if it was the deck of the Gloriana, his regular tanker.

Changing the music to '90s hip-hop, he prepared a meal he knew would impress Aayala, rice and peas with plantains and curry chicken.

When the door swung open, and a tired Aayala walked in with her camera bag in one hand and her pumping bag in the other, Malik's entire body relaxed in her presence, the air crackling with electricity, a current only present when she was in the room.

Damn. He truly needed to keep his eagerness for her in check. There was nothing more here than friendship—at least on her side.

When he noticed the bags under her eyes, his fist clenched, and when Andre wailed and stretched his little hand toward his mama, he knew exactly what the little man was feeling. After all, Malik wished he could stretch his arms and hold her tight until he made her tiredness melt away.

"What's up?" he asked instead of saying the things he truly wanted to say.

"Nothing much. I'm beat, traffic was brutal. I think there was some accident on 595, so shit was a mess. Hold on, baby, mama has to go and change so she can pick you up with clean clothes," Aayala said, her eyes tired but content as they lay on her son.

Then her eyes turned to Malik, and they widened in appreciation, her pupils dilating at the sight of him. Malik watched her tongue sweep across her bottom lip before her upper teeth grabbed a hold of the plump lushness. And he remembered. God, he remembered.

She took a deep breath as if steeling herself from…what? Him? Her attraction to him? He knew there was something there, simmering below it all, but he knew she was adamant not to pursue anything, so the blatant look of need she'd just given him was messing with his brain and other parts of his body. Heat that had nothing to do with the stove flicked his skin, intensifying every spot her eyes touched.

Then Aayala took another deep breath, and her face went from lust to a different type of want.

"Curry goat?" she asked hopefully.

"Curry chicken. I ain't no master cook yet, but soon I'll try some curry goat for you," he answered, still keyed up from her perusal.

"Alright, let me go wash my hands and take off these clothes…and…and…" She stared at him again, her eyes traveling up and down his body, then back to his face. "And I'll be right back down, ok?" The heat in her gaze had him burning up, that warm glow inside of him growing at the mere possibility of what it could imply. If she slipped just once, he was ready to catch her.

"I'M TAKING ALL THE CREDIT FOR THIS DINNER," AAYALA SAID, A smug smile adorning her face. The lines of tiredness were still there, but her eyes shined with a mischief Malik had missed seeing from her.

Aayala might be tired, but it wasn't dire anymore. He noticed that something had shifted these few weeks since he'd been here, and she seemed more balanced. Malik allowed his own sense of smugness to take over, seeing her playful with her guard as down as it could ever be with her.

"Now tell me, Aayala, why you think you can take credit for my cooking?"

"Please, I taught you all you know about cooking!" She smirked. Andre lay in his pack and play next to them, for the moment entertained with his hanging toys.

"You sound mighty full of yourself when you damn well know my mama taught me to cook."

"Well, fine, you right, but I taught you about Jamaican cooking."

"That I can't argue with. You introduced me to everything Jamaican."

"I know. To the point you are ready to become an honorary yardie. I heard that album you were playing last night before bed."

"I told you I was going to get it," he said, bending into the pack and play to give Andre a rattle. Andre cooed at the toy, his hands attempting to grab the item with limited dexterity.

"Yeah, you did. Now you know another Bob Marley deep cut," she countered, taking a sip of her water, her thick lips blossoming into a satisfied smile.

"Aha, but it's not Bob singing, it's—" he started, excited to prove he knew something she might not about Jamaican music.

"I know, I know, Junior Brathwaite. But it's still "It Hurts to Be Alone" by Bob Marley and the Wailers on the record."

"Is there anything you don't know?"

"With a father obsessed with music? I think not. I don't see Winston often, but when I do, all we talk about is music. It's his passion, you know that," she said, shrugging. Aayala made to stand up, and he gave her a look. For once, she heeded his request, settling back down, submitting to his service. She trailed him with her eyes while Malik got up and cleared the table, filling up the dishwasher with their plates. He wanted to touch upon the subject of her father. She rarely spoke of him, always referring to him as Winston instead of dad. The little he had gleaned in the years was that she faulted her mom more than her dad for all the traveling they both did, often away from their only daughter. But the moment passed, and he knew she would close up if he said anything else.

"You know better by now, Aayala."

"And you know better as well. I don't need all this fuss, I can do it on my own," she said, but he could hear the weariness in her voice, the way her words dragged just a little around the ends as sleepiness pulled at her.

"You are exhausted. Go upstairs."

"I need to nurse Andre first," she protested.

"That's alright. Go with him, and I'll be up shortly to get little man settled for bed."

He could feel the push so strongly from Aayala hesitating to ignore his request, the air taut with their clash of wills until the tension released, and Aayala's shoulders dropped, her eyes never leaving his.

"Ok."

TONIGHT, BOTH MOTHER AND SON HAD GIVEN HIM THE hardest time settling down.

Malik's entire back and neck were hard as a rock. He needed to wind down and remembered he still had some of the laundry clothes to fold. He planned to turn his music on, finish folding, and hopefully catch a couple of hours before the baby's first wake-up.

Minutes flew by, and he felt his back and neck dissolve into normal muscle when he heard a loud thud. He quickly scanned the room, his ears straining to detect where the sound had originated, and he quickly realized it was from Aayala's room.

Again?

Caution warred with curiosity and, underneath it all, a desire to be in her presence. In the end, there was no contest. His feet had already carried him outside her door.

He was about to knock when he heard a groan, then a deep, low wail, followed by sniffles. His entire mind and body shifted from tentative curiosity to dragonslayer, ready to resolve whatever was making Aayala cry.

"Aayala? Aayala, are you ok?"

No answer.

He squeezed his eyes shut, his neck and back seizing up again.

"Aayala, I need to know you're alright." In a momentary lapse of judgment, he yanked her door open to find her on her bed, face tear-stricken, wearing black panties and a tank top. Her eyes were wide, chest rising and falling in rapid motion. Her hair was in a silk wrapper, and her clothes were askew. He could see one of her breasts attempting to escape the top. If he squinted, he could see a glimpse of that place he'd only known last October.

Lord have mercy.

His mind cataloged each and every detail, saving the delicious bits for later, focusing on her distress now.

"What's wrong? I was calling your name. I heard you crying. Are you alright?" Malik's feet carried him to the side of her bed, looking down at her, wishing she would confide in him so he could make whatever was wrong go away. His hands itched to reach out for her, but the tears still trailing down her face and the shocked gaze turning into indignation told him he better stay where he was.

"What are you doing in my room?" she hissed.

Deep breaths.

"Aayala, you were crying. I heard a thud. I didn't know if you had fallen and hurt yourself. How the fuck was I to know what was happening here? And I called out for you. I asked you if you were ok."

She went from belligerent to distraught all over again, the whiplash of her emotions jerking him around as well.

"Sorry, I didn't… I didn't hear…" she mumbled, and he finally saw what she was holding in her hand.

A vibrator.

CHAPTER ELEVEN

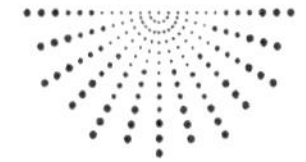

A fucking vibrator was in Aayala's hand. And Malik had been next door, *hungry*.

"Yo, I'mma… I'm sorry, Aayala, I thought you needed help. I shouldn't have pushed in like that," he said, his tongue moving sluggishly in his mouth, his mind picturing and failing to put together a scenario that made sense. Why was she crying? Was her orgasm that good? Had she cried when she came that night before they realized the condom had broken and the night took a turn? Fuck. He would have remembered tears. Something was wrong. He could sense it. The air around them felt strained and saturated with desperation.

What the fuck is wrong, and how can I make it better?

"It's alright… I'm overreacting."

"Don't. Don't minimize whatever's wrong. If you don't wanna tell me, that's ok, but don't." He couldn't help the extra punch his voice carried, but every part of his body tensed in frustration, waiting to hear how he could help her. He wanted…no, he needed to erase the tears falling down her cheeks.

"It's ok, Malik. I'm—" She paused, and he could see her struggling to put up her walls. He rejoiced because it was hard for her. It should be as hard as it was for him to stand here, unable to help her.

"I can't orgasm."

His brain took in the words and did its job of translating and absorbing the data he'd just received. He understood in plain terms what she had said, but again, the toy in her hand fucked with his comprehension, and he had to ask her to clarify.

"Come again?"

She chuckled, the sound devoid of all humor, and he felt the pain behind it deep in his gut. "That's the problem. I can't. Something is wrong with me."

The air stilled, and the desperation saturating the space was cautiously replaced by another feeling emanating from her. He couldn't name what it was, but it constricted his throat, and his hands felt heavier than usual. The steel everpresent in Aayala had disappeared, and she slumped against the headboard of her bed, exhaustion taking over.

"I can't orgasm. I'd never had issues before, never. We've talked enough, you and I, for you to know how I am about my sexual life. Open and healthy."

Malik nodded along, feeling the weight of each word settle on his shoulders. She was right. They had in the past spoken about their sexual lives in a sort of friendly, innocent way that had never felt charged with anything…outside of the few lustful thoughts he'd used in his beat-off sessions. He was no angel.

That knowledge had helped him that fateful night in October. Somehow, his mind had stored each tidbit she'd shared in the past, holding onto the knowledge for future use. Somehow, he'd anticipated without knowing they would always end up falling in lust, even if only for one night.

"But since the birth…" She shook her head and swatted her hand as if waving away mosquitos.

"What happened during Andre's birth? You haven't said anything to me about it."

"It was what it was. Preeclampsia. Licy's mom was visiting with her, and she took one look at me and said something in Spanish. Licy stood up and asked me to get dressed, saying that they were going to take me to the hospital. I refused. I felt fine. But something in my aunt's eyes scared me, so I let them take me. Thank the spirit I did because my blood pressure was through the roof. Less than two hours later, Andre was here. I fought the OB every step of the way. I wanted a natural birth, and… But they did the right thing. He didn't even let me get dilated," she whispered, the last words barely audible.

"Once I got the all-clear after the six weeks, I tried rubbing one out." She shrugged apologetically and smiled, the toy still dangling from her fingers, black and gold glinting in the dim light of her room. "But it didn't work. I did all the usual things that turned me on. And I did get hot and heavy, but when it was time to go over the finish line… nothin'. I've tried everything. Vibrators, dildos, baths…"

He wanted to ask her if she let another nigga touch her, his chest tight with the knowledge that she owed him no allegiance but wanting to know all the same.

"Did you try fucking anyone?" he growled.

She gazed at him, some of her fire returning to her eyes, the heat warming him from where he stood by her bed. "No, but I've thought about it."

"You better not go back to that punk ass Sergio," he demanded, the tightness of his back and neck spreading all around his body.

"What, Sergio?" She frowned, her head jerking back in surprise. "Nah, Sergio is… No, you know that's long gone."

The words from her mouth did good to his muscles, allowing him to release some of the tension at seeing her perplexed look.

"I don't think you need to have sex just yet. And if you do need to fuck, who better than me to help you?" he told her bluntly. He knew whatever was bothering her was more than just not orgasming, but in true Aayala form, she had boiled it down to a tangible thing that had, in theory, a straightforward solution. His chest ached still, and he knew that something else was operating here, but he didn't know if she was aware.

"Ok, here's what we're going to do."

"We?" she asked, her sculpted eyebrows arching up. "There is no *we* in this. I'll figure this out on my own."

"Baby girl…" he crooned and hid a smile when he saw her shiver. He nodded toward the bed, and she granted her permission for him to sit down. "Listen, I told you when I moved in, and I'll tell you again. You aren't in this by yourself. You got me. We are friends, aren't we?" he asked, and she nodded skeptically.

"Well, let me help you. Look, whatever we do, I'll help you…but I won't fuck you." He was glad when he saw her frown in confusion. He leaned into her until he was close enough to see the dried tracks of her tears. Her mouth parted, and he saw that pretty little tongue of hers dart out between those thick, gorgeous lips.

"Yeah, I'll help you with my hands, with my lips, with your toys. I'll help you relax until you get to where you need to be mentally to be able to orgasm. You're probably working yourself up and overthinking that shit too much. It's what you do. Sometimes you just need to go with the flow. Let shit happen. And I'm gonna assist with that. But I won't fuck you. Nah. If you want me inside of you, you'll have to fuck me first," he promised.

He saw her chest rise sharply, but she held that gasp in by the sheer force of her obstinate nature.

"So think about it, a'ight? You know where I sleep."

And he left her in the room with the promise of release on the tips of his fingers.

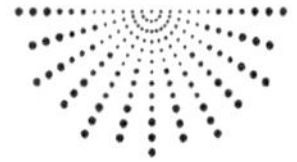

"I'on know why I need to be here," Damian scoffed as he trailed behind Malik into the Center.

"You've taken two years to figure out what you want instead of enrolling in college, so I want you to see what it looks like to have limited options."

The Center buzzed with energy as about twenty students gathered in the great hall around tables, chatting it up. It was a testament to Gabo and Mason's work that these kids gave up their Saturday mornings to come and listen to different lectures about opportunities for college and other high-paying vocational jobs. The work that Gabo and Mason were doing here would allow these sports-oriented students to branch out if they didn't get scholarships like what happened to him all those years ago.

In contrast to the excitement, the sullen energy coming from his brother tried to take over Malik's good humor, but Malik could always find his center and retreat there if needed. With all the energies surrounding him, he locked that shit down.

"Yo, fix your face. You're a grown man now. Come, there's Cap with Gabo."

A series of grunts was all he got from Damian. Malik approached Cap, joy taking over at the sight of the old man.

"Cap! So glad you could make it and come and talk to the kids. So, Bonnie let you out at last?"

"Ha! My boy, Bonnie don't need to give me permission to go anywhere, I'm the captain of that house," Cap said, clapping Malik on the back.

"What's up, G?"

"All good, chillin' here with Cap before the lecture starts. Again, thank you for hooking us up with Cap and the others that have come through. The series about merchant marines has become really popular. The kids look up to you, Malik," Gabo said, face full of gratitude.

The sight of Gabo's face threatened to pull Malik away from the vault he kept himself safe in from too many energies around him, but he couldn't help but let his heart feel the gratitude and be humbled again by the work he'd been able to do with his friends these past weeks whenever Aayala was home with Andre.

"Nah, come on, bruh. No thanks needed." Malik shook his head, dispelling the notion.

"Damian, I haven't seen you in a minute, man. What you up to?" Gabo dapped Damian, who returned the greeting with a lukewarm shrug. Then, showcasing a little of the good upbringing they'd both received, he greeted Cap as well.

"Not much, you know, hustling a bit here and there," Damian mumbled.

Malik made eye contact with Gabo before averting his eyes. Damian hadn't hustled a day in his life, but he was gonna let this one slide and let his brother brag about his overnight job at the old people's home.

"Word? So, taking care of the little old grandpas and grandmas giving you some bread?" Gabo asked him with interest. *The asshole.* Gabo knew the contention between Malik and Damian and the college talk and was just stoking the fire.

The work at the old folks' home wasn't bad. His momma had been doing it for years and loved the job. It was honest work. But he knew his brother, and he knew that wasn't what Damian wanted.

"Yeah, I make good bread there, and I'm working as a bouncer a couple of nights at a strip club. I'm making do," Damian bragged, pursing his lips and shrugging Gabo off.

"Ok. Let's get settled so we can start. Bonnie wants me back home for lunch. She said I gotta take my meds with food. Come, boy, walk with me to the front. You'll help me with the papers that I brought that need to be distributed," Cap announced to Damian, who made a face of resignation but dutifully followed along. A pang shook Malik at the thought of Cap's age showing as he watched the old man walk up to the front of the room.

"Have you considered Cap's offer? Taken a look at getting your captain's papers?" Gabo's whisper followed the thread of Malik's thought as Cap hobbled to the front. Cap was invincible in his eyes and knowing the man was considering retirement was sobering.

"Nah, I have the requirements at Aayala's home, but I haven't done much with it. What I make with the tanker…"

"I know, I know. I don't need a reminder that you are low-key rich," Gabo muttered, and Malik sucked his teeth at the words. Gabo was doing alright as well. He was frugal when he needed to be and had saved up and invested wisely through the years.

Gabo had taught both Mason and Malik how to invest courtesy of his dad's knowledge, and once Daniel came into Mason's life, they'd all learned to diversify even further. But

Malik knew a lot of those savings had gone to the Center. He shook his head, wondering how he could help his two friends and their work.

"But Malik, you got other responsibilities now. Besides, you got money saved, and your parents are good. They have the settlement now from your dad, thanks to your perseverance."

"I know, Gabo. But I need to make sure Damian is set up. I can't let him become a burden to my pops. He overprotects that boy too much. Doesn't deny him anything. Finally, he's gotten justice years later after his workplace accident. I want him to enjoy that money, not have to feed Damian 'til Damian is gray at the temples." There was more to it than that. And it was hard to be so open and vulnerable with his friend, but fuck it, he needed to talk it through.

"Also, the thought of starting over…" Malik shook his head, looking up, trying to find answers to unanswerable questions.

"Yeah, but you won't be starting over if you take Cap's offer. Let's sit in the back so we don't interrupt. But think about it, man. Cap is right. It's time for you to slow down a little." Gabo's words managed to penetrate the vault, and Malik spent the rest of the lecture in conflicted thought.

"That was great, Cap. I really appreciate how real you were with the kids."

Gabo shook Cap's hand profusely. The students had left after the lecture, only the four of them remaining in the Center.

"Young man, did you get anything from it? Thinking of going another route like your brother?" Cap asked Damian.

Malik waited, the picture of nonchalance on the outside,

not showing how he held his breath waiting for his brother's response. All the work he'd done through the years was for Damian *not* to have to take drastic measures like Malik had to take back then.

He wanted his brother to have the opportunities. *All* the opportunities.

Damian seemed more engaged. Cap had worked his magic on him and gotten him to speak a few words after the lecture compared to the early grunts he'd gotten.

"Nah, I'on wanna be away from my mom and pops like that. They need me at home to help, you know," Damian said.

What the... It took everything in Malik not to let his face show his incredulity. There was nothing that was fixed in that house. Everything waited for Malik to arrive. If anything, his parents did more for Damian than the other way around. Malik was relieved Damian didn't want to be a merchant mariner, but it appalled him that it was for all the wrong reasons.

Damian's phone buzzed, and he pulled it out of his pants.

"Look, Malik, I'mma bounce. You don't need to drop me off at home. My homeboy is outside."

"I'll walk out with you if you don't mind. I need to go home to my Bonnie," Cap told Damian, and Damian nodded, waiting for Cap to exit with him. The two left in quiet conversation, leaving Gabo and Malik in the entrance hall.

"Did he really just..." Gabo started.

"Say he helps out at home? Yep," Malik finished.

"Look, I think you need to let Damian figure shit out on his own. He's too grown for you to be steering his life anymore," Gabo said as they walked into his office.

Gabo perched himself on his desk, and Malik unfolded his long frame into the large chair in the corner. Gabo's office had a sofa just like Mason's, but he knew Gabo and Licy had christened the sofa one time too many.

"I know what you are thinking…" Gabo started, pausing as Mason and Daniel walked into the office.

"Why y'all look like that?" he asked, skepticism coloring each syllable out of his mouth.

"Look like what?" Mason asked, staring at Gabo with a hint of defiance.

Malik swung his head between Gabo and Mason and wondered what the underlying tension was all about. To the naked eye, it wasn't noticeable, but he'd known these two since they were pre-teens.

"You know what. Daniel has three wrinkles on his polo." Gabo gestured at Daniel, who did look slightly wrinkled, which was unlike him.

Daniel's mouth twitched, and Malik caught on. Oh, they'd been fucking.

"Corey told me Licy was here last night." Mason quirked an eyebrow at Gabo as if he were slinging it at him. Malik made eye contact with Daniel. Daniel shrugged and smirked.

"So y'all were here all along?" Malik asked Daniel.

"Yeah, we'd planned to listen to the lecture, but…" Daniel shrugged, and Malik guffawed at both Mason and Gabo, now holding a staring contest.

"Y'all keep fucking at y'all place of work. It's getting predictable now. And why do you keep getting mad at each other? You both do it. Just own up to it." Malik shook his head.

Daniel nodded, his face as serious as ever. "I think it's something about the desks and the couch."

"Come on now. We said we would stop!" Gabo threw his hands up.

"You said that, but Licy was here last night." Mason crossed his arms, leaning against the door.

"Yeah, well, yeah, but it was the last time," Gabo said sheepishly.

"So this was ours," Mason lobbed back, gesturing at Daniel, who pursed his lips in doubt.

"Y'all goofy," Malik said, enjoying the back and forth too much. It helped him forget about his worries.

"Hold on, so you're the only one that gets to go unscathed? Nah, bruh. How's your living arrangement?" Mason pulled away from the office door and plunked himself on the couch.

"Yeah, how's Aayala?" Gabo nodded at him.

A tingle started in his hands and spread throughout his arms and legs at the sound of her name. He'd always been aware whenever she was mentioned but only in a friendly sort of interest. But with how things were transpiring with them, suddenly that awareness felt multiplied in intensity.

"Ooooh, that face you just made is very interesting," Mason said.

"I don't think I've ever seen that expression." Gabo chuckled and shook his head. "You're in trouble, my dude."

Malik stripped himself of all outward emotion, not ready to explore with words what was compelling him to offer Aayala assistance in her orgasm troubles. He'd managed to keep his thoughts of her in that same vault he used when he was feeling too much because she definitely overstimulated him.

"Y'all don't know what you're talking about," Malik scoffed.

"Oh, ho, ho, ho! As if we haven't been there, done that. Tell him, Daniel." Mason nodded at his boyfriend.

"Yeah, man, you know I don't join the pile-ons, but you did have a look. Like you're in too deep. And we've all been there, so we kinda know where that's going..." Daniel told him.

A frisson of awareness crackled at Daniel's words, but Malik knew it wasn't as simple as all that for him and Aayala.

There were true obstacles that would prevent them from ever being more than friends and parents to Andre.

"None of you worked away from home over six months a year, so in fact, y'all don't know. But that's a'ight, I'll let you feel that smugness for a minute. I'm not gonna lie and say I'm not feeling Aayala because that would dishonor her, and I wouldn't lie on that woman, but her and I know the stakes, and we aren't looking to complicate things. So, I'm gonna need for y'all to chill. There is nothing more between her and I than friendship," Malik explained while his stomach performed backstrokes away from his center.

"We all thought that at one moment or the other. But we will let you feel that smugness. Because we know we right," Daniel said.

And fuck if that didn't make Malik's heart skip in hope.

CHAPTER THIRTEEN

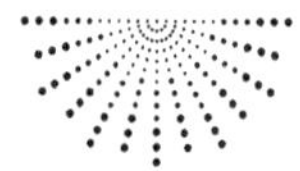

The electronic tone threading through the smooth reggae tunes and vibrating through her wall told her Malik was listening to dub. They were both lucky Andre was a deep sleeper who wasn't bothered by TV or music.

Aayala smiled as her body swayed like a leaf in the wind, letting the music carry her stress away. The years and their friendship had exposed Malik to the best of reggae music, so much he had adopted it as his own. No man she'd ever been with had taken this amount of interest and care of the things she liked. Malik, on the other hand, just by the design of their friendship, had always shown her how much he valued her thoughts and interests.

Their friendship wasn't a boisterous one; it was composed of lengthy messages, exchanges of ideas, quiet support during the hard times, deep confessions, and zero judgment. It was as comfortable and reliable as the terrycloth robe she wore on the nights she needed extra layers to keep away the chill of the late hour.

Right now, she needed that comfort and reliability.

Aayala sat on the loveseat in the corner of her room with an erotic novel in one hand and one of her favorite toys in the other. In a moment of desperation, she'd confided in Licy and Mari about her dilemma, leading to a plethora of recommendations on how to bring her orgasms back.

So here she was, being seduced by black letters on white paper. The book Licy had recommended was hot, straight to the point, and nasty. She loved it, and it had done its job, igniting her nerves with sweet anticipation.

She felt the familiar wetness between her legs, her center pulsating in need. All her nerve endings were on high alert, hoping this time was the one where she'd be able to release all this pent-up force that had nowhere to go.

She'd promised herself she wouldn't use the toy until she was so close to her orgasm that her pussy was clenching in desperation.

Her perfidious pum pum claimed to be ready for tonight but kept whispering reminders of who else was under her roof, listening to one of her favorite songs right next door.

Why not just go to him? All these words and toys couldn't do what he did to us, her punnani reminded her.

"Shhhh," she responded aloud. "What we're not going to do is give up tonight, alright? We can do this together…"

A flash of memory assaulted her: Malik's long strokes keeping her pinned to the car while she whimpered in satisfaction, her cream dripping from between her legs to mingle with her nylon tights, which he'd ripped in a moment of desperation.

Her clit throbbed in remembrance, and she moaned lightly, the sound ripped from deep within her where she kept her desire for Malik at bay.

The bass of the reggae made her walls vibrate on a low frequency that sneaked all the way in from between her legs to the middle of her chest. The music penetrated her entirely the way she wished Malik would penetrate her.

She turned on the toy and placed it between her legs, wishing she could chase away the yearning coalescing deep within her, the buzz of the vibrator melding with the bass of the big tune, making her sigh in relief.

But that sigh was premature, her relief quickly turning to trepidation as she attempted to drive herself further along to her orgasm. The more she wanted it, the more it faded away from her. She picked up the book again, hoping to escape in the pages filled with illicit desire, but nothing was doing it for her.

She heard the song change next door, the bass shifting in tempo to a slower pace, and her heart synched up with the rhythm, bringing her anticipation down to a simmer. The toy stopped working for her, overstimulating to the point of discomfort, so she tossed it to the side.

Aayala closed her eyes, the emptiness that visited her after each failed attempt spreading quicker than on other nights.

The bass shifted yet again, and she could swear the song was calling to her, telling her to go to Malik.

Hesitant and disheartened, she stood up, gathered all her determination, and went to his room.

AAYALA'S HAND SHOOK A LITTLE WHEN SHE KNOCKED ON HIS door, but she pictured the palm trees by the beach in her father's hometown, how they survived all types of hurricanes, and held onto the strength she had.

She hadn't changed, still in her terrycloth robe and her usual black tank top and panties, instinctively knowing if she placed one ounce of thought on what to wear, she would have stayed in her room, dwelling on all the ways her body had transformed after pregnancy.

The music lowered all the way down, and a tinge of trepidation spiked through her.

"Come in."

She strolled in with purpose, finding Malik sitting on one of her office chairs wearing glasses, with a book on his lap, bare-chested in basketball shorts. Her eyes lost themselves in the lean lines of his chest and arms, his taut stomach. Then she went back up to see his glasses, which gave her a rush of tenderness when she heard his snicker.

"Got a good look?" he asked her, still smiling, utterly relaxed. He put the book down on his lap and pushed up to stand, towering over her with his height.

"Sorry, but yeah. Yeah, I did." She shrugged. Might as well start as brazen as she meant to be.

"What's up, Aayala? You should be in bed asleep. But here you are…restless. My offer stands."

"That's why I am here. I want what you offered."

An expression of yearning and triumph flashed on Malik's face, but he quickly hid his feelings behind his eternal mask of nonchalance.

"Are you sure?"

"I'm sure I'm tired of trying and not getting anywhere. Today I took a bath, read erotica, and had a toy. And nothing," she said, the desperation of the night seeping through every pore of her body.

Malik gazed at her with intensity, then went back to his heavy-lidded stare that hid so much. All of her bravado dissipated, and she felt her cheeks warm. Standing here in her office, asking of him what she'd promised herself not to seek, was completely out of character for her. She turned on her heels, ready to walk out when she felt his warm, large hand on her neck. All of her touch receptors sent *yessssss* signals to her brain.

His other hand snaked inside her robe across her belly, and she flinched at the touch of his hardened arm against her soft, scarred stomach, heat searing through his path. His hand clasped her hip, and he nuzzled her into him.

"Today, we start slow. You're so in your head, you can't even relax. Let me help you relax." He whispered in her ear, his warm breath kissing her skin, making all the hairs on her body stand at attention. His scent of teakwood swirled around her, and for a moment, she felt lightheaded, her center of gravity shifting. The promise in Malik's voice. The idea of putting all the effort into his hands was the most tempting gift. And she was going to accept it. Because she was tired of doing it all alone.

"Ok. Here or my room?"

"Your room," he answered while the hand on her neck ghosted down from her chest to the middle of her breasts, pausing there, making her shiver in anticipation.

Where will his hand go next? He shifted it to the side, brushing against her left breast, and she froze. He felt the tension of her body and course-corrected, gliding his hand down the middle of her breasts, circling her belly, and ending on the top of her right thigh.

"Go ahead. I'll follow wherever you go." His lips touched right below her right ear, and Aayala couldn't help but melt against him. The moment her back and ass rested against him, she felt the hardness of his entire body. She felt his dick throb against her, and she couldn't resist but rub herself slightly against all of him.

Malik grunted and tightened his fingers around her hip and thigh in warning.

"Go ahead, Aayala. Now," he commanded. And she'll be damned, she followed his instructions to the letter.

Back in her room, she could feel Malik's heat behind her. She hadn't bothered looking back, confident in the fact that he was right there.

"Do you have any body oil?" His voice sounded deeper than normal. It reminded her of *that* night. Her pum pum tingled in recognition. If her pussy could talk, she would have purred a *Hi, Malik* in response.

"Yeah, on my bathroom counter."

She heard him rummage in her bathroom and return with something in his hands. Still, she refused to turn around and look at him, reminding her of that balmy night last October when she took everything he had to give, still trying to deny in her mind that she was fucking her best friend.

"Do you want to do this with clothes or without?"

"What is it we are doing?" She jumped when she heard the cap of the body oil open in the quiet room.

"I'm going to give you a massage."

"Oh, I forgot. You are a master masseuse, courtesy of your ex in Indonesia." She couldn't help the current of nervousness that made her voice threadier than usual. She cleared her throat, intent on finding her steel.

"She isn't my ex. We were never together, but yeah, she taught me a lot. Clothes on or off?"

"On. I mean, I'll take off the robe, though," she answered, dropping the robe. Still, she stood facing her bed, refusing to make eye contact with him, making the moment intensify with mystery. The air swirled with contained desire and temptation all wrapped up in Malik's scent. Her room suddenly felt so much smaller with him inside it, and she had to take deep breaths to calm her racing heart.

"I can't say I've forgotten how beautiful you are because I haven't forgotten one second of that night. And now I can see you with better lighting. You're extraordinary," Malik said, awe coloring every word, but at the reminder of lighting, she shrunk a little, glad that her lights were dimmed and she had agreed to keep her tank top and panties on.

"Whatever made you slump like that, get it out of your mind," he commanded. "You. Are. Magnificent. I wish I could see your face right now, but I can tell this is a lot, and I promised we would take it slow. Lay down."

Her body seemed to be his poppet because before she could register his words in her mind, she was already laying down, her face turned to one side, propped up on her pillow.

She waited, breath caught in her throat like a dragonfly in amber, waited to feel those large hands on her trembling body, but he had other thoughts.

"You know, I dream about you at least once a week, if not more," he told her, using one of the calming techniques she used on her boudoir clients, talking to them until they relaxed. There was a little voice in the back of her mind reminding her not to enjoy this too much. She was liable to get used to this good living, and he wouldn't be around to provide it any time she was too stressed. Then a louder voice interjected with *shhhhh, just let me enjoy this!* It sounded very much like that backstabbing pussy of hers.

"There are some nights that I wake up and I'm rock hard, my dick throbbing in my hand, convinced your out-of-this-world pussy was surrounding it. When I was at sea, and I had a few hours to myself, I would close my eyes and just play all the memories of that night on repeat. I haven't ever jacked myself as much as I did these last six months, not even when I was a teenager." His deep, low voice kept her lying still on the bed, her ears straining to catch each inflection and change of tone. Everything he was feeling, he transmitted to her via his words, activating them like weapons of pleasure, and she hadn't been prepared for the assault.

"There were nights at the tanker that I would wake up sticky and warm in my own cum, my dick still pulsing with the need to be inside you again. To hear your mewls, your pleasure, to feel your warm, silky skin under my hands. To be in your presence once more," he confessed, and she couldn't help but mewl in echo of the memories he evoked. Her complete attention was zeroed in on him, her body attuned to his every breath, every word.

When his warm hands, lubricated by the oil, met her shoulders, she became one with the bed. Thoughts swirled around her mind about that fateful night. Somehow, the music was back on, and the smooth tunes of "Night Nurse" by Gregory Isaacs greeted her ears.

Malik's large hands glided and kneaded her tired muscles, the oil softening her skin with the heat he created. He slipped his hands under her tank top and worked on each knot in her back, washing away all her worries like waves on a sandy beach. Her mind refused to focus on anything but his hands, the memories he evoked, and the music. Her pussy tingled in excitement, ready for the race once more, but Malik's soft words of encouragement reminded her to relax and unwind.

"You're tensing up, beautiful. Let go. Relax for me. You know, when you told me this wouldn't happen again, I believed you. But I want you to know I'm prepared for the honor you bestowed upon me today. Rest assured, every time you let me help you, I will make it worth your while. Because I've been here with you so many times in my mind," he whispered as his hands traveled down her back toward her ass. He slid his hands under her panties and kneaded her ass like he was working on troublesome dough, and Aayala purred in pleasure, pushing up to receive more of his ministrations, his words lashes of wind against her palm tree.

"Good, beautiful girl. That's what I like to see." He growled, and Aayala felt it deep down in her stomach.

His magical hands continued their work down her thighs to her calves, which he lovingly caressed down to her neglected feet. She tensed up a little when she tried to remember the last time she'd had a pedicure but forgot all about that when she felt his thumbs press a point on her sole that had her heart slowing and her mind quieting down.

"That's it. Relax, baby girl," he whispered as he continued to knead her feet, then made his way to her arms. He worked on her arms with the same loving attention he'd paid the rest of her body, and with each muscle he touched, with each part he massaged, Aayala's eyes fluttered closed, and her breathing slowed to match the easy pace he used to treat her body.

His deep baritone hummed along with the soft reggae music coming from his phone and the vibrations of his voice traveled through his fingertips, adding to the entire multi-sensory experience. Malik's oiled hands worked their way to the sides of her torso, trailing next to her breasts, and for the first time since the birth, she didn't mind the sensual touch there. His fingers lingered on the outside of her tank top, and she nodded her permission, her eyes still closed. Somehow, he'd realized how sensitive she was there and waited for her approval, the mind reader.

He exhaled, his warm breath tickling the back of her neck as she felt his fingers trailing her breasts closer to the nipple, and all of her froze in sweet anticipation of the touch. But just when she thought he would, his hands traveled outward toward her shoulders, ending on her neck, which he massaged, accompanied by playful touches to her ears until her eyes completely closed and her body surrendered to Morpheus's hands. The last thought in her mind as she fell asleep was that it felt good to let go and trust Malik with her troubles.

CHAPTER FOURTEEN

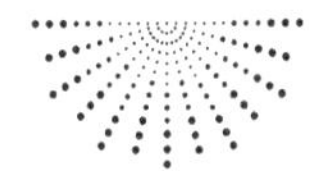

Aayala woke up disoriented from a deep sleep. She gazed around her room and groped around her bed for her cellphone. Her heart pounded inside her chest at the sight of the time.

Ten in the morning!

She hadn't slept this late since before giving birth to Andre. What was she thinking? What the heck did Malik do to her that she completely conked out like that?

And her breasts, the ache in her chest, reminded her she hadn't pumped for over twelve hours. She pulled her pumping machine and strapped it on, feeling immediate relief when the machine started making its tell-tale repetitive sound, which she secretly thought said *suck, suck, suck,* but then again, half the time she was pumping, she was slightly delirious from tiredness.

After emptying her breasts, she went in search of Andre and Malik. She found Malik on the large sofa in the family room folding clothes, and the relaxed manner in which she found him folding her panties made her want to scream.

"What are you doing?" she asked, not liking the fact that it felt damn good to see him sitting there like it was their place and not just hers. After dropping all her defenses the previous night, she was due some rebuilding. She was hastily placing bricks around herself, her vulnerability too over-whelming to keep out in the open.

"Folding your clothes. Did you sleep well?"

"Well, I overslept! Where is Andre? I need to feed him."

He stared at her with interest, taking a second too long to answer her. She felt his bedroom eyes focus on her face, then glide over her body, and she trembled.

"So, where is Andre?"

"It's his morning nap time. You know this. Here, let me put that milk away. You ended up pumping more than he drank, so you're good."

"Don't tell me I'm good! I shouldn't go this long without feeding him or pumping. My supply…"

"Aayala." He turned around after putting the milk away and leaned against the fridge. He was wearing a floral shirt and jeans today, and for some reason, this look was doing it for her. She swallowed hard and focused back on his face, fighting the inevitable pull she felt when around him. He was smiling, the devil.

"Aayala, you look rested. One night that you slept more than normal won't stop your milk production. Andre is good. He needs you well-rested. I need you well-rested. So, I made sure of that."

"I didn't ask you to help me rest." She fisted her hands on her hips. "I asked for help getting me to orgasm."

Yes, and just that. Just orgasms. Nothing else. Nothing like helping her relax and listening to her body and whatever else he did last night. Not him making her ache for all the things they could be if only… That was not what she'd signed up for when she walked into his room.

"Yes. And I don't think you'll be able to do that without

relaxing and getting your mind to slow down and de-stress." He tilted his head, waiting for her rebuttal, and she wanted to scream in frustration. It had to be that because it couldn't be anything else. It couldn't be that he was right.

"Baby girl," he whispered, and even though that was one of her nicknames from her family, the way he said it sounded so different. It spoke to her deep-down buried needs.

"You like it when I call you that, don't you? I remember you told me once you have a bit of a daddy kink. And you know about me. I'm not like our friends who go play and then turn it off. I didn't even know to call it a kink until you told me what it was."

Aayala swallowed, keenly aware she had come downstairs in the same tank top and panties as last night. The way his words were making her wet would be apparent very soon.

"I like to be in control. Nah, that sounds soft as fuck… I *need* to be in control. I need to know you're taken care of, that you're good. And since that night last October, that need drives me every day. I don't want to tell you what to do or what to think, but I do want to ask you to slow down and let me take care of you. I need that control because you are so focused on everything else and not yourself," he said again, talking to her as if this was a walk in the park and they were just shooting the shit or something. His words mesmerized her, painting a picture she wasn't sure she could trust, but oh, she wanted to, so badly.

"I remember what you told me that time when we were writing to each other about what we liked. You said you like to be told what to do on certain occasions. So, I have a proposition for you."

She shifted on her feet and stood straight. She knew she wasn't ready for whatever he had to say, but she couldn't let him see that. Not now. "Go ahead, ask."

"You let me take care of you like I need to…so that this

urge to throw you over my lap and spank you until you listen to me subsides. And you, in turn, be a good girl, and maybe, just maybe, I'll let you call me daddy." He raised his hands when he saw her wanting to speak. "But I won't fuck you. And I'll only help you come, but nothing more...unless you ask."

The conceited...

"You have to be ready, Aayala, and you aren't ready yet. And I'm not looking to push you past any of your limits," he said, and the entreaty in his eyes calmed her raised hackles. That look in his eyes softened her enough to say the truth. The truth that kept emerging when she searched deep within herself and checked in with what she really wanted from him.

"Alright. Let's try all dat. But what happens when you leave? You just get to wreck me?" she asked, speaking into existence the major deterrent to letting Malik have such power in her life. A flash of her fifteen-year-old self raced through her mind: Aayala pulling at her mom at the airport, asking her to stay in Florida with her this time... Asking her to pick *her* this time...

"Aayala... You know this ain't easy for me either. And I wish I had the right answers to reassure you, but what I do... it's what I'm good at. I'm looking to see if I can change my plan to tighten up that timeline so I can be here for you and Andre, but..."

"But you have your family and us to think about." She nodded, an ache spreading through her at his words, but none of them surprised her. Malik was responsible and dedicated to his family. All this kinky talk would not deter him from his responsibilities. And it shouldn't. But where did that leave her and Andre?

"I know it's not what you wanted to hear, but... But I can't lie to you." He shook his head, and the rawness in his voice tugged at everything inside of her that wanted to make him feel better. It tugged at everything inside of her that woke up when he suggested that she gift him her submission. She took a tentative step toward him, wanting to erase the sadness in his eyes.

"I know. It's ok, it's still a yes for me. I'm tired of fighting it, you know. Take care of me to your heart's content. And I'll be good, I promise. And maybe, just maybe I'll gather the courage to let you do more to me. Because Malik?" She whispered now, standing a breath away from a kiss. Her heart pounded in her chest as the air crackled with the unresolved passion between the two of them.

"I, too, dream of you at least once a week, if not more," she confessed, and Malik grabbed that confession, yanked her into his arms, and ravished her. Her heart slammed in her chest at the touch of his lips.

The kiss started as passionate as that night in October, his tongue fighting for dominance and her body and heart surrendering to his touch. His lips devastated her, claiming her with every lick of his tongue. He savored her as if he'd never tasted anything as delicious as her, and when they finally parted enough to breathe, her legs buckled, the passion between them so potent she felt weak at the knees.

With harsh breaths, he rested his forehead against hers.

"Damn, I wasn't ready for that kiss… Baby girl, you're gonna make it so hard not to fuck you every moment we are together. How am I gonna resist you?"

"But what if I don't want you to…daddy?"

Aayala knew the one in trouble was her when Malik made a noise that could only be described as animalistic, turned them around, pushed her against the fridge, and kissed her until he stole her breath away. Because she couldn't wait to tempt him to oblivion.

"ME CAN'T SEE DA BABY FACE!"

The sound of her mother's voice boomed in the family room, mingling with Andre's giggles. His little hands gravitated toward the forehead on the screen, which was all they could see from Aayala's mother.

Aayala wondered who had thought of this great idea... Oh, yeah. Malik.

"Linda, the phone is too close. Yeah, you're too close. Yo! Push back a bit," Malik said, and Aayala knew he was holding back a bark of laughter. Her chest tightened at the tenderness she felt at seeing him interact with her mother so well. Finally, her mother got it together to place the phone somewhere where they could see her entire torso and face, and she, in turn, could see her precious grandson.

"There's ma boy. Oh, he getting plump. What you feedin' him, Aayala? Did you start giving him some plantain porridge?"

"Mum, he's not six months yet." Aayala raised her voice enough for her mother to hear her where she sat on the opposite sofa, shaking her head at Andre and Malik.

"I didn't wait 'til you were six months to give you some porridge," Linda protested.

"I know that, Mum. Different strokes for different folks. Nothing wrong with that."

"Ok, Yankee girl. You do your fancy thing. Sooo, Malik, how you enjoy living with your boy and my girl?" Linda pivoted, her voice full of trouble. Aayala couldn't help the groan that escaped her at her mother's words and aimed a threatening gaze at Malik, who smirked, then winked back at her. Aayala bit the inside of her mouth to stop herself from laughing out loud at his humor.

"I love living with your daughter, Linda. I was looking

forward to spending some time with you too, though," he continued, supporting Aayala with that faint admonishment to her mother. She was grateful but could have told him to save his breath. Nothing ever fazed that woman, not even the pleas of her young daughter back in the day.

"You know, I can't believe I hadn't met you 'til now. And we always missed each other when you've come to visit Aayala in the States," Malik said, handing Andre his new toy.

Aayala stood up, going to the kitchen to prepare her work lunch and check that all was ready before heading out, movements jerky as she kept one ear focused on the conversation in the family room. As Malik's hands were full with Andre, she also started his coffee. She'd noticed his cup was already low.

"I know, boy, I know, you don't have to tell me too much. That girl of mine there has told me plenty of times. *'Mum, you've never met Malik, you know?'* But let me tell you what I tell her. I know I've done right by Aayala. She wasn't a rolling stone like her fada and I am. I wanted to be where her fada was, and I thought she would want that too, but that life didn't suit her. She loved the States, and when he started having opportunities to travel more, she asked to say behind. So, we let her. Between her aunties and my mother-in-law, they took care of her. And my brother always kept a close eye. Aayala nevah wanted for notin," Linda said, as she always said on this subject, finding defense in the knuckle-headed decision she had made to travel the world behind a man that loved her but couldn't offer her fidelity and stability. As always during this topic, an icy chill fell over Aayala to know how disconnected Linda was from the reality of how she had truly felt.

"So yeah, I know there's some censure in your tone about us nevah meeting, but you know, you haven't stayed still in one place for me to meet you eitha, not since you became a lickle man, so there. Pot can't be calling kettle," Linda finished, then made a funny face, and Andre erupted in giggles. On top of the chill she was already feeling, a frisson of unease ran through Aayala to hear the comparison that her mum had just made.

"I miss you, my lickle man. I can't wait to hold you again, ya hear?" Linda's brusque tone mellowed as she spoke to Andre, and Andre again tried to reach out to the phone, recognizing his grandma's voice.

"Listen here, you two. There's no one way to do things, ya know? There ain't no book that tells you what's correct and what's wrong. There are plenty ways to do things. Remember that." And with that sage advice, her mother ended the call.

Aayala turned to Malik, eyebrow raised, shaking away her concerns.

"What? You gotta call your moms, she has to stay connected to Andre, *ya hear?*" Malik said, his last words sounding eerily like Linda. She placed his refilled coffee cup in front of him and saw his eyes flash with something, and that something echoed in places inside of her she couldn't focus on right now. Then he smiled.

"Oh, oh, you got jokes like that, I see. Next time you want to call my mother, can it not be when I'm trying to leave the house to go to work?" Aayala said, grabbing her cooler bag already containing her bottles and pump machine. Her camera bag and supplies rested next to the door, courtesy of Malik's attentiveness.

"I know. That was my bad. We just keep postponing calling her and…"

"Yeah, I know. I'm still a bit vexed with her for leaving so soon, but you are right. I want Andre to talk to her on the regular."

"You got everything?" Malik asked, taking the cooler bag from her hand even though she hadn't offered it to him. In return, he handed her a large bottle of water. He'd been on her case about staying hydrated, to her amused annoyance.

With a dexterity often seen in fathers of two or three kids, Malik juggled her pump bag, her camera bag, and Andre effortlessly. Her mouth watered a little, and she swallowed deeply, trying to dispel her thoughts.

"Are you trying to show off? I'd be struggling with just Andre and a baby bag to get out of the house." She shook her head and followed behind him as he walked toward her car, stopping for a moment to admire how natural little Andre looked, peeking his little face over the top of his father's broad shoulder. The usual tension of the morning faded away, her posture softening as she took a second to take in the two most important men in her life.

"Gotta practice. I take Andre to my mum's the days you work, so him and I have our routine down pat."

"Ok, father of the year. But for real, thanks. You don't have to do all of this."

"Nonsense, I told you I do, and next time you say that to me again, I *will* spank you. And I *will* enjoy it. Now get in the car and go to work before Andre and I hit you up with our double charm and convince you to play hooky."

A thrill ran through Aayala, both at the promise of a spanking and because she'd never been tempted not to go to work before.

She loved what she did. *Loved it.* But the picture of a tall, dark, rugged Malik, wearing black basketball shorts and a ribbed sleeveless undershirt…looking at him hold their son, who had managed to grab Malik's ear and hold it like a shiny new toy, had her reconsidering her whole day.

Her feet felt three times heavier than usual as she entered her car and started her engine. As she drove away, her eyes focused on her rearview mirror instead of what lay in front of her.

Ninety minutes later and Aayala had arrived at the latest hotel for the lifestyle photo shoot. This property was nestled along the coastline of the most northern point of the South Florida area, making the hotel feel like a hidden treasure in the middle of the bustling cities along the way. Aptly named Le Refuge, the two towers that made the hotel sat side-by-side surrounding a lower flat circular building that made up the valet area, lobby, and various restaurants.

Aayala exited her vehicle, greeted by the soothing voice of the valet attendant as he offered her assistance with her bags. Again, she relinquished her items, happy to follow behind the kind gentleman, the lingering feeling of well-being still with her after her drive.

She immediately sensed a pleasing aroma of fresh jasmine, lily of the valley, and citrus and realized that tasteful arrangements of the flowers surrounded the entire lobby, evoking an exquisite and calming arrival. She let the lobby speak to her, taking all the imagery in, already picturing some shots she wanted to capture with their models.

They'd set the photo shoot schedule in a way that provided Aayala and Sergio time to explore the space together or separately for the first thirty minutes while the models had their makeup done. During the first shoots, she'd appreciated doing the walks with Sergio, but lately, she'd sought solace during her tours, sensing Sergio's increasing need to reconnect with her, a need that wasn't reciprocated.

Today she was in luck and could explore the grounds of the hotel to her liking. By the time she arrived at the extensive suite set aside for the models to use as a green room, Sergio was already there, lounging in the sitting area with a cup of coffee in hand.

"Ohhh, so glad you made it. For a moment, I thought you were gonna stand me up," Sergio said by way of greeting.

All Aayala had to give Sergio was a gentle lift of her lips

upward, hoping her eyes matched the gesture, but she knew she was probably failing. She had no beef with this man, but his odd persistence in being close to her during the shoots and prying into her personal life had her surrounding herself with her armor.

"Hey, Sergio. I've been here for a while. I took my time walking the grounds."

"Oh, I see. I looked for a bit, but I figured I'd leave the bulk of it for when you arrived."

"Nah, I figured each of us is focusing on a unique look, so it would be ok to do our walks separately. I mean, it's worked the past few shoots."

"For you," Sergio mumbled, and she pretended not to hear him.

"Ok, so are the models ready? How do you want to map this out?" Aayala asked, all business, a sense of urgency coursing through her. A flash of broad, dark shoulders and the cutest baby cheeks and eyes greeted her, reminding her of what awaited her back home.

***

Aayala had started her break early, going to take care of her pumping while Sergio took his turn in the pool.

Sitting down for lunch, she opened up the compartment of the bag, and where she usually placed her lunch, a note lay over the sandwich of the day.

> *Aayala, you are magic. You are strength. You are extraordinary.*
> *PS. Andre says gaaaa. Little Man trying to steal my thunder.*

Aᴀʏᴀʟᴀ ʜᴀᴅ ʙᴇᴇɴ ꜰᴇᴇʟɪɴɢ ᴡᴇɪɢʜᴛʟᴇss sɪɴᴄᴇ ᴛʜᴇ ᴍᴏʀɴɪɴɢ. Nothing, not even Sergio's odd mood, had brought her down from that little high, and she had nursed and tended the feeling with gentleness, realizing she hadn't felt this carefree since before Andre had been born.

She always walked with a brimming heart nowadays, her love for Andre immeasurable, but layers of concern, stress, and feelings of loss fluttered around her, weighing her down.

The start of her day had kindled a hope for more. More than the mundane everyday minutia she'd always try to excel in, more than the average goals for an average life. She dared to want more, and what was scarier was that *more* had a name and a face that had flashed through her mind throughout the day.

Without additional thought, she whisked her phone out of her bag and called Malik.

"Yo, I was about to text you. How's the shoot?" Malik asked.

"It's going well, actually, I really feel in my bag today. Actually, I feel so good I took a boudoir booking for next month." She whispered the last words, afraid of saying them too loud. Too early.

"For real? That's what's up! I know you've been feeling a bit off about doing those since the birth… I hope this means good things for you."

"It means I feel inspired again. Not sure if all is back to regular, but at least my eye is going back to some type of normal… I saw your note."

"You did? Good. You need to remember that every day. And Aayala?" Malik's voice deepened.

"Mmm?"

"Don't forget, you can still make magic within you as well, and if you need any help, you know I'm here."

A sigh came out of her, and she felt languid and malleable, his words the hammer to the white iron that surrounded her.

"Ok, I'll keep that in mind."

"Ok, baby girl. Keep having a good day. Oh, by the way, I figured out the dopest family costume for Licy and Gabo's Halloween party that we can reuse after trick or treat with Andre."

This man really was waging a full-on battle for her heart.

"I can't wait to see them. Talk to you later," she said and felt a presence behind her.

She turned around and found Sergio scowling at her.

"Are you done with your little phone call? The break is done, and we've been waiting for you," Sergio admonished.

"Sergio. It's eighteen minutes from when you called a break. Your bad mood does not need to sour my day. Whatever this is, please do less," Aayala said.

"That was your baby daddy? So, he's staying around for a little longer for you? Not running away again?"

Aayala froze, hating the fact that Sergio knew enough of her and Malik to know how to hurt. Just like that, all her concerns returned, and she remembered why she needed to hold onto her defenses.

"You need to mind your business, Sergio. And just to be clear, I'm not your business." She said it with no inflection in her voice, but inside… Inside, she wished she could go back to five minutes ago when everything seemed possible.

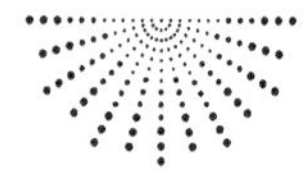

"Are you sure you're alright with this?" he asked her again, Aayala's nervousness seeping into his veins and making his heart trip a couple of beats.

"Yeah, yeah. Yeah, I'm good." Her voice, usually modulated and serene, was currently high-pitched and—he'd never dare to say it out loud—high-strung.

Aayala had embraced his costume idea, going all out to find all the accessories needed to make them as real as possible. The costumes were not easily recognizable, and as they parked in his parents' driveway and were greeted by his dad, he could tell they'd have to do some explaining throughout the night.

"Who you supposed to be?" his father asked in his husky voice, standing by the door, tall and imposing as ever. Here was a glimpse of Malik's future. If he wanted to know how he was going to look once his sixties visited him, he only needed to look at his pops. They shared the same dark, smooth skin, his dad's still barely wrinkled with minimal blemishes, the same eyes that conveyed security and dependability, bolstered by the same tall, lean frame. The only difference besides age was the clipped shirtsleeve to the shoulder, the accident that changed everything.

"Pops, come on now! I would think you knew. You have some of their LPs!"

Aayala smiled and held tighter to Andre, who had on a soft knitted hat in the Jamaican colors with some fake dreads attached to the end. Aayala wore a seventies-inspired outfit with a fitted leather jacket, shirt, and slim pants that flared at the bottom. Her hair was all pulled up underneath an oversized cap. She even wore a fake beard. That left him wearing a similar getup as Aayala with a dread wig on his head.

"Are you tellin' me you dressed up my grandson as Bob Marley and the two of you are The OG Wailers?"

"See, Aayala, I told you Pops would get it."

"Alright, you win this one, but I don't think the rest of the crew nor your mother will. You still not won this bet, chill."

"Come on, Peter Tosh, let's go in and get Andre settled before we head out."

The moment they walked into his parents' house, a ball of tension formed in the pit of his stomach, but he knew it wasn't coming from him, so he breathed out the sensation and placed his hand on the small of her back, giving some of his sense of calmness back to her. The smile remained on her face, stoic and brave, but her eyes told a whole story. She was about to shit bricks about leaving Andre with his parents for the night.

"There's my babeeee! About damned time y'all got in. I have the guest room all ready with my baby's crib, and I have a little bed there where I will sleep right next to him in case he needs anything from his grandmama during the night."

"Woman, are you telling me I'm sleeping by myself tonight?" his father protested, settling himself in his favorite recliner, while his mother took Andre from Aayala. He watched Aayala's hands fist, then relax as they found themselves empty of their precious load.

"Damn right you're sleeping by yourself, you lecherous old groping ass. I don't need you tryin' to do nothing to me tonight. I need to be focused on my babe."

"Yo, Momma, for real? Do you really need to say all of that? Aayala and I don't need to know the details of your..." He gestured between his pops, who was wheezing with laughter, and his mom, who had a giggling Andre in her arms.

"How do you think you made it here, son? Also, were you not there when you made Andre? What the fuck type of prude are you?"

"Mom, language!" he said at the same time Damian strolled into the living room, echoing his words. Damian approached Aayala, who quietly nodded hello, then plopped himself on the opposite sofa from where his pops was sitting.

"Hush, both of you. This is my house."

"Yeah, but him right there, that's my son, and I ain't teaching him all those bad words." Malik pointed at Andre, who stared at his grandmama in fascination.

"Alright, alright. Only reason I'll temper myself is because I can see Aayala standing there ready to yank Andre back from my arms and run far away from the house, and I've been waiting for this day since he was born."

"I would never do that." Aayala shook her head.

Momma raised an eyebrow in patent disbelief.

"Nah, for real, Ms. J, I wouldn't. I just wouldn't have shown up at all. If I'm here, it's because I'm ready." Aayala shrugged, and he felt some of the nervous tension dissipate with her words. If there was something to say about Aayala, once she decided not to dig in her heels, she moved swiftly.

"So, what y'all supposed to be? Rastas?" Damian asked.

"No, son, not just Rastas," his father interjected.

"Yo, Damian, I thought you were working at the home tonight?" When planning this night, Malik had asked his mother about Damian and if he would be here to help her, and she'd explained he had a shift. He'd been disappointed as he preferred for his mom to have a backup, and his father wasn't that dexterous when operating in the middle of the night.

"Nah, I quit that joint," Damian drawled.

"You…what? This is the fourth job you've quit this year. Mom and Pops need you to have a stable job. Moms can't do it all!"

Damian shrugged and looked down, some shame darkening his cheeks, but he lifted his eyes defiantly, the momentary lapse gone. That shit pissed Malik off. He couldn't believe how irresponsible Damian had become.

"Nah, Pops got that money from the settlement with his old job. He got bread now. And what he don't get from the settlement, he gets from yo—" Before Damian could end the sentence that would set Malik the fuck off, his mother interrupted.

"Come on now, y'all gonna be late! Didn't the party start a half-hour ago?" His mom rushed them out with the efficiency of a defensive linebacker. Her father followed behind, amused.

"Mrs. J, if you need anything, *anything*, please just call me, alright?" Aayala spoke over his mother, who kept up a stream of words he couldn't even follow. Malik knew what his moms was doing, and he didn't appreciate it one bit.

"Ma, I'm leaving, but this conversation with Damian is not over. You should have told me," he scolded her from the car.

"Fine, we'll talk tomorrow when you pick Andre up. But for tonight, just have fun, you two, alright? Just enjoy. Being parents is fucking hard. Y'all need some rest."

"What I need is for y'all to stop babying Damian."

"Son, I hear you. But you gotta let Damian's future go and let him figure things out. He's a man now. He'll either get his shit together, or he won't. But it's not on you, it's on him. And you know we are ok here," his father told him.

Malik shook his head, then said his goodbyes. His parents were ok because he worked hard to ensure income was always coming in. The decision he'd made when he was eighteen years old had weighed differently through the years, but never as heavy as it felt right now.

CHAPTER SIXTEEN

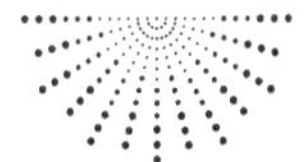

"Whatever you are doin', keep doin' it," Mariana said between bites of chip and dip, standing in her Cleopatra costume.

"Could you chew…less loud?" Aayala replied, ignoring Mariana's original comment.

"Why are you trying to come for me?" Mariana protested while she popped another chip with the smoked fish dip into her mouth and proceeded to chew loudly.

"Because you're doing that on purpose to get on her nerves, that's why," Licy, dressed as a Dora Milaje, responded from the entrance to her kitchen, bringing an empty platter to be replenished.

Alicia and Gabo's house had become the crew's primary location for hangouts, their large backyard and pool area ideal for all types of entertainment.

The odd sensation of not being tethered to Andre's schedule had her adrift during the beginning of the night. Malik stayed by her side, making her smile and bringing a sense of security that washed her worries to the corner of her mind. They weren't completely gone, but they'd agreed to retreat for the time being.

"You need help, Licy?" She stood up and grabbed the platter away as Alicia opened the fridge one-handed to pull out more cheese and charcuterie.

"When did we become so fancy that we entertain with charcuterie boards?" Mariana asked, shaking her head.

"Who is *we?* When's the last time you invited us to your apartment?" Licy asked, arranging the platter to her liking while Aayala added crackers from the pantry.

"Ah, it's like that, Licy? Anytime you entertain here, I come and help you set up and clean up, so I include myself, a'ight?"

"If you say so. I mean, Daniel has that nice enormous apartment. You should host dinner one of these nights," Licy said.

"You say that now, but the moment I plan something, you gonna try to take over." Mariana rolled her eyes.

"She ain't lying," Aayala mumbled to herself, smiling.

"Ok, Aayala, you're going to take Mari's side, I see. It's every cousin on her own. We need Migue for the tiebreaker!" Licy laughed while finishing the platter. Migue, their good friend, was currently in Aruba with his husband and couldn't chime in on this current debate.

"Nah, I'm just kidding, but you can't deny you have the hosting locked down, and even if we were to try to plan away from your house, you'd take over." Aayala glanced at her, making her fake eyebrows jiggle.

"That costume of yours, y'all really got creative!" Licy slapped Mariana's hand away from the charcuterie platter just as Mason dressed as Julius Caesar and Daniel as Marc Anthony walked in, followed by Gabo dressed as M'Baku—which Aayala suspected was Licy's idea because she'd been thirsting after Winston Duke's character since the movie released—and Malik.

"Why y'all hiding in here and having us doing all the hosting?" Mason asked.

"We're not hiding. We are talking about Aayala's creative costume," Licy reiterated.

"Ooh, yeah, see how it matches Malik's? Like they are…" Mason trailed off.

"Yeah, I noticed that too." Gabo walked around his wife and wrapped an arm around her midriff with one hand, taking the platter away from her with the other.

"This is getting too crowded for me," Aayala said, walking toward the living room, feeling the intense regard of her cousins and friends as they looked between her and Malik. He stood next to Daniel, beer in hand, completely relaxed under the scrutiny of his friends. This was quintessential Malik, always unbothered.

"That's ok, we'll just follow behind you! Yo, babe, grab some beers for all, please," Mason said, giving Daniel a quick peck before following behind Aayala.

Shit. Mason's observant ass had spoiled her smooth escape, and now the entire crew relocated with her to the terrace, where most of the other guests were mingling. She sat on one of the large sofas, and everyone naturally found spots around her, the magnetic pull of the core of their group keeping them close by. She loved these hangouts, she truly did, but since Malik and she were in this gray space, it had become increasingly uncomfortable to be under everyone's inspection.

"So who came up with the costumes, huh, lover boy?" Mason asked Malik as he accepted a beer from Daniel. Mari was sitting on Mason's lap, and Daniel sat on the arm of Mason's chair, the three of them the picture of synchronicity.

Watching them was like watching a trio of musicians that had been playing for years, each aware of the others' place and part. The dull ache in her chest had nothing to do with the fact that she'd felt some of that with Malik these past weeks.

"I did. I know Aayala loves Bob and the Wailers, so we dressed like that so we could take pictures with Andre before we left," Malik said, sitting on the opposite side of the large sofa.

"This feels like the same type of interrogation we've done in the past when…" Mariana started.

"When something is brewing somewhere!" Licy laughed as Gabo attempted to cover her mouth, and she scooted away from him.

"I thought we said we wouldn't mess in anyone's business after Mason, Mari, and Daniel?" Gabo fake-whispered.

"I know, but this is fun," Licy fake-whispered back.

"See, the difference between those times and now is that y'all got flustered and shit under pressure. Aayala and I are not bothered. If something happens, it will happen on our terms, in our time. No amount of messing with us will change that." Malik stared at Aayala while delivering his message.

"True." She nodded back at him. "If anything happens—and that's our business if it does—we'll let y'all know so you can crow, but in the end, we'd be winning, anyway." She shrugged, holding his gaze without wavering. His bedroom eyes felt intense on her, and with each second that passed, he tattooed on her skin the reminder that everything between them was all up to her. She only needed to ask. She remained stoic under his perusal, but inside, she felt as if her stomach had lost its mind and joined the fictitious Jamaican bobsled team.

"Alright, then. That wasn't as satisfying as I thought it

would be. Y'all too mature for this to be fun," Mason said with undisguised disappointment.

"Nah, that's what's up. Y'all both on the same page, and y'all both know we have your back. That's all that matters," Daniel said, his sage words surrounding them with the love and support of their family and friends.

CHAPTER SEVENTEEN

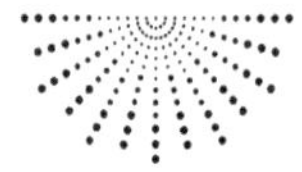

Nothing could be heard in the house. After a night of jokes, music, and drinks, they finally returned to her townhome to catch a good night's rest before picking up Andre in the morning.

Malik, forever in tune with her, asked her if she wanted to get Andre before driving home, but the thought of having to wake him up in the middle of the night seemed frivolous and selfish. She knew her boy was in expert hands with his grandparents.

After a hot shower, Aayala moisturized, taking time to reach every corner and crevice of her body. Her skin, where it used to be taut and firm, had yielded to softness, her stomach riddled with lines and scars that refused to budge no matter how much cocoa butter she applied each morning and night. Her hands glided over her hips, thick from carrying Andre for eight months, their shape forever transformed and redesigned.

Her ass, always her best asset, seemed to have expanded and attempted to move into a new zip code. Her breasts, modest at best, had grown and become too unwieldy, and the pleasure they'd brought in the past had changed to a mental mix of responsibility and nourishment that didn't seem compatible with the previous way she'd enjoyed touching them.

Ayala wanted to love her new body. She wanted to irrevocably discover all the new facets and fall helplessly in love with herself. She knew and saw the beauty in her new lines, saw her lush curves under the beams of moonlight. But she couldn't reconcile her rational understanding of how to embrace her new body to the visceral state of disappointment she felt each time she saw herself in the mirror.

She had considered removing the mirrors from her room —at least until she'd tackled her insecurities and had a healthier view of herself. She was helpless to the dissonance that came from seeing herself and not immediately recognizing the body in front of her, but lately, the urge to remove them had diminished.

Tonight, with the glow of moonlight still on her and the laughter of her friends lingering in her ears, she felt generous to herself in ways she hadn't in a long time. The hands gliding across her body took stock, and the narrative in her brain shifted. She visited the dip of her waist, thickened with little rolls that felt comfortable under her fingers, thighs almost meeting between her legs to greet each other like long-lost lovers. Her hair, loose and wild, coiled down her shoulders in abandon, her collarbone with its elegant slopes dipping down a line to the middle of her chest where her heart beat steady and strong, her body a testament to all the battles won through the years.

As she stood unguarded to her own disappointments and gentle praises, she shivered, remembering Malik's eyes on her today as he assured all their friends that whatever was meant to happen between them would happen at their own pace and time.

She didn't know if it was the company or the drinks and fun, but in the moment when he spoke to her directly while he answered their questions, she had been completely dialed in to his every word and believed them with a naïveté that hadn't visited her since she was a young adult. Since those years when they'd both started writing to each other because she'd wanted him to still feel at home, no matter how far he was.

And now he had offered her his own cure to help her find the things she'd lost, and she was tired of fighting herself and denying him the opportunity.

Before she regretted her decision, she picked up her phone and texted him, asking him to come to her room.

The second the text left her cellphone, she felt a thrill rush through her fingers all the way to the middle of her, heating her up in the process. Her fingers tingled, and she saw herself, still naked in the mirror, and hesitated, uncertain if she'd made the right call.

Aayala's insecurities bum-rushed her, and she searched desperately in her drawer for something to wear before Malik answered her text.

She pulled out one of her black panties, hopping on one foot to get them on, and a black cotton teddy that she hastily threw on when she heard the knock on her door.

Malik hadn't even answered her text. He'd just come right over.

"Come in," she said.

She stood by her window as Malik's presence filled the room with his calm. He stood by the threshold wearing his basketball shorts and ribbed undershirt, all black, just like her. As if they'd planned this shit or something. Why must he look so utterly relaxed? *And those eyes.* Those dammed eyes that saw everything.

"You texted?" His gaze stayed on her face, but somehow,

she knew he was taking her all in. She didn't shrink back from his perusal. She felt that thrill again and felt emboldened by her decision. Her perfidious pussy was down there doing some deep stretches as if she was getting ready for a race or something. The faithless hussy. No loyalty to Aayala whatsoever.

"Yes."

"What can I do for you?"

"You know what."

"Actually, no, I don't. Your text was vague as fuck, so I'mma need you to spell it out for me."

"I said, 'I'm ready to continue.'"

"Come on now, baby girl, you can do better than that."

In for a penny...

"I want you to help me orgasm. Tonight. I want to orgasm again."

Malik appraised her, and her skin heated, but the strength of tonight's vulnerability held her in place. Here was a man that truly knew her, truly understood her inner workings. Someone who'd learned how to anticipate her needs and words and was gentle with her, even though she always portrayed strength. She let herself relax, the ever-present steel dissolving into bones and flesh.

"I see you... Come here, baby girl."

She padded softly to him, relinquishing her cares.

Aayala stood in front of him and felt the warmth of him caress her body. He studied her intently, his bedroom eyes fully alert, drawing her in. He moved so stealthily that she was in the air before she could register the fact that he'd swept her up in his arms and, in a few steps, deposited her gently on her bed.

"Ok, relax," he said, and his voice trembled a little.

Was he nervous? No...couldn't be. Not her calm and collected friend.

She relaxed as he asked, not that she needed the prompt. Putting this on him had removed all her responsibilities to reach that elusive pinnacle. Now, it was all in his hands, and she didn't have to worry.

Firm hands slid over her calves, the gentle massage reminding her of the last time he'd touched her—and his words.

"You know, when I left your room after the massage, I had to go to the guest room and relive each touch of your skin in my brain. I was so fucking hard I thought I would pass out."

Fuck. Again with his words and the seduction—he didn't need to even touch her to make her feel so much. His hands glided up her legs, the whisper of his touch raising goosebumps along the way. Her pussy clenched in commiseration while her stomach did a lazy flip at his words. This man could make her so soft. So, so soft.

"Lift your hips for me, baby girl. Be good for me now."

She closed her eyes, shuttering the visceral way she wanted to surrender and comply with his words, the way her arms and legs trembled at the gentle but firm command. She did as he told and was divested of the panties that she shouldn't have bothered putting on.

A loud groan escaped his mouth at the sight of her pussy.

"Look at you. You're already ready for me, aren't you?" he whispered in a rough voice, and something about his tone made her realize he was indeed nervous. Her chest expanded, and that little organ inside felt ready to escape at the knowledge.

"It's ok if I don't come, it's ok," she assured him.

He wrenched his eyes away from her glistening pussy, and the determination in his gaze left her breathless.

"As long as you trust yourself and me tonight, I'll make

sure to do the utmost to end this streak for you. Do you trust me?"

Aayala nodded, transfixed by the earnest way he was looking at her.

"More important, do you trust yourself?"

"I do…when I'm with you." The words escaped her without her giving them much thought. The rawness that followed them made her feel self-conscious for the first time tonight, and she hated that feeling.

He squeezed her left thigh, sensing her retreat, anchoring her back to this moment. She resisted at first, trying to bring back her protective armor, but Malik's eyes… They commanded her full attention.

"That's my good girl. Now, the only way this works is if you follow all my commands, a'ight?"

"Yes."

"Yes who, Aayala?"

"Yes, daddy."

"That deserves a reward." And Malik dove into her pussy, his lips greeting her with a deep, passionate kiss, taking the entire hood of her clitoris into his mouth in a sensual caress that had her hips thrusting off the mattress. *Bombo—he can really eat pussy.*

She turned into another substance under his skillful mouth, viscous and, by the muffled words coming out of Malik's lips, succulent as well. The usual powerful steel that held her together had transmuted into a thick syrup that she couldn't contain. Aayala was spilling all over figuratively and literally while Malik's long, thick tongue made its way into her and his finger played with her clitoris.

The firm way he touched her bundle of nerves was exactly what she didn't know she needed. Before, she'd found pleasure in indirect contact with her clit, direct stimulation over-sensitizing her. Circles over her closed labia had been enough to make her come like a freight train in the past.

But now, it seemed things had changed, and the map to her pussy's treasures had been bestowed on Malik instead of her. She suspected this was the work of that disloyal coochie of hers, but right now, she couldn't be mad. The way Malik was making her feel…

"Ah, right there!" Whatever he had done with his tongue inside of her tightness had made her squirm in delicious abandon, her legs quivering, attempting to give up on her as she held them open for his ministrations. She pushed her lower body against his mouth, wanting to hump that clever tongue of his until she came all over him, searching for the high that seemed to approach.

Like molasses, the promise of her orgasm was thick and slow to arrive, and for a moment, she worried it would take her too long and Malik would get tired or annoyed.

A draft greeted her pussy for a second, all stimulation stopping before her clit was surrounded by hot, wet heaven as Malik sucked it into his mouth, using his tongue in an unholy way that would ban him from his Momma's church forever.

"Fuck!" She screamed at the contact, the heat in her body intensifying, the viscous substance liquifying, her entire body opening, exhaling, waiting to accept the next surprise from Malik's talented mouth.

"Stay with me, Aayala," Malik practically growled at her. She always made fun of Alicia's books with all the growling the men did, but shit, that gravelly thing he just did must have come from his diaphragm, and she soaked her bed when she heard him. She guessed she had some apologizing to do next time she saw Licy.

"Ok."

He pinched her clit. *He pinched her fucking clit.* Her legs clenched as the throbbing pain traveled from her clit to her legs, down to her toes currently gripping the sheets.

"Fuck! What was that for?" she protested, all the while the blooming pain blossomed into a delicious pleasure-pain mix that had her rubbing her legs together to chase the sensation.

"Stop that. Open your legs again."

She whimpered and opened her legs.

"Wider, baby girl."

She opened wider, exposing herself again to his onslaught.

"That pinch was to remind you that when you answer me, you answer 'yes, sir,' or 'yes, daddy.' We ain't playing games right now, baby girl. This is the real deal, we put what we wanted from each other on the table, so let's not forget again, ok?" The masterful way he spoke to her made her gush again. At this point, her pussy had probably transformed into a glass of water.

"Yes, daddy."

"A'ight, then. Focus on what I'm doing and how it's making you feel. No other thoughts allowed."

And he went back to business.

His tongue did things to her that had no name, no description in the dictionary, no rational explanation. And Aayala didn't try to understand. She just lay in her soft silk sheets, which she fisted in her hands and gripped with her toes, and held on for dear life. Three fingers were now inside of her pussy while his tongue did unspeakable things she'd remember when she was one hundred years old.

She was liquid heat under his powerful hands that held her legs open for his pleasure. She was malleable alloy, ready to be strengthened as she held onto his shoulders, back bowed in pleasure as her mouth opened in silent screams. She was renewed as his tongue lashed one last time, and the scent of her arousal, tangy in the air, mixed with his woodsy musk, a combination so alluring and potent her mouth watered.

Just as unexpected as when Malik swept her into his arms, her orgasm surprised her, splashing and spilling over every corner of her body, the force of it so powerful that she sobbed from the breathtaking beauty of her climax.

"It's alright, baby girl, you came so good for me. So good, that was stunning. Shhh."

A dam opening its walls, no longer able to contain anything inside, that was Aayala. She cried and cried, unable to explain to herself or Malik what was driving this intense need to let go. Tears streamed from her eyes unbothered as Malik embraced her, their backs against the headrest of her bed. She was glad for his arms because she felt lightheaded, and her chest caved in at the release of so much.

Once all the tears in her body had departed and there was no more water to produce, she quieted, letting the slow rhythm of Malik's breathing soothe her rawness.

"Feeling better?" he asked.

"I wasn't feeling bad, I just— I don't know…"

"It's been a wild year between the pregnancy and everything else. Think about it. We found out you were pregnant right after Halloween last year."

"You're right. Even so, I didn't realize I was holding so much in."

"I did. I did the moment I saw you by the ship. It's been a lot and…and I wish I'd been there for you every step of the way. But I'm here for now, and I—"

"I know. I know you're here, and you'll do everything in your power to be present these months. I know. And you asked me to trust myself, and I did, and I trusted you. And here we are." Her body still quivered from the life-changing orgasm she'd had, and her insides felt delicate. Same as her heart.

They stayed quiet for a while, the house settling around them with its familiar creaks and clicks, until Malik spoke again.

"Was it good, though? 'Cause let me tell you, baby girl, I like tears in certain moments, but not the type you just cried after coming…was it good for you?" The vulnerability in his voice wrapped around her heart, squeezing it and filling it with tenderness.

"Of course, it was good! I almost passed out, it was… Good is so not an adequate description of what that orgasm was. Thank you, Malik. Thank you for getting me out of my head, and for…" She sniffled and buried into him.

"No need to thank me, baby girl. Now lie down, time for you to sleep."

She felt like protesting. She wasn't Andre's age to be told when to go to bed, but she felt him tense as she turned to tell him so. Then she remembered. She remembered what he needed from her, and she turned back, letting him big spoon her, and she closed her eyes, drifting away in minutes.

CHAPTER EIGHTEEN

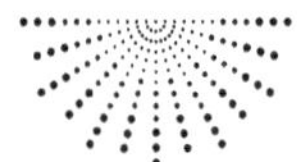

Slack deck rope had nothin' on his muscles right now. Aayala's bed was the softest yet firmest mattress he'd slept on in his life. Wherever she bought this joint, he needed it. Better yet, he needed a place in her bed now and every night he was on land, though he might be biased about the mattress because of the company next to him.

Aayala had contained herself to her section of the bed, still sleeping on her side after all these hours. She'd stayed in his arms, and his hands had tingled for minutes last night, full of her lush curves.

He'd been nervous. Shit, he'd been in some fucked up, scary situations in his life, but there was something about the responsibility to help her orgasm that had humbled him and roused all his fears. Fears that he couldn't give this woman everything she deserved.

How could he? He didn't even have a home to call his own. All these years he'd been single-minded in his focus to save enough money for his parents to have a good retirement, for his brother's college, and for his own future. A future that had always looked blurry in the corners and intangible, but he'd been unconcerned about the lack of clarity. He'd always thought he'd have time to create that future once he retired early.

By deciding to become a merchant marine, Malik had made a conscious decision to grow his wealth through long yearly voyages while also knowing that it would be virtually impossible for him to leave the work without having built the financial cushion he wanted.

But now, here Aayala and Andre were offering him a future in 4K and the best surround sound, and he no longer could remain unbothered about the time he spent away from home. He knew he couldn't give them all they needed, no matter what route he took.

He'd avoided fully thinking about all this because it only created distractions he didn't need right now. He wanted to be fully focused on Andre, on Aayala, and his family and friends. This time was his to reconnect, and the worries that flooded him lately were overwhelming him and taking over his usual peace.

He'd avoided tossing and turning, not wanting to wake Aayala, who'd soon have to wake up to pump. He thought he wouldn't be able to fall asleep, but the gentle sway of her breathing finally lulled him and his troubled thoughts.

Somehow, even with all the nightly worries that stormed him last night, he'd woken up in a great mood.

The lushest ass he'd ever seen in his life against his hard dick had a lot to do with it.

He couldn't help the jerk of his hips against her softness as she stretched and resettled, then fell deep asleep again. Malik wanted to stay right where he was cradling Aayala until she woke up on her own. She needed the rest. Her breasts lay heavy under his arm, and he knew soon enough they'd serve as her own personal wake-up alarm, but for now, he just wanted her to sleep. His bladder, unfortunately, had other plans, and soon he had contorted himself to get out of this slice of heaven and relieve himself.

After he finished in the bathroom, his brain, as it did every morning, went into task mode, and with a last longing look at Aayala, he left her room, hoping she'd take advantage of the quiet house.

He took a quick shower, checked Andre's hamper and put his clothes in the wash, emptied the nursery's diaper genie and replenished the diapers underneath Andre's dressing table, ran downstairs, turned on the coffee, and started breakfast.

Each task, each step taken gave him the sense of contentment he needed, his muscles relaxing after all the tension and worry after Aayala came and fell asleep. He whistled while preparing pancakes and eggs and missed when Aayala finally came downstairs.

"Well, you are in a good mood today," she said, still wearing her panties and teddy, two wet spots forming around her nipples.

"I am, and you look like you need your pump. Should I run to pick Andre up?" he asked, loathe to cut their time alone short but knowing Aayala's preference for breast-feeding over pumping.

"Nah, we left your moms with enough milk until tonight. Maybe we should let Andre stay there longer. She's been asking me for so long, and I felt so conflicted at first, but..." She shrugged.

"It feels good to have a day for yourself?" He nodded while placing the pump and clean bottles on the table for her.

"Yeah."

"Mmm, I hear hesitation."

"You do because there is. I shouldn't want to be away from Andre. He's not even one, for God's sake."

"Are you for real? The little man is attached to your hip

anytime both of you are in the same room, which is most of the time. It's ok to want a break, Aayala, it doesn't make you a terrible mother."

The frown on her face made Malik want to put her over his knee and alternate between spanking and fingering her until she let go of all that guilt and just enjoyed the day, but even though she knew what he was like, he didn't know if she was all ready for that. Instead, he settled for taking care of her in other ways.

"Here."

He placed a bowl of fruit, two pancakes, and eggs in front of her with a large glass of water.

"From now on, your water intake and meals are mine to keep track of," he said, wanting to clear her mind of her concerns.

An eyebrow climbed all the way up her hairline, and he was afraid she was going to hurt herself.

"Is this part of your needs?"

"Yes."

She watched him while he cleaned up. There really wasn't much more to say. They'd both shared what they wanted from each other in different ways during these past weeks. If they were planning to move forward with whatever this was meant to be, then he might as well lay the foundation.

"Yeah, and sleep, seven hours at least. No staying up late trying to come anymore. I make you come, I cook your meals, you drink water for me, and you stop thinking silly thoughts like you being a bad mother. And every time your mind goes there—and trust me, I'll be able to tell—I'll make sure to spank you and finger you until you come."

He walked over to her, a thrill running through him. He couldn't wait to make sure she took care of herself properly.

"Close your mouth, shorty." He tapped her chin, and she

closed it. He smiled at her delicate gulp while her eyes never left his face.

"And if I do all of that and...obey your commands, what's in it for me?" she asked over the weird noise of the pump machine.

"Rest, balance, and unlimited orgasms."

She chuckled and shook her head.

"I can't believe I'm saying yes to your rules, but alright. We'll do all of that—not that you weren't already doing it, but it seems you need it to be official. I mean, I'm still going to do me, and you know it, but you're welcome to try to bring balance, and I'm all here for the unlimited orgasms."

"Yeah, because now you know if you don't obey, you'll get punished."

"Oh, ok, I heard that. And what if I like the punishment?"

"Try me, Aayala, and you'll see."

Aayala squirmed in her seat, all her attention on him.

"Ok. Ok. Oh, fuck!"

She looked down and realized the bottles in her pump were almost full. She disengaged from the machine, removing the bottles, and he quickly closed them and stored them in the fridge.

She removed the pump bra and went back to her breakfast as if nothing had happened. As if she hadn't agreed to be his submissive, at least in the privacy of her home.

The pride he felt in the moment, knowing she agreed to his rules and knowing he had the care of her and his son filled him with a sense of awe. Maybe there were ways he could be enough for her. Just maybe.

AAYALA'S FEET RESTED ON HIS LAP WHILE SHE FOCUSED ON HER laptop. After breakfast, they cleaned up the kitchen together and convened to the family room to shoot the shit for a while. They agreed to call his moms and let her know they'd be getting Andre tonight. His momma was ecstatic screaming into the phone, something to the tune of, "About fucking time!" The woman had zero care for language, truly.

Malik was navigating the state's website for captain permits, something he'd promise Cap he would look at. Cap intended to retire this year and wanted Malik to take over as the captain of this rich white family luxury yacht, but the pay was less than his current one. Not bad at all, but it would have him retiring way later than his original plan.

Still, the need to be around Aayala and Andre was becoming louder and louder as the days went by, and he couldn't imagine how difficult it was going to be to get on that ship come February.

"You know, you look sexy with those glasses." Aayala's voice was a welcome interruption.

"For real? You never said that before."

"I wasn't trying to put a move on my friend before."

"A'ight, I'll wear them for you whenever you like."

She chuckled and kept typing.

"What you doing?" he asked curiously. He loved the way she pursed her lips in concentration and was tempted to reach across the sofa and kiss those soft, big lips of hers. Just as he thought that, her tongue slipped out, and she slowly licked her bottom lip, then bit it while she kept typing, and he went from relaxed to fully alert, the move so quick he felt lightheaded.

"I'm working on a concept for the couple I told you about, the one for the boudoir shoot. Can I tell you I'm a bit nervous? I don't know what's gonna happen that day. My inspiration has been better lately. I've felt inspired to capture and had great shoots at the different hotels, but this… This is more intimate, more demanding. I don't know if I'll do good, at least not to their expectations."

"Ok, then, how can I help?"

He felt Aayala jerk to attention, her focus shifting from her laptop to him. At the same time, her feet flexed and met hardness underneath.

"How do you want to help?"

He stood up and took his time pulling off his t-shirt. Aayala remained static, a beautiful smooth sienna statue.

"Go get your camera, baby girl."

CHAPTER NINETEEN

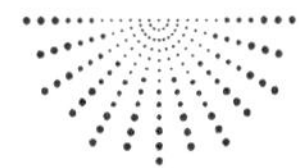

Aayala's tongue made an appearance again, and she licked her lips slowly, her eyes trained on his torso before slowly drifting down to where he was hard and desperate for her. Malik had made her a promise, and he wasn't about to break it. He wouldn't have sex with her. Nah, she needed to make the move.

"Ok." Her eyes went back to his face, and the smirk she gave him had him adjusting himself in his sweatpants.

She glided next to him, her green scent, her eternal summer smell making him hungry to be wrapped up in her warmth.

"I'll be right back…"

Aayala disappeared for minutes, then she sauntered back to the family room with her camera in hand. His eyes spotted those sexy shorts he loved and an off-the-shoulder t-shirt that showed the strap of one of her nursing bras. The way she circled him, eyes appraising, had him squaring up to give some space to things down below.

She was gorgeous. He could see the trepidation in her, the way she bit her lip as she decided how to approach this impromptu shoot. She zeroed in on his crotch, and his dick couldn't help but grow even more under her careful regard.

"I don't know how you do it," she said, clutching her camera while she held him captive with her gaze.

"What is it, baby girl?"

"I don't know how you carry all of that between your legs so gracefully. Look at that, it's so…" She licked her lips again, and he clenched his fist. Man, if she kept up with that, she was gonna get fucked—forget his promise.

This was exactly what had happened their first time. She kept appraising him like this while they danced together, the whole night throwing vibes at him she'd never exhibited before. When he couldn't take the teasing anymore, he'd bluntly asked her if she wanted to get fucked, and her answer had been a resounding yes. But he couldn't do that now. He needed to keep his head, so he wrenched his eyes away from her and looked up.

"So fucking thick, so present, and so large, and… I mean, look at how it shows in your pants. Lawd."

"So you gonna torture me or take pictures of me?" he said, still looking up.

"Oh, shit, sorry. That whole stream of thought shouldn't have come out of my mouth."

"Nah, shorty, that's ok. I don't mind being objectified by you, but only by you."

He hazarded a look, and her cheeks were red, but there was a fire in her gaze, and she stood with her hip cocked out, her foot tapping lightly.

"Ok, then, sit there on the sofa like you usually do at the end of the day when you are watching TV…"

He followed her instructions, sprawling on the seat, one leg extended while the other bent at the knee. One arm he rested on the sofa side, and the other he brought up to the back of his neck. He heard her hiss, then she got to business.

There was no awkwardness as she took pictures of different angles while he sat relaxed, following her with his eyes. That cute frown was back, and she pursed her lips in concentration as she took several shots until she was nodding to herself in liking.

"Ok, get up and stand by the fridge as if you are looking for something."

"So you've been fantasizing about me while I'm innocently looking for something to eat?" he asked as he strolled toward the fridge.

She padded behind him, a smirk on her face but no answer besides that. He did as she asked, the cold air of the fridge blasting against his chest and nipples. Aayala got closer, this time taking what felt like a hundred shots until she told him to close the fridge again.

"Here, let me bring your sweatpants a little lower…" She put down her camera and approached him. The warmth of her hands greeted the residual cold on his belly. His flesh jerked at the contact, and she looked up, searching his eyes.

"You alright there?" she asked.

"Yeah, are you ok?"

"Oh, yeah, I'm here fulfilling a fantasy of mine."

"Oh, really now? So, you been thirsting after me before October?"

She laughed as she dragged his sweatpants lower on his hips, arranging them to her liking. His dick, which had been hard since the beginning of the shoot, had been calming down, but the contact of her hands and the scent of her hair as it brushed against his chin had him hardening again.

"I've always found you attractive, and I wondered here and there, but not until that night did I decide to make a move."

"Why was that night different from the many other nights we've been out together?"

"I…" She let go of his pants and nodded pensively, that damn tongue again making an appearance, dragging against her lush lower lip.

She picked up the camera and knelt in front of him, her face getting up close and personal with his hard-as-fuck dick.

He could feel her warm breath brushing against the cotton fabric, her breathing growing labored. She took a couple of shots as she knelt close to him.

"I'd been feeling lonely. I had broken up with Sergio for a while, and even though I'd had the occasional fling, nothing felt satisfying. Before that night, I had gone without for four months, and enough was enough. I'd jazzed myself up to wear the most revealing of Mari's designs, wanting to celebrate my body and her success. And somehow, I felt freer than I'd felt in many years. And you—always there, my best friend—somehow, that day you seemed…tempting. Alluring. Something in my gut told me I didn't need to look far and wide. Here was the person who would break my drought. So, I just followed my gut. It was as simple as that. The attraction between you and me…"

Throughout her speech she'd kept taking photos, getting up slowly, capturing close-ups of his body until she was standing again.

"It's always been there."

"Yeah, but we've never…"

"Nah, we always left it alone. The friendship was more valuable."

"Exactly. But that night, I felt reckless."

"Are you feeling reckless now, baby girl?" The way she was so serious while working and so focused on her craft had him ready to beg her to fuck him. If that's what it took, pride be damned, he'd do it. He needed to be inside of her. It wasn't a simple want, it had morphed into a need as important as nourishment. He needed that magical pussy to surround him again and make him whole.

"I'm feeling like I want you to stand by that window, bracing your arms against the frame."

He detangled his thoughts away from Aayala's pussy and did as she asked, gripping the window frame for good measure. He heard her breath hitch, and a flash of satisfaction ran through him. His breathing was labored too. Having her so close to him and not being able to touch was torture.

He heard the camera click several times, then stop.

"Are you comfortable with some nudity? I promise I won't share any of the pics if you're not good with me posting on social media."

"Nah, it's alright, as long as my face is not in them, I'm cool. Don't want to give my moms a reason to cuss me out."

"Cool, cool," she replied and, in a quick motion, brought his pants down enough to reveal the top of his ass while still keeping them around his hips.

He heard more clicks of the camera, and then silence. The silence had a distinct quality. There was a charged stillness, similar to the calm before a storm, where the wind stopped and everyone on deck was on high alert.

Malik stayed where he was because he could smell her arousal, that earthy scent mixing with her light green tones that reminded him of the early sun when they were close to shore. He needed her and was about to embarrass himself and beg when he felt her warm palm on his shoulder.

Goosebumps erupted under her soft hand as she drifted down his back, then reached the curve of his exposed ass.

"What are you doing, baby girl?"

"I just wanted to touch you a little…" she breathed against his back, and he trembled, his dick thumping inside his sweatpants.

"I'm the one that calls the shots here," he reminded her.

"Yes, but you told me when I was ready, I would have to fuck you. So, this is me shooting my shot," she whispered, her voice quivering.

"Touch my dick, baby girl." He invited her to take charge, if only for a second.

Warm hands reached from behind, circling his hips and gliding inside his sweatpants. A chill traveled from the top of his back all the way to his feet and back again, his body completely tense with her every move.

Malik had been dreaming of this moment for months, a year. To be touched by Aayala, to be so close to her he could smell the flowery shampoo she used. He'd imagined it all.

His imagination was a poor substitute for the perfection of her touch as her hands took hold of his dick. He wanted to weep in thanksgiving and frustration.

"Fuuuck, baby girl. You know how long I've waited for this moment?"

"Yes, I've waited too."

The quiver in her voice made him turn around to face her.

Malik liked tears. The very few situationships he had in the past where his partner was into the same shit he was into had taught him there was a bit of a sadist inside of him. But he only liked certain tears, and the ones silently falling onto Aayala's cheeks were not the good type.

"Why are you crying, baby girl?"

"I'm afraid what happened with you is a one-time thing."

He'd started getting in the habit of picking up Aayala whenever he could, and this was no exception. He carried her from the window and deposited her on the sofa.

He knew what Aayala needed right now more than anything was gentleness. She needed to be reminded of how extraordinary she was and how lucky Malik was to have her in his life. Malik kneeled in front of her, his hands bracketing

Aayala's legs on the sofa. He whispered low encouragement to her as he attempted to remove her top, but one of her hands stopped him.

"I don't want to take my top off…just my bottom."

He was hungry to see her, all of her in her glory, but he knew when not to insist. Being in charge of the power dynamic meant he needed to recognize when it was ok to push and when it was not.

He helped her out of her shorts, the two working together until she was bare from the waist down, and her glistening pussy greeted him like a long-lost friend. At this point, they were.

"Why are you looking at me like that?" she said with a watery smile. He leaned back on his knees to have a better view.

"I'm just taking the time to admire that beautiful, mouth-watering pussy."

Not able to help himself, he pushed closer to her, ran his tongue down up her slit, and played with her clit a little. She squirmed, then divesting herself of all reserve, she held onto his head and ground her pussy against his mouth.

He took the gesture for what it was and dived in, licking and slurping all her tangy goodness. He held on to her thick hips and pushed her even closer. God, the earthy smell of hers enveloped him, and he could live just to eat her pussy every day. Fuck the sea, fuck the voyages, fuck the money.

All he needed in his life was Aayala.

He feasted on her, making her yelp in surprise at first, then getting her to grind to the rhythm that best took her to an orgasm. He had her pleading and begging as she rode his face, bringing him so close to coming his own spine tight-ened in response.

"Fuck, Aayala. Baby girl, I need inside you."

"Oh, oh, oh, yes! Right there, Malik, I'm so close."

"Then come, baby girl."

"No, I wanna come with you inside me." She caressed his close-cropped head, and that shit felt as if she had run her palm over the head of his dick. Who knew his head was an erogenous zone?

"Baby girl, are you ready to take me? Are you sure? Do you have birth control?" he asked, needing to be certain she was good.

"Yes, please, yes. I want to wait 'til I come with you inside me. I got an IUD after Andre."

The raw need in her voice propelled him. He sat on the sofa and did one of his favorite things, lifting her so she could settle that magnificent ass on his lap, facing him. His dick was nestled between them, kissed by the wetness of her sex, and he was ready to risk it all to be inside of her again, but no drastic measures were needed.

Aayala lifted herself slowly, all the while smirking as she noticed how desperate he was.

That spark of recognition, that unadulterated joy, was coming from her, and it spread inside of him, becoming his as well. Her happiness seeped in everywhere until he grinned like a simp.

"Don't play with me, baby girl, sit on this dick." He squeezed her hips and groaned into her mouth as she kissed him.

Her kiss held sunshine and summer, and he reveled in her sweetness, surrounded by her clean green scent, and the soft wetness of her pussy, which felt just as he remembered, squeezed his dick from the moment it met his head all the way until she sat fully on him.

Their lips parted at the same moment as his dick throbbed inside her triumphantly in its return, his entire body wired, every particle of his being fusing together wherever his flesh touched hers. Aayala's mouth opened in pleasure. She was so fucking beautiful, unguarded, and vulnerable, just for him. He felt her shiver and sigh against his mouth before she started a languid roll of her hips that threatened to finish him with a quickness that would embarrass him.

He wasn't going out like that, though.

He held onto her hips as he thrust up and forward, the wave of his own pelvis lifting her up and hitting that spot inside her he knew would make her wild. Malik closed his eyes, remembering that fateful night and how her mewls of pleasure were the sexiest soundtrack he'd ever heard. He lost himself in her, the memory of them together meshing with the present as he kept a relentless tempo, hitting that spot every time.

Her pussy tightened around him like silky rope made just for his dick. His feet were planted on the floor, and that was the only place he felt grounded. Everything else was suspended in air, everything tingled.

Aayala had grown oddly quiet, and he opened his eyes and lifted her chin to check on her.

"Are you ready to come, baby girl?"

A tear escaped from her, and she gasped in horror. Her pussy clenched again, and she held onto his shoulders, pushing herself down on his dick over and over, her face contorted in desperation. The tingling sensation in his body transformed into a coldness that spread all over, yanking him back to earth.

"Nah, Aayala. Aayala, slow down." He held onto her again, trying to stop her from grinding against him, but she kept up that mechanical movement as tears ran down her face.

"I can't come, Malik, I can't. I…it feels different. I used to be able to come like this and now…fuck. It feels good, but I can't!"

Each tear and sob felt like ropes snapping loudly in his

head. Each time he tried to hold onto the rope, it snapped and slipped mockingly through his hands. Each tear that fell from her face cut deep inside of him. His dick, still not getting the message, was hard as fuck inside of her, but this wasn't it. These were not the tears he wanted from her.

"Aayala, baby girl, stop. Please."

She must have heard the determination in his voice because finally, the mechanical movements stopped, and she lifted herself off him, sitting next to him on the sofa and breaking down right in front of him.

He sat there helpless as Aayala wept her soul out, his arms open on his lap and his wet dick hard and sad, the reunion he'd dreamt of a nightmare instead. If he'd had any doubts about what he could do for her, today told him that he could do nothing for her. Nothing at all.

CHAPTER TWENTY

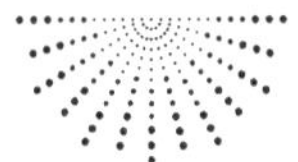

When Aayala had come under Malik's expert pussy-eating skills, she thought in the back of her mind that the occasion had been a fluke. But who the fuck thinks those types of pessimistic thoughts? So, she'd shoved that feeling of dread to the back of her mind and left it for tomorrow's Aayala. She'd deal with it when the time came.

The time was now, and present Aayala was pissed at her old self for not dealing with that shit then and there. Here she was, sobbing her eyes out in front of Malik, not knowing what to do but let this ball of unresolved feelings flow out of her like a river at the end of a waterfall.

Things were not right. Something wasn't clicking, and she didn't know what to do. The moment her pussy met Malik's dick, that feeling of joy slipped away from her and dread started growing in the back of her mind.

The feeling of his dick moving inside of her was so fucking good. He hit her spot so well, but the crescendo that usually came of that type of phenomenal dicking did not happen. The wave did not wash her all the way in. Instead, she was stuck ashore with her boat, and nothing moved for her. No resounding waves took her away. She knew without a doubt that if she'd had this same sex before birth, she'd come after a couple of strokes, no additional help needed.

Strong arms surrounded her, and she rested her worries on Malik. He placed her on his lap, and she vaguely realized his pants and shirt were back on. All the water in her body must have left through her eyes, and she couldn't stop the flow. Again, emotions beyond the moment threatened to overwhelm her with their complexity. She had no definition for what she was feeling outside of a complete sense of helplessness.

Aayala went from being fully in charge and in control of every aspect of her life and body to chaos. No set schedule but what Andre dictated, sleep-deprived, touched out by the end of the day, her hair had thinned out at the front and was finally returning, and just a week ago, she'd braved jeans again. Her creative inspiration was all out of whack, coming and going as it pleased, and the man who had the potential to completely sweep her heart away was leaving in a few months. Nothing was going as planned.

"I know, Aayala, but maybe we don't need to plan right now. Maybe the plan is we go with the flow for a while?" Malik asked, his low baritone tentative.

"Sorry. I don't know what I said, but that was another stream of thought that was not meant to be said out loud," she whispered, all tapped out from crying. She was exhausted and thirsty, and her body ached, and yet her double-crossing pussy still throbbed in faint anticipation.

"You just said nothing was going as planned, that's all. You've been crying for a while, on and off, and I just needed to hold onto you because that's all I could do for you right now. But rest assured, Aayala, I will find a way to make this better for you."

"You don't need to promise that. You can't control every-thing, same as I can't. I think that's just it, that's why I lost it. I guess the way I used to come before has changed, and that's ok…"

"Yeah, but that don't mean we can't explore together, I know you make fun of me for reading all the pregnancy books and shit, but I read some of this, and if you let me, we can figure some things out together."

"I'm willing to try…"

"But?"

"Nothing, it's just… Even with all this crying, even though I feel wrung out, I can feel the edge of the orgasm still trying to reach me, and it's driving me wild." Being in proximity to Malik was not helping things, either. He smelled like his shampoo and teakwood, which was fast becoming her favorite scent.

"I think maybe we try later, not now," was all he answered. She could tell, even in her fogged mind, that Malik was hurt. She wished she had the strength to reach out and be a balm, but she'd just placed a tiny bandaid on her gaping emotional mess, so she didn't even know where to begin with him.

"Please, daddy…" She couldn't give him words and couldn't give him an explanation, but damn it, she could give him this. Stubborn wasn't her middle name, but it was a second last name.

"Fuck, baby girl, you just broke down in my arms, on top of my dick. I need a minute," he said, but she felt him growing hard against her again. They needed each other right now, both equally hurting for different reasons. Let their connection, no matter how fragile, be the remedy for their pain.

"I need you," she whispered, telling the entire truth in

those three words, a truth more encompassing than she could explain.

"Me too. Always," he whispered back. Then he sat up, bouncing her in the process.

"Get on my lap facing the window."

Aayala did as she was told, the soft command working overtime, making her pussy vibrate in anticipation.

"No overthinking, no expecting to come. You do as I say and only that."

She nodded, eager to let go and trust again.

As if Aayala wasn't solid weight on his lap, he maneuvered her until her legs were hooked behind his so he could control her position. Then he proceeded to open her wide.

"Take off your shirt and bra."

She hesitated, not wanting to lose the protection of the cotton over her, but the edge in Malik's voice told her they were way past the point of no return. He'd been a prince today, taking care of her needs and consoling her once she'd lost herself. With trembling hands, she reached for the hem of the shirt and peeled it off quickly. Her bra left her body with the same speed, and she was glad she'd pumped right before this.

Her nipples, which had become tools instead of points of pleasure, woke up, sensing something different today.

"Touch yourself."

Each command was short and to the point, as if all patience and relaxation had left Malik's body and all that he had left were short sentences to communicate.

"Where do you want me to touch myself?"

"Your pretty wet pussy. Show me how you like it." He breathed the words into her ear, making her shiver again.

Aayala touched herself, going with her tried and true method. She wanted to prolong the sensation of anticipation.

Malik pulled on the hair at her nape.

"Fuck!" The nape of her neck landed on Malik's shoulder, and he grasped her chin and turned her face to meet his smoldering gaze.

"You want to come?"

She nodded.

"Then stop playing games and show me how you like it."

She trembled at his words. The mint on his breath made her want to taste his mouth again. The whole day she'd been dying to kiss him, and he didn't disappoint. He met her lips with a savagery that ignited a dormant feeling deep down in her belly. Something that had no name but had been simmering since she'd had Andre and her whole life spiraled into a new plane that didn't respond to any of her usual control.

She was left gasping after the bruising kiss, and her pussy grew wetter in less than a minute.

She played with the wetness, then tapped her clitoris, hitting it directly, the nerves traveling all down her legs and back up to her sex.

"Fucking heaven, baby girl. That's how you like it. Stop trying to do things the old way. Things have changed. Embrace the chaos." Malik's words carried more meaning than the way she liked to masturbate, but neither of them was ready to have these conversations. Better to focus on low-hanging fruit, on the thing where they both connected and saw eye to eye.

On their passion.

She stimulated herself, touching and caressing with the same firm touch Malik had used last time, her body surrendering to the sensations growing from her sex and her heart. The connection was inevitable as she rested her back against Malik, secure knowing that he would hold her 'til she came.

"Touch your tits, baby girl."

Her hands moved quicker than her brain, but she caught

on and paused when her fingers were a breath away from her nipples. She braced herself for the uncomfortable reaction that greeted her every time she'd tried to switch gears with her breasts since birth. She wanted to feel sexual, a full—

Malik pinched her nipple, eliciting a yelp from her, then his warm breath ghosted the nub, which extended itself, begging to be licked and suckled. Her hand quickened down below, the hunger to let Malik take over and make her feel fully sexual again making her mouth water.

"Touch your tits," Malik commanded against her nipple, then blew on the tip, and her head crashed against his shoulder, a needy whimper escaping her lips.

No hesitation this time. Her hand met her breast, and she cupped herself, pushing one breast against the other, her right hand never stopping as her entire lower body started clenching for the inevitable finish.

"Every morning, I wake up and I thank the stars I came inside of you that night." Malik's low voice dragged more moans out of her. "Every night, I ask that I'm able to take care of you the way you deserve."

"Oh, Malik." She plucked at her nipples, not caring for the slight bit of milk that appeared, the tingling sensation that warned her of her letdown feeling different while she sat on Malik's lap. Now, at this moment, she owned everything that happened with her body. She was in control. And all she wanted was to come apart in his arms.

"Every day, I wonder how I can be the man that you need me to be, to provide for you as you deserve." The agony in Malik's voice made her gasp. He was cracking himself open for her, divesting her of all worries and laying his on a platter, exposing his fears.

"I want to be everything you want and desire," he confessed, voice ragged, dick hard against her ass as she rolled her hips on him and rode the crest he created with the rawness of his confession.

"You're so fucking gorgeous. God, look at you. I don't deserve you. Come for me, baby. You can do it. You're doing it all by yourself."

She cried out, the stimulation of her breasts colliding with the throbbing from her wet pussy, creating a collection of sensations that took her breath away. Then feelings sizzled through every part of her, and her body tensed then released, the strength of her orgasm shattering all her barriers.

At the end of it all, she lay bare on him with his heart in her hands, knowing that no matter what he'd given her today, she couldn't hold onto it for long. He would leave soon enough.

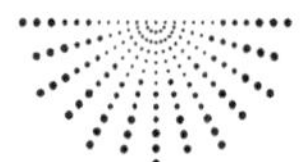

ayala had packed and repacked her camera bag at least five times in the past hour and found herself doing the same exercise once more. The clock told her she had a few hours before the boudoir photo session was set to begin, but she hadn't been able to stay still since she'd woken up that morning in Malik's arms.

Last night had been… She couldn't truly process all the feelings she had about last night. How her body was on board with everything, then when he penetrated her, things went haywire; how he made her come with his words and his encouragement; how he held her until she fell asleep.

In the back of her mind, though, she wanted to try again, to try to have him inside her without losing her ever-loving shit. She didn't want it to be like this. Maybe it was a matter of trying again. This was, after all, the first time she had anything inside of her since she had given birth. Maybe, just maybe, she could give herself a little pass.

And it helped to focus on the physical with him, not the ache in her heart that bloomed each and every time she remembered he would leave for the sea soon. Her breath skipped at the thought of how life would look without him in the everyday flow of things.

Better to focus on her plan, on her goals.

She went through her mental list: four lenses, compact flash cards, tripod just in case, her two cameras, all in.

All this nervous energy needed an outlet. She needed to have her shit together before she walked into that studio. Her clients were the sweetest, shyest couple, and every year for their anniversary, they gathered the courage to do a boudoir session to celebrate their love. This was the fifth year she had the privilege of photographing them, and she wanted to do justice to their experience.

After acknowledging to herself she'd find no peace in the house, she rushed to get her key from the hook by the door, and her stomach dropped when she realized it was missing.

Shit, where did she see it last?

Oh, the last time she had it was…

Fuck.

She plopped down on the sofa in the living room and dialed the number by heart.

"What's up, baby girl?"

"I'm so sorry. I know you and Andre just left not too long ago, but my car key is in the baby bag."

"Ok, don't you worry, I'll turn right back around. Let me just settle Andre with my moms."

"Alright."

The moment she heard him, she felt better, his voice acting like a calming agent to her agitated soul.

The wait was brief. In less than twenty-five minutes, he was back at the house.

"Alright, here we are," he said, dropping the key into her hand and leaning down to give her a soft kiss, lingering on her mouth, pressing soft pecks all around, then nipping at her bottom lip.

"I can see you were worrying yourself while I was out," he murmured against her lips.

"Yes." She smiled against him, basking in the house's quiet and the quiet of her heart while she was with him.

"You want to take me to the shoot?" she blurted out, and once the words were out, they felt good. They tasted as sweet as his presence.

"I thought you'd never ask. Come on."

"OK, HERE WE ARE, BABY GIRL."

They sat in Malik's SUV. The potent smell of glue, that new car smell she loved, permeated the space. She'd been psyching herself up throughout the drive and felt more centered than even half an hour ago.

Her creative eye tingled with curiosity, noting how the sky shined a perfect bright blue, which translated to beautiful natural lighting. The studio was a loft on the twentieth floor that boasted floor-to-ceiling windows with views of the Fort Lauderdale city line. The strong afternoon sunshine would be the perfect enhancement for the shoot.

She needed a boost, something to clear her of the nervous current suddenly running through her, making her hands clammy and her heart pound so hard in her chest she was afraid it was audible.

She turned to Malik, who sat quietly, giving her the space she required to get her head straight.

She was early, arriving an hour and a half in advance to the appointment by design. She knew she needed time for herself and to set up the loft to her liking.

Which meant she had time… Time to explore the thing that had been nagging her in the back of her mind the whole morning.

"Daddy…"

"Baby girl, whatever you're tryin' to start, please be kind. I have to drive back hard as a—"

She stopped his words by placing her hand on his lap. She found he was already hardening under her touch, and that made her insides shiver at the knowledge. Suddenly, she had an urgent need to feel him inside of her that she couldn't shake. Aayala's mouth watered at the thought of his dick inside of her.

Her hand caressed up and down the soft fabric of his basketball shorts until she got him good and hard.

"There aren't a lot of cars in this parking lot…" she whispered as she snaked her hand inside his shorts and underwear to find that silky rock-hard shaft. She felt like a siren, luring him and his dick to sin. As much as she loved him taking charge, right now she felt reckless and ready to take matters into her own hands…pun intended.

"No, but—"

"And I mean, you are out here riding with the deepest tint, just asking for a fine…" she continued, her voice husky and sure. Whatever was driving her, she trusted the feeling. It was the same sense of sureness that drove her that October night. That this was the right thing to do. That connecting with him like this, trusting herself fully, would spark the passion for creating that had flickered on and off these past few months.

She pulled his dick out of his boxers and shorts, and he lifted his hips to assist her in her endeavors.

"Eager much?" She chuckled.

"You are topping right now…" he warned, voice deep and raspy. His hands were clenched on top of his legs, but he didn't move besides that indicator that he was way more gone than he wanted to show.

"And what are you gonna do about it?" she prodded while

she slowly bent toward his lap. She heard his breath hitch once he realized her intentions, and her warm tongue sneaked out to meet his smooth, hard head.

"Mmm," she murmured, licking the top of his dick, and felt him jerk. She smiled and, in a move she knew he didn't expect, glided all the way down his thick, long shaft until he met and passed the back of her throat.

"Fuck, baby girl, I...fuck!" He groaned, and his hips thrust up, making her eyes water. He felt so big and thick in her mouth, and she loved the taste of him, clean and musky. She pulled away, spit trailing her tongue, then she went right back, slurping down his beautiful dick.

His hand went into her ponytail, and he held her still.

"Ok, if you want to play with me like that, then I'm gonna let you have it," he said with a menacing tone that made her panties disintegrate. In this moment, she felt powerful both in what she gave him and in her submission, and Malik, for all he taunted her, was at her mercy. They both knew it, and it exhilarated her to have him so gone right now.

He fucked her mouth with precise thrusts that she met like a champ, opening her throat up to accept everything he had to give. And in the process, she opened herself up and let her fears go. She focused on herself and the moment she was living and didn't overthink.

"Oh, yes, baby girl...yes, oh," he mumbled, and she felt his legs trembling underneath her hand. A surge of pride hit her when she realized how quickly she'd driven his arousal, but she knew she had to stop, or he'd come inside of her throat. And as much as she wanted that, she needed him inside of her pum pum. Right now.

She pushed away from his hold, his dick leaving her mouth with a pop.

"Daddy... I think you should punish me for taking the lead," she said while she watched Malik. He looked so scrumptious: his chest heaving with big breaths, his shorts past his hips with his veiny dick shining with her saliva, still wearing his t-shirt, his face a picture of stern longing. A flood of warmth traveled through her, and she had to stop herself from moaning out loud.

She never broke eye contact with him.

While she shimmied out of her panties, the sense of security and sureness drove her every move. Her heart was racing inside her, and her pussy throbbed in anticipation. She didn't know if her pum pum was gonna get with the program today, but for some odd reason, she didn't give a damn.

"Fuck me, baby girl. I'll make you pay for topping from the bottom, but you clearly need this, so I'm going along for the ride." He pulled his basketball shorts up and exited the car. She was confused for a second, then realized what he was doing.

She watched him settle himself in the back of the SUV, where there was way more space. His shorts met the floor of the car, and she patted herself on the back for picking a tank top dress today.

"Get your sexy ass back here right now," Malik commanded, and her punnani purred and gushed in response. Aayala wholeheartedly agreed with the sentiment.

She finagled herself to the back of the car, demonstrating a dexterity that she thought had deserted her after she gave birth, and wasted no time climbing Malik the way he deserved. It seemed with proper incentive, she could be very, very flexible. And Malik's dick was more than proper incentive…way more.

Her wet, warm center met his slick shaft, and they both gasped when she slid down his length in one delicious move. She had to work to accommodate him, but God, was the labor worth it. The way his girth and length stretched her was a delicious torture she'd missed. Last night she'd been too much in her feelings, too happy at first, too aware, then too sad, and her mind had wandered away from the moment activating her body's response. Today she was fully present, and she meant to stay that way.

"Ok, then, baby girl, you started this, so you better show me what you got," he said with a smirk, sitting back and planting his hands on her hips, making her tremble in need.

"Oh, I'll show you," she whispered against his mouth, then did just that.

She wasn't a yardie for nothing. Her waist had its own talents, and she showed him how good her own swirl and whine could feel. Each time she sat fully on him, she heard her wetness meet his dick, a testament to how much she was into it all. The windows were closed, and they'd steamed up. The heat they were creating inside was greater than the Florida heat outside.

"Mmm, right there, baby girl. You feel too good." Malik's raspy words traveled to the base of her spine, making her shiver in anticipation.

He played with the top of her dress and figured out a way to expose her bra. He tweaked her nipples, then took one of her breasts in his warm mouth, sucking with a pressure that connected with her nerve endings down in her pussy. Whatever he was doing, it felt too damn good. She pulled his face to her chest while he licked, nibbled, and suckled her breasts, taking turns between the two of them. None of the concerns that usually worried her came this time, and she let herself enjoy to the fullest, lustful moans mixing with the laughter bubbling out of her.

She'd completely left her worries in a box to be inspected after, and her creativity was sparkling in the back of her mind. Ideas crystallized in her subconscious as she rode Malik, letting his gasps and groans guide her movements.

"Fuck, baby girl. I need you to slow down, I need you to

come too…" Malik said in a strangled voice as she picked up her pace, using the strength of her legs to ride up and down now, holding herself on his shoulders, pressing her body against his, and capturing his mouth again for a sloppy, sensual kiss that had zero finesse but was so full of passion it would end up in her top ten best kisses ever.

"Mmm, baby girl, you're about to make me nut, but you need to behave now because you need to come too." Malik grunted and let go of her hips, one hand transferring to the bottom of her asscheek and the other going in between them.

He pressed his hand on her clit, and it felt like he'd turned on her body to its fullest setting. Her breath caught when he flicked it with enough force to make her clench around his dick, and he muttered a curse but kept at his purpose. He dragged the wetness between the two of them and circled her nub while she continued with rolls of her hips, his hard dick throbbing inside of her in abandon.

"Sailor, I think I can come without you playing with my clit," Aayala said, gasping for air in between words.

"Are you sure?" He moaned as she clenched around him in response. He took a hold of her ass and started pumping in short, fast strokes that left her speechless and holding onto his shoulders to keep up. It was all him now, and she felt her ass and breasts bounce and jiggle to the force of his thrusts. Sweat trickled down her back, and the smell of sex and their intermingled scents permeated the car so strongly she could almost taste it.

She tightened her thighs around him and enjoyed the ride, but that switch Malik had activated with touching her clit was missing. Instead of dwelling on it too much, she decided to take action.

"I'm gonna…. I'm gonna need for you to touch my clit to come." She moaned while he kept up a steady and impressive pace.

"Fuck, baby girl, that ask just earned you a big reward. I'll make sure this ain't the only time you come today, alright?" he said, bringing his hand back to her clit. Again, her entire body vibrated at his touch, and the sweet urgency of her impending orgasm returned.

"Oh, right there, Malik… I'm close." She begged him, and he grunted, shifting his strokes to that swirl of his that destroyed her each and every time. He captured her left nipple in his mouth, licked it, then bit her, making her scream, the sound bouncing against the doors of the car. He licked it again, then suckled her nipple, and at the same time, he tapped her clit one, two, three times while he rolled his hips, giving her all his dick.

"Come for me, baby girl. You've earned that orgasm. You fought for it."

The mix of sweet pain, relentless pleasure, and Malik's brand of dominance were all she needed to surpass all her settings and go beyond high. Her orgasm grew from her clit, radiating out toward her limbs. The intensity of it made her legs shake. Her arms slackened around Malik, and she slumped onto him. The only thing holding her to him was her weight and his hold on her ass.

He nestled his face on the exposed side of her neck, and with three more hard thrusts, he roared his pleasure into her.

The car was a mix of AC pumping cold air, valiantly attempting to cool the steam created by their fucking, and the pants and gasps from both of them, louder than the music, which she'd only now come to realize Malik had left on. Damn, she had been so greedy for his dick, nothing else mattered.

They straightened their clothes, smiling like loons any time she caught him staring at her or vice versa.

"Well, that was…"

"That was fucking glorious," she said with a nod.

"Fuck, I'm so glad to hear you say that, baby girl. Last night broke my heart, and for a minute, I thought it had broken my dick too," he whispered, and the pain in his voice broke her heart a little.

"I'm good. It's good. Clearly, there's more for me to uncover about what works and doesn't work…but you were right, we just need to keep trying different things." She shrugged, pulling her camera bag to her. The high of the afternoon was still very much in her, and she was planning to ride it the whole session. Her creative eye sizzled and tingled with excitement.

"Ok, so I should be done around five, alright?" she said and stretched back to capture his mouth in a sweet kiss, biting his bottom lip at the end. The grunt he gifted her made her pussy tingle, and if it wasn't for the appointment she had…

"You better leave because I'm about to take you again in five seconds unless you walk out and go kill it in that boudoir session."

Her laugh escaped her, and she pressed her lips once more against him, moving quickly away, but he was faster. She found herself back on his lap again.

"You've pushed all my buttons today, baby girl. This is the last time you do that." Then he kissed her until she forgot her name, his, and that they'd just christened his new car and seemed well on the way to a second ceremony.

Twenty minutes later, she sauntered out of the car, leaving a disheveled Malik still with his semi-tumescent dick out. He'd given her another orgasm with his hands and dick that had her walking funny. She felt on top of the world.

This would be a good day.

CHAPTER TWENTY-TWO

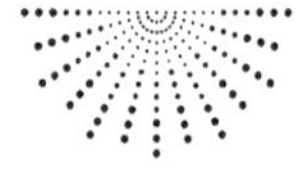

The afternoon smelled of barbecue and freshly mowed grass. The sounds of the water in the pool and the faint bass line of a reggaeton song from a distant neighbor's of the Millers filtered through her consciousness.

Aayala's entire body had that delicious ache you feel after having a great workout. That's what happened when you were getting dicked down on the regular. She was getting the equivalent value of five hundred squats and pushups per day. For the first time in a long time, her sneakers posted up in the corner of her room didn't seem like a failure anymore.

Malik and Aayala had gotten into a tentative groove, both careful not to disrupt the balance they'd found together. Their relationship didn't need a title because they weren't the type of people that were hung up on appearances. They both knew without a doubt that their bond had undergone a transformation since the night he massaged her, and it progressively came closer and closer to a situation…a situation with no type of explanation.

"Since you got here, you've been spaced out. And on top of that, you didn't bring my baby, so I'm mad at you," Alicia protested, sitting opposite her on the lounge furniture on the pool terrace.

"Licy, I love you, but if you don't stop just asking for Andre and dismissing me, I'mma stop coming through." Aayala remained relaxed in her chair, her eyes closed, enjoying the warm breeze that touched her skin.

"Wow, hey! You know I love Andre, but I loved you first, right?"

Aayala wanted to ignore the entreaty, too caught up in her relaxing child-free afternoon to bother wanting to have any type of verbal tussle with Licy.

"Yeah, I know. I know."

"Didn't sound like it. Sounded like you were accusing me of putting Andre first."

"Well…"

"I do not!"

"Yes, you do, but I get it. You want to be Auntie Extraordinaire. I try not to take it personally."

The sliding door hissed open, and Gabo appeared as if godsent. Maybe now Alicia would drop the subject because Aayala knew she was right. Furthermore, it made her wonder if Licy was certain she didn't want to have kids. The way she fixated on Andre was…interesting.

"Gabriel Ernesto, Aayala just accused me of prioritizing Andre over her!" Alicia said in outrage.

"Well…" Gabo scratched his nape, looking everywhere but at his wife. "Aayala may have a point, Ali. I mean, first thing you do when she walks in is ask for the baby."

Aayala nodded at Gabo in solidarity, secretly smug. "I rest my case."

"Gabo, that's not—"

Gabo interrupted the flow of words with a well-placed kiss on Licy's mouth. "I came out to check if you wanted a drink or snacks."

"I'd love a lemonade." Aayala jumped at the offer. Her sundress was in the process of adhering to her back, the warm afternoon taking its toll.

"Ok, how about you, love?"

"Just water, thank you. And don't think I will forget you took Aayala's side."

"That's ok, Ali, I'll be ready for whatever you wanna do to me."

"Ugh, y'all nasty," Aayala said, shaking her head.

Gabo swaggered back into the house while Licy cackled.

"Listen, I'm sorry if I made you feel any type of way. It wasn't my intention. You know I love you, and that excitement for Andre is just an extension of my love for you," Licy said after she calmed down.

"We good. Don't sweat it." Again, Aayala attempted to leave the subject alone, her shoulders bunching up to meet her ears, the slight pain across them a sign that the topic was well past its due date.

"You know, you are so good at giving advice and being there for people. But as a true Firecracker, you just clam up when it's time for you to be supported by us."

"Licy…" she warned.

"No. You're struggling, but we're all pretending you aren't. And I don't know why. I mean, in the year of our Lord Beyoncé 2022? For real?"

Nothing that Licy had to say would be alien to Aayala. She was certain nothing that came out of Licy's mouth would be something she hadn't rehashed over and over in her mind. She didn't want to go *there*. Not again.

"You like these moments when you're apart from Andre."

The statement was a slap in the face. This was not what Aayala was expecting. She reared back as if Licy had truly hit her. The nerve of Licy to imply that she wasn't a good mother…

"I'm a good mother."

"I didn't say you weren't," Licy said gently.

"Licy, tread lightly."

"You always got me to back off with that sentence in the past, but you're hurting. You know, I've been talking to my therapist about the confusion I've felt since Andre was born. I thought I was 100% certain I didn't want kids, but the love I feel for that little boy… Ugh, it's just overwhelming. But in talking with the therapist, I realized that love, although larger than life, wasn't enough for me to give up my independence."

Confusion made Aayala pause in her indignation. She wasn't certain where this was going.

"And I see you, and I know how independent you were before Andre, traveling everywhere for your photo shoots, doing all of these things, and change is hard, you know? It's ok to say that, it's ok to want space sometimes… To do things just for you. How was the boudoir shoot?"

The sliding door opened again, and Gabo appeared with drinks and some chips and dip, which he placed on the low table between them. He kissed Licy, then retreated back to the house.

"Licy, stick to one subject. You're making me dizzy!"

"How was the shoot?" Alicia insisted.

"It was good. Actually, it started absolutely great. It was…" Aayala said, not wanting to go into too much detail about how she'd pumped herself up. In the middle of the shoot, after building amazing energy and getting great shots, her overthinking started taking over, and the second hour became a stilted mess, the couple feeding off her energy. Malik had taken one look at her, drove her home, brought Andre to her to nurse, then tucked her in for the night.

"I fucking cried worse than Andre in Malik's car after it. I felt so…hesitant. Fuck," she finished, feeling that same sense of helplessness as after the photo shoot. Would she really need dick therapy each time she needed to do a boudoir shoot?

"Yeah, and you're a badass, so I can only imagine how foreign that must have felt for you. Everything these past months has been new. Including Malik."

"I'm truly dizzy now, Licy, you're rambling."

"No, you know I'm not. I'm just highlighting all dem ting you avoid speakin' 'bout."

"Oh, you're pulling out the big guns, huh?" Licy knew her too damn well, knew that Aayala's steel armor didn't allow her to break down in front of her. She was a thug, she was yardie. She came from the bush in Jamaica. She couldn't afford all these tears and feelings that kept overwhelming her…

"If I have to. Have you called your dad?"

"Now you just playing dirty."

"Yeah, I am. Before you leave today, I want to give you the number of my therapist."

"Licy… You know me, no need no 'ead docta."

"Aayala, stop, you know better."

She shifted on the sofa, folding her arms. Her stomach quivered at the thought of going to a therapist. Licy was taking it easy on her. If the roles were reversed, she'd badger her with rational sentences until Alicia saw reason. But all the things Alicia was bringing up were things that she didn't have full control over. Her stomach tanked at the thought of talking to someone about all her troubles when she couldn't wrap her mind around what her troubles actually were. It all felt so overwhelming. But Licy was right. Something needed to happen.

"I do, but I don't at the same time. All dem tings…they weigh heavily. You're right. And when I'm ready, we'll talk."

CHAPTER TWENTY-THREE

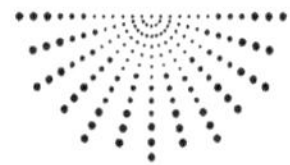

"Boy, if you hammer that nail one more time, it might travel at the speed of light through the fence."

Sweat dripped down Malik's back, and he was glad for the glass of cold water his pops brought him from inside.

"I asked Damian to help me with the new fence, but when I got here, he was gone."

"Yeah, your brother met a new lady friend."

"I wouldn't call the women Damian meets ladies."

"Oh ho, I'm old, and I know that comment is wrong in many ways. Come, don't make me stand for too long. I walked for a while this morning. Let's sit."

His pops pointed at the bench underneath the mango tree. He had installed the bench for his mother when he bought the house for her. He always said the meaning of the bench was a special secret between his mom and him. Many nights, Malik had found them here sitting, laughing together after they thought Damian and Malik were asleep.

After his pops' accident, when he lost his arm, he'd find them here, speaking in harsh whispers, the concern of losing their house palpable in the quiet night. Malik had known it was his turn to take care of his family.

He'd never regretted his decision…but he'd been questioning his motives lately.

Malik sat next to his old man, his pops making a show of unfolding his tall frame onto the bench.

"You know, we knew you used to come and stand behind us and eavesdrop. Your mom still thinks it was the sweetest thing. But I always wondered and worried that you felt you needed to be watching over us as if you were the caretaker…then you up and left us and joined the merchant marines."

"We've talked about this, Pops. It was what I knew. It was your career."

"I would hesitate to call it a career, but it sure as hell provided for this family. Bah! I wish you hadn't left. You were so young, and I'd worked so hard so Damian and you didn't have to bust your ass working like I did—like your grandpa did. I wanted you to have one of them office jobs and be in the AC, and hopefully tell some folks what to do. But you up and went and became a merchant marine. All because your pops lost an arm."

"Pops…" Malik closed his eyes and took a deep breath.

"And then after that, you followed even further in my steps by obsessing about money and future plans. How much is in the bank now?"

"You know how much is in the bank." He dragged his hand over his face, wiping away some of the moisture gathered on his brow after the hard work of the afternoon.

"You're damn right I know, which is why I don't understand why you're still planning to take another voyage. That money is yours."

He had to stand up. This conversation had happened so many ways, but ever since he'd found out Aayala and he were expecting, his pops had dialed up the intensity and frequency of his particular brand of stubbornness.

"Old man, I've done told you. That money is for you and moms, and the rest is for Damian."

"No, it's not. I got my settlement. That ship company finally did right by me and my lost arm after all these years because you pushed and prodded and made me pursue the lawsuit, even though I had no intention of bothering with it. And you supported this family throughout that entire time. Now I have enough from that settlement for your mother to retire in peace."

"But…"

"No buts, boy, I can be as hardheaded as you can be. Now, about Damian—"

"That's nonnegotiable," he assured his father. Whatever Pops had to say about the money he'd saved and grown through the years, him and his momma didn't get to decide what Malik would do with the money he'd saved for Damian. If Damian was so inclined, he could go to one of the top universities in the country. Malik had made sure that Damian had a choice, unlike him. He'd worked hard and loved basketball, and in the end…

His pops stared at him, realizing that he'd put in some hard work and pushed a boulder uphill today. But the boulder had no more room to budge.

"Alright. You keep saving for that boy. Whatever good that does anyone."

MALIK COULDN'T THINK OF A BETTER WAY TO SPEND HIS Sunday than holding Aayala and listening to whatever deep cut she picked to keep on schooling him about reggae. They were playing house, and somewhere along the line, it had intensified into a real ass relationship.

He knew Aayala well enough that labeling what they had would spook her, so he wasn't rocking that boat. Besides, as his father gently reminded him today, Malik wasn't planning to stay for much longer.

He needed to stay true to his plans and continue working and cashing in so that he could retire early. He wanted to be there for Aayala and Andre, but he knew he was more valuable to them by providing. Aayala needed financial flexibility to be able to create to her heart's content without having a spectrum of bills hampering her vision. She didn't need to take jobs she didn't want to take because she had him.

He'd activated other avenues, but none of those had borne any fruit, and time was ticking closer and closer to February, so he had reached out to his union and signed up for his usual ship, hoping it was a contingency plan and not his full reality.

"I'm stopping at Daniel's for a couple of hours, then I'll be home." *Home*. He'd started to call her house his home without realizing it—a habit he'd loved creating not for its repetitiveness but for how right it felt saying it.

"Ok!"

"Aayala, what's up?" That tone of her voice, that chipper falsetto, was a dead giveaway that something had gone wrong in her day.

"I'm fine, I just spoke with my dad today. He's planning to leave for Geneva in a couple of weeks. And my mom doesn't know."

"Shit."

"I know. I'm not surprised. All these years, and he's still trying to slink off in the night and see whatever lady he has in a particular new city. Ma has actually slowed down on following these last years, but who knows how she'll react this time?"

"Are you good?"

"I'm straight. Nothing they haven't done in the past. And she already left me high and dry with Andre, so it's water off my back."

"Well, that paid off, didn't it?"

"If you mean I gained a bossy baby father tryin' to tell me what to do, then yeah, it paid off and then some."

"You got jokes because that baby father has you coming on the regular. Is Andre asleep yet?"

"Oh…you're giving me your bossy voice. You know when you deepen your voice like that, it makes my pum pum tingle?"

He grabbed the steering wheel with force.

"Don't play with me, Aayala, I'll turn this car right around. Is Andre asleep?"

"Yeah, he's down for the night. And I'm all by myself."

"Did you eat?"

"Yes, daddy."

"And did you drink your eight glasses of water? Whenever I'm not there, you slack on that."

"I drank ten."

"Fuuuck. Good girl."

"Mmmhmmm, I've been the best of girls."

"Ok, when I get home from Mason's, I'll give you your reward, but in the meantime…go ahead and draw a bath for yourself, turn on some of the candles I got you. Decompress."

"Nah, I think I'm going to edit some of my—"

"Aayala. It wasn't a suggestion."

Silence. He took the next turn, the road a way to get to Aayala's house because he wasn't about to let her get away with not taking care of herself tonight.

"Ok. Yes, daddy. I'll run that bath."

"Mhm. I'm of a mind to come home and make sure you take care of yourself."

"No, you need some dude time, and you'll break Daniel's heart if you don't go, then I'll have to hear Mariana complain for a week that Daniel is moping around because he didn't get to chill with his BFF."

"You really got all the jokes tonight. But don't you worry, I'll make sure mixed in with your reward, you get a little punishment for making me re-route twice with your sexy self." He joined in her mirth, knowing he would get the last laugh.

He finished the call with Aayala and turned to the recently-turned Torres, Braithwaite & Robinson driveway. He guessed once he finally finished taking long voyages—if Aayala would still have him—the transition to her home would be seamless. Malik only had his clothes to move. That shit used to sound practical in the past, but now, he couldn't shake the hardness in his gut that came with the thought.

"Ok, ok, so I think that whoever gives the best head should be the one that gets the largest amount of space in the closet," Mariana commented.

Malik let himself in the house and was greeted with that statement. The space was full of extra furniture and extra tension. For the third time tonight, he contemplated turning back and going home.

"Fuck, Mari, how do you suggest we decide that?" Mason asked, turning to her as she got up from the dining room table, car keys in hand, to greet him. Malik bent down to receive her kiss on the cheek and then interjected because he couldn't help himself. That, and because the tension in the room was giving him a headache.

"Y'all should pick categories and give points for first, second, and third place. Then rank the answers, which should be given anonymously."

Mariana stood back, staring at him. On the other side of the family room, he felt Daniel's amusement cutting through the tension. Mason sat in the dining room, mouth open at Malik's idea.

"I don't know if you're kidding, but that's actually brilliant. I'll come up with the categories while I'm at Mummy's and Pa's, so when I come back, y'all betta be ready." She went to Daniel and gave him a sensual kiss on the mouth, then approached Mason and ran kisses all over his face, ending with a slow lick of his lips.

These three stayed horny…. He wondered what Aayala was doing right now. Was she in the water already? Naked and slick with bubbles?

"Why the fuck would you give her that idea?" Mason complained as Mariana sauntered out of their house to go visit her parents.

"Well, it seems you've been at it for a while? And I love messing with you." He plopped down on a chair in the middle of the action.

"I don't know what I saw in you." Mason shook his head, and Daniel snorted.

"Of course, you know what, you playin' yourself? I'm a fucking catch. And if I was gay, I'd be the best fuck you'd ever have. Best believe."

"Yeah, we heard, is all about the stroke with you. Mariana wouldn't shut up about it for a week, talking about, 'if Aayala says so, you know that shit is good.' As if Aayala is a dick connoisseur or something."

"Yo, check me out, I know you're out of sorts, but no need to speak about Aayala in any type of way."

"Don't mind him. He definitely didn't mean it as it came out. He's cranky he's having to move his things around, but inside, he's secretly thrilled we've moved in. He can't make up his own mind on what to feel more—annoyed or excited,"

Daniel said, strolling toward Mason and putting a hand on his nape, massaging his upset away.

"Fuck, sorry, dude, you know Aayala is like a sister. I didn't mean it like it came out."

"I hear you," Malik said, knowing Mason didn't mean any harm. Still, he wouldn't let anyone disrespect Aayala, not even his closest friends.

"Speaking of Aayala, are you staying?" Daniel cut to the chase.

"He's just asking because he has a fucking friend hard-on for you. Gosh, it's like all the men close to me have other best friends. It's annoying as fuck," Mason said.

"Dude, did you have dinner already? Do you need to eat? Do you need a Snickers bar?" Malik inquired.

"Nah, sorry, it's just I don't like it when Mari goes out late at night." Mason scrubbed his face.

"Since when?" Malik stared at Mason. He was acting very weird tonight.

Daniel closed his eyes and sighed, then kissed the crown of Mason's head.

"Can we get back on topic? Did you get your Captain's papers?" Daniel insisted.

"Not yet. And as I've told you, I haven't been officially offered the job, so I'm continuing with my normal plans until I hear different. And when they offer, I'll have to analyze it objectively. I have a plan."

"Yep. We've heard the plan. But maybe you should hear Daniel out. He's been trying to talk to you about your Captain's papers for a minute now," Mason added, exasperated.

"Listen, I can go." The energy coming from Mason was more than annoyance. He was…worried and anxious. It checked out, what he said about Mari, but Mason wasn't like that. Mari was super independent. Hell, all of them Firecracker cousins were, so something else was at play here. And what about Daniel's odd insistence on his Captain's papers? He was sure Daniel had plenty going on in his job to be worried about Malik's problems. The dude was cool, but the weird intensity wasn't adding up to him.

"No, man, we planned this the entire week," Daniel protested, and Mason gazed at him with a hint of a smile, then nodded.

"Yeah, I'm being an ass. I'll get my shit together now. Besides, Gabo is on his way. He just texted me."

"Alright, you just let me know. I get being under pressure and shit." Malik relaxed back into the chair.

"So you're gonna leave if you don't get the offer from the family? Are you open to exploring other opportunities?" Daniel again asked, an odd intensity that Malik had no energy to decipher today. Between Mason's off-balance remarks and Daniel's marked questions, he was putting up his energy blockers to protect himself.

A chime cut through everything, and he took his phone out to find a picture of Aayala's toes. It was a close-up as they peeked out of abundant bubbles. His fingers tingled as he answered her text message.

Malik: Beautiful, baby girl, keep relaxing. I'll be there soon.

Aayala: How soon? I want you now.

Malik: When I say so.

His breathing intensified as he put his phone in his pocket.

"So?" Daniel asked, both he and Mason staring at him oddly.

"So...so what?"

"Are you gonna leave?" Daniel asked again.

"Oh shit, sorry. Am I... Yeah, well, yes, you already know."

"Who texted you?" Mason asked suspiciously.

"Mind ya business."

"What's up! Y'all can relax now. I'm here," Gabo said, sauntering into the house, a smile on his face. Malik calculated that he could make a gracious exit about twenty minutes from now.

Another chime.

"Who is it?" Mason asked.

Another picture. The hair of his arms raised when he saw Aayala's collarbone and a hint of her breast. Another close-up. She was teasing him. Fuck, he was going to let loose with her tonight. It was time.

"What's up, Gabo, you good?"

"Yeah, I'm straight. Alicia is on her way to her uncle and aunt, and I'm with my dudes. All is well in my world."

"Damn, one out of three," Mason mumbled.

"For real, babe?" Daniel scoffed.

Daniel and Mason shared a look, then Mason's face turned to a mask of contrition. *What the fuck was going on?*

"So, Malik, are you gonna stay? Did the family offer you the job?" Gabo asked, essentially pushing the last button he had to give. Why were they all fixating on this topic? Didn't they understand he had no other choice but to leave again? The captain's papers would come, but the reality was that making the choice to take a less-paying job would delay his timeline.

Tonight of all nights when he just wanted to bask in Aayala and enjoy the time he had left with her? Fuck it. He was going to do just that.

"I'mma head out." His phone chimed again.

A picture of Aayala's plush lips, slightly open, with her tongue peeking out. He felt lightheaded as all the blood left for normal functioning went straight down to his dick.

"Yeah, whatever you just got there, based on your face, I would leave if I were you," Daniel remarked.

"Word," Mason said.

"You ain't lying," Gabo replied at the same time.

He marched out, ready to punish and reward his baby girl.

"Huh. So, that's the face I was making when I was messing with Daniel and Mariana? You're right, it looks like constipation," Malik heard Mason whisper, and Gabo guffawed in response.

His friends ain't shit. But he still loved them, though.

CHAPTER TWENTY-FOUR

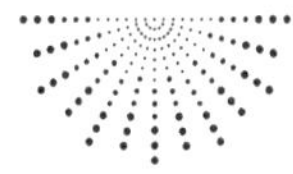

The knowledge of what awaited him propelled his every step to get closer to Aayala.

Malik opened the door to her bathroom after he knocked, and his breath took off without permission.

Aayala submerged in bubbles, illuminated by the flickering candles around her, was a sight he'd remember 'til the end of his days. Malik had mental snapshots of her through the years, but this…this was the crown jewel of his mental collection. Mellow reggae tunes greeted his ears, and the scents of jasmine and chamomile seduced him.

"Hi. You sound…agitated," Aayala said from the tub, sounding breathless. His eyes followed every movement she made as she slowly lifted one leg out of the water and onto the ledge of the tub.

"I'm not agitated. I'm breathless." He said the simple truth.

Aayala's laughter warmed him, the sound delicate and brief.

"I'm a little breathless, too. I guess you stopped by your room for a second?" Her eyebrow lifted high as she inspected his bare chest and basketball shorts, the black ones she loved.

He ran a hand over his chest, attempting to calm the ache from how quick his heart was racing.

"Get out of the water."

"I was hoping you would help me clean up?" She again let out that self-deprecating laugh that covered her nervousness.

"Aayala. It's me. No need for nerves."

"Who said I was nervous? I'mma thug, I'm good." She rolled her shoulders, her fake cockiness endearing. It reminded him he needed to be gentle with her. He thought of the punishment he'd painstakingly planned on his way here —and the reward—and realized he needed to shift gears.

"Alright, thug. I still need you out of the water."

"Yes, daddy."

She stood up with no artifice. No intentional seduction. She didn't need to try, he was conquered without her having to try. She stepped out of the tub, then in a sudden rush of shyness that made her chest and cheeks redden, she grabbed a towel and wrapped it around her body.

"I didn't ask you to dry yourself," he chastened.

"Oh... I... Yellow." She flushed darkly, and her shoulders slumped in defeat.

He knew it. He fucking knew it. Usually, her need to come overrode her need to hide herself from him, but tonight... Tonight, they would have this talk. Once and for all.

"Alright. Come, step closer."

She hesitated, then approached him.

He picked her up and held her close to him, then strode to her bed, placing her gently on top.

He saw the standing mirror by the corner of her room, and the plan quickly rearranged itself in his mind.

"I was going to have you do some lines, then spank you. A little easy punishment to start slow, but I realize that's not what you need tonight. That's not what either of us needs tonight. So, when you are ready, let me know, and we will switch gears."

"I'm ready. I just didn't feel like taking off the towel at the moment. Can I put on clothes, daddy?" she whispered in the room, the soft reggae tunes filtering from her bathroom. He wanted to let her stay in that comfort zone. He truly did. His dominant instincts were out of whack with her, but she needed to face her demons.

"No."

"Excuse me? Did you say no?" The flash of insolence made him harden. He wanted her to show some of her steel. It was part of who she was.

"You heard me, baby girl. No. When you are ready to take off your towel, once you've dried and warmed up, we'll start."

"No, no, that won't work for me."

"Are you safing out? You can and should if this doesn't feel right for you."

"No, no, I don't want to safe out, I just don't feel comfortable naked, ok? It doesn't feel…" Aayala's eyes filled with tears, and he was ready to safe out himself.

"Look, we better—"

"No, no, I— What did you have in mind?"

"I need to tell you some things, and they will be hard to hear. I want you standing in front of the mirror naked. I also don't want to force you to do anything you truly can't take."

The next song on her playlist started, the low bass vibrating into the bedroom. Aayala sat, deep in thought, until she jumped up from the bed and let the towel travel down to the floor. His fingers prickled with awareness of their proximity and how badly he wanted to touch her. But they weren't there yet.

"Where is that vibrator you were using the other night?"

"Why do I need a vibrator when you are here…daddy?"

"Don't you worry. Go get it now, baby girl."

She approached one of her drawers and pulled out the small device, handing it to him.

"Stand by the mirror."

Aayala padded to the spot he pointed at, her sienna skin making the tip of his fingers tingle in need. She was perfect, but he knew he'd not be able to convince her without putting in the work. She kept her eyes closed, not wanting to start.

"Open your eyes, baby girl. Remember who is in charge," he said, standing behind her, capturing her neck in his hands and pulling her face back to meet his.

Ragged breaths escaped her even though he'd barely touched her. He wanted to feel as breathless and swept away as she was. He couldn't help but ravish her juicy mouth, licking her bottom lip one last time before moving away. After the kiss, she was thick molasses in his hands, ready for what he wanted to do to her.

"Tell me, what do you see?"

"I see…a tired mother." Her voice trembled.

"What else?"

"I… I see your beautiful dark hand on my chest, holding me up," she said, and his hand pressed against her soft, dewy skin, still warm from her bath.

"Good, and what else?"

"I… I see stretch marks," she said with a little more confidence, and his hands trailed down to her belly and hips to follow said marks.

"Me too. You know what I like about them?" He breathed in her ear, making her shiver.

"No…" she moaned.

"I love that they are a roadmap of the strength of your body. A reminder. What else do you see?

"What else?" he insisted. He squeezed her hips and nipped the side of her neck exposed to him, then licked it slowly, not able to resist having all of her lushness in his arms. He needed to taste and caress. He felt lightheaded, the scent of green and flowers coming out of her body mixing with the earthy fragrance of her.

"My sad tits…which confuse me, now that you are here." Her breath hitched.

"Well, calling them sad is a fucking crime. Can I touch?"

She nodded.

He moved both hands, cradling her heavy, full breasts. They didn't look sad to him. Fuck, just having the privilege of touching her was heady. Malik knew she was sensitive here. He'd read up on what could happen when someone breastfed and felt a disconnect with their body.

He willed himself to take his time, massaging, circling, and teasing her thick nipples until he heard her gasp.

"Do you still think they are sad?"

"When I'm with you, they are not. When I'm with you, I feel sensual again."

"I want you to feel that way every day, not just when I'm around because that's who you are. You can be both things, sensual and nurturer. There is space for both."

"I see flab." Her words made him jerk back in surprise.

"Really? I…won't tell you something you see is not there, but I see thicker hips than before, and your ass… Lord have mercy on me with this ass." His hand ghosted down her soft hip to her left cheek and squeezed and massaged until she rolled her hips back against his hard erection. The touch of her plumpness against him hit him hard, threatening to fell him like a mast hit by lightning on a stormy night. "But truly, what I see the most is strength mixed with comfort," he said.

Aayala stood stock-still, her eyes brimming with emotions that he wasn't sure he was prepared to handle. His toolbox was limited at best, and the mantle of responsibility settled heavily on him.

"I see a woman who is conflicted about her new responsibilities as a mother."

There. He didn't even have to push. The true disconnect below it all. He accepted her words and held them close, a precious treasure to protect. These were difficult words to say. They were difficult words to hear.

"Tell me more."

"I want it all. I want the old me back. The me that could pick up and travel anywhere. The me that could take jobs at the drop of a hat. I want the me that fucked and came every day, the me that loved running and going out. I want the me that felt creative pleasure in working with other sensual creatures. I want to get that me back and still have it all. Have Andre, be a great mom, and love him how he deserves. Instead, I have this new me, overly concerned with not fucking up this little person who will be shaped by each and every move I make. I'm leaking every three hours. My pum pum forgot we were partners and has gone haywire. I create, but I have to use all the technique and my knowledge now, it doesn't flow the same. Generational trauma is biting my ass. Where did I go?"

A tremor started from deep within Aayala, and it took over him. He let the seismic consequences of her words travel through the room and do the damage; they'd rebuild what they must.

"What do you need?"

"I need time and space, and I have none. When you leave... It's just me."

When you leave... She didn't wonder or hope. It was a done deal for her, and her absolute certainty grabbed him by his throat, making it hard to swallow. This was why he didn't let external emotions overwhelm him... He closed his eyes, needing a moment to process it all. He remembered the mantle he'd accepted tonight, the one he'd accepted when he was eighteen years old, and stood tall, holding her closer, making her body flush against him. He could provide here, on this. And later on, by leaving.

"What do you want?" Malik grunted, squatting to align himself with her as Aayala nestled herself against him with a shimmy that made his dick end up cradled between her ass cheeks.

"I don't want to talk anymore because you know. Because you know me. And I see what you do, and I feel the support, and I know…" She paused, voice strained. "If only…"

He swept her into his arms, turning her around to capture her lips again and stop the words that were about to tumble out and probably destroy them both. Because he did know her, and he had noticed. And he wanted to answer that she should be able to do all she'd described. He knew it was absolutely unfair that she was the one to change her life the most for a decision that they both made.

He would never regret his decision, but he'd fucked up. He'd miscalculated when he assured her they could do this because when he thought of it all, he saw himself as a distant provider. And that's not what Aayala needed. But that's all he had to give.

He poured all his rage at himself and all his lust for her into this kiss. She whimpered against his lips, taking all he had to give her like the truly good girl she was. She needed him to take care of her; she needed that support, that solace…to have realized it now after all these years…

"I need you to fuck me 'til I can't think anymore," Aayala begged.

That begging…fucking shit. He couldn't think straight when she begged so pretty.

He pushed her down to the floor, arranging her until she lay on the carpet, her body draped on her side, her head lying on her left arm, as he grabbed her right thigh and dropped that leg over his, giving him unfettered access to her wet sex.

He could see both of them in the mirror—Malik holding himself up with his left arm on the floor, his right arm still holding her open for him as he pushed inside her tight pussy. He watched his length enter her, inch by inch, and it took all of him not to spill inside of her at the delicious contact.

He shivered at the sight of them together: Aayala laying languorous and open, soft tits bobbing to the rhythm of his thrusts, her pussy glistening as it received his thickness, her big lips parted in ecstasy, her hypnotic eyes never leaving his. The position allowed her to surrender completely and let him take control, and he fucking needed to take control. He was right behind her, his fingers splayed on her thigh, his long, strong legs tangled in between her soft ones, making sure she could take it all. He didn't break eye contact with her, his chest expanding each time his dick hit bottom and he swirled inside of her.

He grabbed and squeezed her right thigh as she whimpered. The smell of sex, longing, and her bath soap surrounded them as he started to thrust faster inside of Aayala.

The melody of her noises guided him, telling him he was on the right track with each plunge deep inside her, each swirl of his hips grinding them together. She was gone; he knew that because her hand left the floor to caress her tits. She tormented her nipples, and he felt each tug by the way she hugged and squeezed the hell out of his length.

"Keep playing like that, baby girl, and you are going to get fucked 'til you sleep until noon tomorrow."

"Aah, Malik, please," she begged. He held her hip and rewarded those pretty words, shifting his thrusts to a hard, punishing pace that made her gasp in astonishment. Aayala had to let go of her tits and hold onto the floor because he was fucking her so hard, she started sliding on the carpet.

"Don't run now, Aayala. You asked for this, and you're going to take all I have to give. This is what I can do for you, baby girl, if you only let me…" His voice cracked. Fuck, he didn't intend to let her pussy make him forget himself so much.

"Yes, daddy. No running." She hooked her right leg over his right thigh, opening herself even wider, and then she rolled her lower body against him.

"Fuuuck." Her voice, that deep husky moan, made the hairs of his arms and leg stand at attention, made his dick jerk and grow harder inside of her. He was starting to feel lightheaded with all the sensations coursing through his body.

Out of self-preservation, he shifted his body to hers, turning them into an open spoon, her legs still spread open, all the while never slowing down. His hand cradled her breast again, and he buried his face in her neck, biting her as they shifted gears to a filthy whine that reminded him of all the dancing they did that fateful October night.

Sweat sprouted between their bodies, the skin-to-skin contact creating slickness that aided the easy slide of their bodies as they met together. The wet sounds of his dick gliding in and out of her made his spine tighten, and he had to slow down because Aayala's rolling hips and ass were about to make a punk out of him.

"Turn on the toy and put it against your clit." He ran his tongue over the outer shell of her ear and nipped her there, making her groan. He needed her to come, same as he needed water. It was that simple. He'd taken her orgasm situation personally, one thing to do for her that no one else could do. One thing to make right in the long list of things that had changed for her.

"It's ok if I don't come every time. If this is the new me, then so be it… I'm at pe—"

"Stop. We agreed to try new things."

"Yes, daddy."

She did as told, like the good girl she was, and he felt the instant she went from enjoying and present to moving by instinct in rapture. If what she had been doing before was addictive, what she did now would have him joining a cult to venerate her, no question.

Her body molded against his, and her pussy fluttered and squeezed as she pressed the toy to her clit. She drenched him with her need, and when she screamed his name, she allowed him to forget for a minute that this wasn't forever. She allowed him to forget himself and his self-protection. His love for her pulsed out of him, and as she gripped him tight, words spilled out at the same time he filled her.

"Fuck, Aayala, I love you."

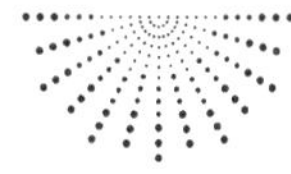

CHAPTER TWENTY-FIVE

"I love you?" Aayala asked him as he dragged himself slowly out of her. For a moment, it seemed he'd planned to camp inside her. Her pussy still throbbed with the aftermath of the orgasm they'd just created together. Aftershocks were going on inside her chest, Malik's words echoing in her room, not settling until addressed.

Malik rolled over on his back and laid still, staring at the ceiling. She wanted to shake him until he spoke but restrained herself. The cold air hit her, her nipples contracting and seeking shelter where there was none to be had. She stood up and searched in her drawers for something to wear, hating how vulnerable she felt.

"I wish you wouldn't," he growled.

"What?'" she asked, turning to face him while she slipped on her sleep shorts.

"Put clothes on right now. You're beautiful, and I'm in love with your body. Same as with your heart. I think I might always have been and didn't realize it."

Blood rushed at double speed through her veins, the

movement so fast she could hear it, feel it, her ears pounding at the beat of her heart.

"You playin' with me right now."

"No, I'm not. And I'm not trying to make this a big declaration either. This is just reality. I crushed on you in school, and as we kept writing to each other, it just grew in my mind and in my heart. I don't think I ever thought to put a label on my feelings. I don't know why you're surprised. I've been telling you things I tell no one for years. And I'm not a talker."

"I..." She was left without words. Thoughts swirled around with no place to go. "I..."

He chuckled, but she knew he wasn't amused. "Be easy, Aayala, you're gonna strain yourself tryin' to say something back. I don't need it. You and I, we're together, and we'll remain together until you say different." He stood up in one swift motion, elegant in his nudity, and she stood poleaxed, wearing her shorts and nothing else, heart thumping wildly inside, eyes basking in the view.

"Ok."

"Good girl." He nodded as if that was all that needed to be said.

***

Time had an interesting quality to it when things were good in her life. Usually, it flew by when Aayala was having fun, traveling, and living the good life. But what was happening these past weeks was beyond good.

The memories Aayala and Malik were creating together and with Andre were the type that became indelible. The type of memories that had a scent, a rhythm to the beat of a song, a physicality to them that no matter where you were when they came back to you, they made you stop and relive the moment.

Time was behaving oddly, accelerating when she didn't need it to and slowing down at unsuspected instances. The slowdown inevitably was when she was overthinking her situation with Malik. The declaration of love from weeks ago had made Malik step fully into himself. In the process, he'd fully embraced the man he wanted to be with her, demanding she take care of herself, prioritizing her, and sexing her up and down that townhome, finding innovative ways to keep her on her toes and make her come. It didn't always happen, her orgasms selective and finicky, but each pleasurable minute was worth it because it was with him.

Through their explorations of what worked best for her now, they'd realized that her pelvic floor was weaker than before, so she'd started Kegel exercises, which had greatly helped. She still couldn't come vaginally. She had lost her privileged spot as God's favorite, but the sensation created by his fingers felt as close to heaven as it would get.

They'd finally indulged in impact play. The playful spankings he gave her when she missed a glass of water or hadn't eaten lunch while working always led to steamy encounters late at night. And she was always hungry for the relief only he could give her.

The one thing he refused to do was talk about what he'd said that night. He wasn't shy about reminding her he loved her, but he didn't want to answer the many questions she had about it. Inevitably, he would distract her with a command, and they'd end up fucking, which was why, many weeks later, they had unresolved topics to tackle with no progress in sight.

With the passage of time came the change of seasons, and the holidays had arrived with a quickness most parents could understand. One moment she was putting away the

Halloween costumes, and the next second they were putting up lights on the tree.

For Andre's first Christmas, Alicia, who had self-appointed herself the matriarch of their generation, had planned Nochebuena for all the family. Alicia had cajoled with Gabo's support until all the Firecrackers and significant others agreed to stay at their house to receive the 25th and open gifts together.

"Are you awake?" she whispered in the quiet room. Malik lay behind her, spooning her with his tall, lean frame. They had gone to bed after three in the morning, drinking and dancing the night away.

"Yeah, I'm awake. You want me again? You know I'm always ready for you," Malik whispered back.

"Stop playin'. We shouldn't have done that here!"

"Why not? They stay having sex in the Center, they don't care. Besides, Alicia took one for the team and had Andre sleep with them, so we should take advantage of that…" he crooned in her ear, his hand snaking underneath her tank top, cupping her breast.

"Is this ok?" he asked.

"Yes, it's ok." She pressed back to him, meeting his hardness and undulating against him.

"Fuuuck, if you keep doing that, I won't let you out of this room until you come."

"Ok."

A groan. "Drop your panties and spread your legs."

"Yes, daddy."

A shiver ran through her as she answered him. She thrilled at being a good girl, at knowing someone would take care of her. The satin covers dragged across her back, decadent in their texture against her skin.

His hand returned to her breasts, where he pinched and tweaked her nipples hard, creating a direct line of sensation from his fingers down to her pussy. He took his time, whispering in her ear, telling her about all the things he still wanted to do to her.

He plumped her breasts, and she leaned into his hands, sighing with her entire being. She loved being petted and played with. She wanted to be treasured, his favorite toy. He pinched her again, then soothed the sharp spike with languorous swipes of his tongue. He had the audacity to look up at her and wink, then bite her nipple, making her yip loudly.

"Shhhh, you're gonna wake everyone up. Be quiet. You can't say a word until you come."

She nodded because she knew he'd reward her, and she was right. She always was.

Her smugness soon turned to thrashing and begging just like he loved. He slid his hand down the satin sheets until he found her wet and ready for his magic hand.

She turned her face to look at him, his bedroom eyes brimming with intensity, connecting with something inside her chest that had lain dormant and was waking up just for him. Chills of pleasure ran through her, to be so precious to him, to be seen so well… His thumb pressed directly on her clit. At the same time, he placed three fingers inside of her.

She froze, every single molecule in her pausing to enjoy how right it felt to be touched by him, a flash of heat blossoming from her chest outward.

He played with her, whispering in her ear as she bucked and moaned, the sounds of her wetness loud in the morning lull.

"You hear that? Do you hear yourself? Such a good girl, how wet you get for me. Feel how your pussy grips my fingers. She's crying for some dick."

"Ahh, yes! Right there."

With expert movements, Malik kept up a strategic attack

against her clit and pussy with his fingers until she came all over his hand, sighing as her orgasm washed through her.

"Mmmm. Merry Christmas, baby girl."

"Merry Christmas, daddy."

After their lovely interlude, they showered and went downstairs in search of the rest of their family and friends.

"Merry Christmas! I tried to let you sleep as much as possible, but little man over here woke up a few minutes ago and wants his breakfast." Alicia sat at the kitchen table with Andre dressed in red PJs that said "Santa is Coming to Town" and a cute red Santa hat. A pang went through Aayala as she'd brought another set of PJs for him to wear. These were clearly ones that Licy had bought. Aayala had worn a matching set to his and had convinced Malik to wear a t-shirt that matched the black and red colors.

Andre squealed when he saw her and Malik, and as she held him, his warmth spread from her arms into her heart, filling her chest up as she accommodated her clothes to feed him.

Even though she was annoyed as fuck at Licy choosing different PJs, she tried to let it go for the sake of their morning together. Reading her for filth right now wouldn't be a good start to the day, and she was glad to find her center so easily and see that the gesture from Licy was one of love.

Fucked up and wrong as hell, but still coming from a place of love.

"You're gone for her, aren't you?" Mason said as he sauntered into the kitchen, holding Mari's hand.

"Was that supposed to be a whisper?" Malik asked, crossing his arms over his chest and winking at her. Those bedroom eyes were still brimming with whatever emotion he carried from their morning together, and she felt a tingling at the back of her neck, her arms prickling at the cold temperature of the kitchen.

"Nah, I don't do that…unless I'm fucking, then I whisper in my lovers' ears all they want." Aayala grinned at Mason's words and Mari's outraged face.

"Ay, Dios mio, Mason, for real?" Mari asked, grabbing a banana next to her and peeling it.

"What? You love me like this."

"That I do." Mari stretched from her perch on the countertop and kissed him on the lips.

"Baby girl, didn't you bring matching PJs for Andre? You want me to go get them from the room? I know you were excited for the three of us to match today." Malik asked the innocent question rolling off his tongue with such ease. The devious, amazing man. Her pum pum, that duplicitous lady of the night, throbbed in agreement.

"Oh, yeah! Sorry, Aayala had given it to me for him to wear, but I had bought him this little gift for today. I didn't know you guys had outfits planned. I should have known. I'll go change him." Licy stood up, reaching for Andre, who had become a master at eating and was done with his breakfast. Aayala smiled at her cousin, who had taken the gentle rebuke from Malik with poise. She couldn't stay annoyed at her after that. Well, she could, but she wouldn't.

As Licy rushed out with Andre, Daniel and Gabo walked in, whispering in low voices.

"It's Christmas," Mason said, voice cutting. The temperature dropped a few degrees, and not from Licy's AC. Aayala flickered her eyes toward Malik, who stood watching Mason like a hawk.

"We know," Daniel answered, grasping Mason's hand as he walked up to him.

"It is. Merry Christmas, y'all, but this conversation—" Gabo started.

"Should wait 'til we are back in the Center after the

break," Mason admonished, pushing closer to Mariana, who seemed resigned to the situation.

What's happening? Having a baby had fucked up her radar. Usually, she'd be in the know. Either Licy or Mari would have told her and looked to her for advice. Her belly knotted as she searched Mari's face, not quite knowing how to help. She hated this feeling. She knew her cousins thought they were protecting her when they kept things from her after Andre was born, but it was hard to reconcile how disconnected she felt from them sometimes.

"Is this about…" Malik started.

"Yeah," both Daniel and Gabo answered.

"Well, y'all know my proposition. And I presented the spreadsheet before the holiday party, and it adds up. Those were just the people who have approached me that would be willing to pledge monthly. And we all have friends and colleagues that would help too. It's worth trying. Let's focus on mutual aid instead of waiting for rich assholes—not you, Daniel—and do the right thing." At Malik's words, Aayala's puzzle pieces snapped together, but there was still a gaping hole in the middle of it. Something else had Mason bent out of shape. This couldn't be it.

"Fuck, y'all can't let it go. I told you I don't want to ask the community to pay for the Center's work when it was created to alleviate the needs of the community. It makes no sense." Mason pounded his right hand on the kitchen counter.

"Love…" Mari held his left hand, which he fisted on her lap. Aayala saw the grimace on Mari's face and knew from conversations with her and Malik that the Center was in dire straits. All of them were helping and agreed with Malik's plan, but Mason kept blocking the final move. Gabo, out of respect for his partner and his friendship, wanted to wait until Mason was on board with Malik's plan.

She'd been so proud when he walked her through what he

thought would be the saving grace of the Center—a plan for the professionals and members of the community that were doing well and owned businesses to pledge a monthly payment to the Center, and in return, the Center would provide them with tax donation letters to assist small Black-owned businesses.

The pledging was voluntary, and there were tiers. Depending on the tier, you also received privileges to host complimentary events in the Center space during nights when there was no scheduled programming.

Malik had created a full business plan, and it worked. She'd already budgeted her pledge. She wondered if he realized how well he'd built his presentation and overall project, how his plan would probably save the Center, and what that meant for him, stretching himself to look at other opportunities outside of being a mariner…

"Why are you being closed-minded about this? This is the best foot forward. We are bleeding money, you and I, and we have other responsibilities. We need to shift perspective," Gabo reasoned as Licy returned with her baby. Aayala held her arms out to Andre, wanting his solid weight as comfort. The heaviness in the room didn't care that it was Christmas morning, and if someone didn't back down soon…

She gazed at Malik again and saw how rigid he stood. His usual calm demeanor evaporated with the tension. She ached to go and stand by him and hold his hand, but she knew he prided himself on his calm.

"Is this about the Center? If we're talking about Malik's plan, I agree. I mean, why not listen to him? The Center was opened because of the impact him not getting a scholarship had on you and Gabo," Aayala reminded Mason, needing to support Malik by any means necessary.

"Yeah, you'd think my idea had some merit," Malik said, still resting against the far corner of the kitchen, his face a mask of neutrality. But she knew. She knew how difficult this conversation was for him. How much his life had changed by not having that scholarship, and how close he felt to the Center and the kids there.

"Nah, y'all say all of this. All good talk, but only Gabo and I are putting in the daily work."

"That's fucked up," Daniel said.

"He didn't mean it like that, babe," Mariana pleaded, getting down from the counter, faltering on the way down.

"Oh, he did." Malik sat shaking his head, flashes of emotion running through his face.

"Fuck, you gotta be careful, sweetheart, you can't be doing shit like that anymore!" Mason exclaimed as Mari stumbled and held herself against the kitchen table.

"Enough!" Daniel bellowed, and everyone stood silent, shocked at his outburst. Daniel, the calm and collected one of the crew after Malik.

"Mason. You don't let me help you. You don't want to implement this plan, which is the best thing for the Center and the kids. You want this to flourish, but you're holding onto a romantic view of what the Center should be instead of the reality of what it is. Malik's plan is solid. He has the backing of the community. They all love him and know him. Why not work with that? And we all know of young professionals looking to help out in tangible ways. Let's do this plan. And you gotta let us help. And you gotta let Mari breathe."

Aayala studied Mari's face, and a cold certainty settled in the pit of her stomach, ready to ignite based on Mariana's next words. She shifted her gaze to Malik, wanting someone to confirm. He nodded pensively, unsurprised.

"Are you...?" Licy asked.

Mari nodded, eyes misting with tears.

"Ahh!!" Both she and Licy jumped up from their chairs

and scrambled to Mari, who greeted them with a watery smile.

"And it's twins," Daniel said proudly, eyes shining bright.

"Gatdamn," Gabo said, hugging Daniel, who was grinning wide. She'd never seen him smile for so long. Losing his temper first, and now this. What a Christmas morning.

Gabo hugged Mason next, their whispering and low laughs mingling with Licy's exclamations and rapid questions. Aayala just held Mari's hand, wanting to give her an anchor while everyone swirled around them. The noise rose as emotions settled from an uncomfortable high to a jolly one.

Malik dapped and hugged Daniel, his face pure happiness, then he turned to Mason. "Dude, I knew you were acting weird as fuck and had my suspicions. You could have just said you had a million worries on you instead of acting like a dick. We got you, man, we always got you. We'll figure this out."

Malik embraced Mason, and she saw Mason's shoulders shake with emotion. A tear escaped her eye at the scene.

Childbirth truly had made her soft. Damn.

"He's been a mess since we found out. All worried about it being a geriatric pregnancy and all the shit that comes with multiples. I've never felt better, but he don't listen. Same as with this Center thing. I swear he has a Superman complex, so I'm just patient with him," Mari said, happy tears streaming from her eyes to match the emotion brimming out of her and Licy's.

"Don't they all?" Licy said, voice low. "That's why we gotta stay close and pay attention because they'll keep that shit inside, and we'd never know. Even though Gabo is doing much better at communicating since we've been together."

A sense of dawning flooded through her as she looked at Malik and paid attention to all his actions these past months.

It was like someone had turned a bulb on in the middle of darkness.

His involvement with the Center, his insistence on getting his captain's credentials. Was she missing something? Was there an opportunity for more? She knew he was shouldering more than he should, but he refused to let go of the load. He seemed proud to be able to carry it all, and somehow, she'd gone from self-sufficient to trusting he could carry some of hers too.

She gazed at him as they all walked out of the kitchen to go open gifts. But then she thought of how open they were with each other and remembered there hadn't been much they kept secret since they were in their twenties. The light bulb dimmed, and she avoided eye contact when Malik returned her gaze, feeling numb after the rollercoaster ride her insides had taken with her suppositions.

When he gave her his gifts—a collage of pictures of the three of them to hang in her office, and three new vibrators, which he whispered they'd play with before he left in February—the feeling of numbness spread to full heaviness until the bottom opened and she started falling.

He was still leaving. Nothing had changed.

And even though her heart was already his, she couldn't give it to him and have him leave with it. She knew she would not survive with the two of them far from her.

A flash of her father's voice telling her he was leaving again sparked dread in her. It would be so easy to succumb to whatever Malik could give her, but she had firm examples of why long-distance love wouldn't work for her. She would probably grow as obsessive as her mother, and that couldn't happen. Andre deserved a mother that was present and dialed in.

Not a heartsick one, waiting by the window every day.

CHAPTER TWENTY-SIX

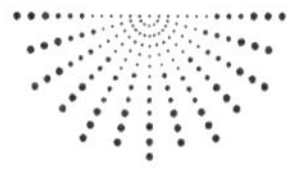

The calendar, that piece of paper that gave her so much hope months ago, was mocking her now. There wasn't much left of her six months, and her list of goals grew dust on the sticky note on her board.

Be a great mom? If you were to ask Andre or Malik, it was a yes, but she still battled the dissonance of her experience as a mother.

How could she balance the burning desire to pave the entire way in soft wool for Andre so that he might never experience pain, to have all the time in the world to listen to him giggle, making her chest expand with love? To teach him to be a good, kind young person and break all the generational curses she thought she'd dodged? Of course, she hadn't dodged them. They'd all hit her in the face these past months. On the other hand, she wanted her independence, to not have her day scheduled around the times she needed to pump, or just be able to pick up and take a booking in L.A. or New York without worrying about childcare. So, was she a good mom, or was she just treading water?

Get back into boudoir? So-so.

She alternated between great bookings where she'd taken bomb ass pictures and days where she cried herself to sleep because she couldn't quite capture the essence of the person. Malik assured her she was being too hard on herself, but she knew what she could give, and what came of her camera some days wasn't cutting it.

Learn how to be a single working parent? Big fail. Every habit she'd wanted to create went in complete opposition to what Malik wanted from her. His presence in her home had shown her how great it could be between them if only…if only he wasn't the most responsible man she'd ever met. And that was saying something with examples such as her uncle Clinton, may he rest in peace, and Mariana's father and the boys. Malik would not rest until he knew his family, she and Andre were settled, even if it meant working 'til he was sixty.

The romantic in her wanted to commit to the long-distance situation and just enjoy it. Anyway, she'd done it in the past with Sergio. She'd never lost sleep because of it.

But the thought of being apart from Malik… He'd awakened in her something she hadn't realized had been inside of her. She wanted to be cherished, loved, and love back. She knew it wouldn't be easy being away from him, and driving him wild with demands would sour their relationship, and Andre didn't deserve that. He deserved parents who were smart and kept it simple so they could be the best co-parents.

A bolt of familiar heaviness fell in her chest as Malik's departure loomed closer and closer.

She sneaked into the office, aka Malik's room, even though he spent all his nights in her bed, to put away some of his laundry, which she'd started washing early in the morning before he woke up. The exasperating punnani whisperer refused to let her do anything else in the house. He'd probably spank her then finger her 'til she screamed his name once he realized she'd done the laundry for everyone.

Oh, well…she'd have to take it. She smiled at herself, anticipating the funishment. She had to take advantage of all he had to give to her.

Her phone went off, startling her, her hands shaking as she answered it. She hoped the noise hadn't woken either Malik or Andre up. It was the crack of dawn, and there were still a few hours of sleep. She was planning to return to bed and see what Malik thought of her doing the laundry.

"He left!" A high-pitched scream rang in her ear, and for a second, Aayala searched around, crouching, fists balled, concerned someone had broken into the house and the alarm system had gone off to alert them.

"He left me again and…have you heard from your Da?" The suspicious tone of her mother's voice told Ayala she was in a nasty mood.

Relaxing her posture, Aayala breathed.

"Ma, I don't like to get in bet—"

"You ingrate, you should have warned me!"

A chill ran through Aayala, and her mantra every time this happened activated in her mind. *She doesn't mean it, she's just hurt.*

"Ma, I didn't know any details. You know how Da is about things like this."

"Exactly, why you don't tell me, huh? I could have talked him out of it, ya understand? He just needs some reasonin'. Now he gone, and I need to figure out how to get to him again. Just 'cause you can't hold a man for long don't mean you need to ruin it for me too."

Aayala's hand shook. She'd dropped Malik's ribbed undershirts on the floor.

"Ma, get a hold of yourself!" she hissed. "I know you are hurtin', but you can't be callin' me blamin' me for Pa. It ain't fair. I worked hard to stop judgin' what you both do or do not do. If you mad, call my fada. Don't call me. And if I don't criticize you…"

Her mom scoffed on the other line but otherwise stayed quiet.

"Then you shouldn't criticize me either. No more, Ma. Let's stop that once and for all."

"You right. I'm mad and taking it out on ya. I'm sorry, ya hear? I know you right and I should let him go, but your fada is my life. He's the love of my life. I can only hold onto what I know is mine."

A busy signal beeped loud in her ear. Her mother had hung up.

ANOTHER DAY AND THE CALENDAR WAS TRULY MOCKING HER. In less than two weeks, Malik would leave. And… Fuck it, she was Aayala Powell, from Kingston, Jamaica, via Canarsie. She could ask a man what his plans were.

She was no punk.

Gathering her courage, she walked out of her home office, ready for the day.

Downstairs, she found Malik sprawled on the floor, holding Andre while their baby bounced up and down on the chubbiest, most yummy legs in the world. As always, when she saw Andre, she was hit with a burst of pure joy and love to see him growing so happy.

"Hey, boss man, look who's there?" Malik said to Andre.

Andre kept up his calisthenics, up and down, his balance only possible by Malik's hands holding him. The two of them were so alike, truly the same bone structure, the eyes, cheeks, and nose. The love was overflowing and making a puddle around her. How could she not ask Malik to stay? She didn't want to vocalize it, afraid to put it out into the universe, but she'd be a wreck if he was leaving.

These past six months were supposed to be about her learning how to perfect parenting while still keeping herself intact, but instead… Instead, she'd realized she had feet of clay, gave the best hugs to her son, and was completely in love with being dominated by this man in and out of the bedroom.

"He's too busy for his mama, but wait 'til he gets hungry…" she said with a laugh.

"You're in a good mood today."

"You say it as if it's a surprise."

"Nah, not surprised at all. I mean, not to brag, but I know I'm keeping you well-supplied. But I have the impression that you've got something else on your mind."

"What are you planning to do come February?"

Silence. Malik watched her carefully as if she held a bomb that needed disabling or it would be the end of the world. Her stomach plummeted, and everything that was loose and easy after her morning shifted inside of her.

"I—"

Her phone rang, and she was prepared to ignore it but saw it was Sergio.

"Sorry, I gotta get this."

She strolled to the living room for a little privacy and was greeted with a bellowing Sergio.

"Where the fuck are you?!"

"Calm the fuck down, Sergio, that's not the way you greet me." She hung up and picked up when her phone rang again.

"Fuck, I'm sorry, it's just we got an email asking for a status update, and I thought the calendar said we were starting at 9:30 a.m. But it's 9:45 and you're not here yet."

"No, no, the calendar says 11:30 a.m. for this one because it's overnight," she assured him.

"Aayala, that schedule changed a week ago. Didn't you get the email...oh shit..."

"What email? I didn't get an email," she said. When she didn't get a response, she took a different approach.

"Are the models there?"

"Yeah, their call was 9:45... I was supposed to send you the change..." Sergio sounded apologetic now. She, on the other hand, was holding onto every imaginary handle at her disposal to avoid going off on him like a banshee.

"I'll be there as soon as I can. It's a drive, but I'm hitting the road now," she said calmly, none of the turmoil from inside reflecting on the outside.

Malik chose that instant to walk into the living room with Andre in his arms and her pump bag and camera bag in hand. The sad smile on his face told her he'd heard her side of the conversation.

"Sergio fucked up and didn't tell me there was a time change. I gotta go now, but can we talk? We need to talk when I'm back tomorrow, alright?" She wished she could stay and hash out their next months together. What would it look like if he actually stayed? He'd be able to get a place to live, they'd keep on co-parenting, and during their nights, they could... Best not go there. Her mind couldn't go there right now.

"For sure, we'll talk when you are back. Drive safe, though. Andre and I'll be waiting home for you."

CHAPTER TWENTY-SEVEN

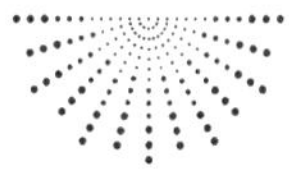

The rich dark red of the model's bathing suit contrasted beautifully with the hotel's chic lounge seating in this exclusive adult-only pool. Greenery surrounded the small crystalline pool, together with navy blue lounge seats, which looked so thick and inviting that Aayala could take a nap. She might have to hit up Michelle and ask her for a stay. Of all the resorts they'd visited, this one was the most beautiful.

The adult-only pool nestled in lush greenery was a photographer's dream, and her inspiration had roared back with vengeance. A bursting swirl of creativity mixed with nervous anticipation carried her through the shoot. This hotel was far away enough and had so many rich details as one of the crown jewels of the collection of hotels that the shoot would be divided between two days.

Her fingers itched on the camera button, and her mind raced to her brief conversation with Malik.

Two weeks left.

Time was slipping by, and they'd kept playing house and avoided some hard conversations. Neither of them were cowards. Lord knew she wasn't one, but the procrastination had been natural, so easy to slip into, and she suspected it was the same for Malik. Now her stomach was in knots, awaiting his words and thoughts on how they would figure out how to move forward together.

She had twenty minutes for this particular shoot, and she made the model move around the space with precision, squeezing shots until the last minute she had allotted.

Lina, the model, was a beautiful Black and Asian-American plus-size beauty, and she worked the camera so well. They had already exchanged phone numbers, wanting to work together in the future. Their synergy was kismet.

"You're on a roll today." Sergio glided next to her during their quick lunch break.

She walked into the suite, trying to keep a brisk pace that would encourage Sergio to hang back.

No such luck.

"Can I eat with you?" he asked.

She kept walking.

"Damn, preciosa, I know you are mad at me for the way I goaded you the last shoot, but…"

She kept walking around the buffet station surveying fruits, sandwiches, and salads, unconcerned about whatever imaginary drama Sergio had with her.

"No buts, Sergio, you know me well enough to know I'm not one with the bullshit. What do you want? You've acted like a brat these whole months, and I am counting the minutes until I don't have to shoot alongside you again."

"Damn, it's like that?"

She raised an eyebrow, then grabbed a water bottle and walked out to the suite terrace where they'd set some tables for them to eat.

"Can we talk? Please?"

Aayala sighed, and the breath gave her enough clarity to

realize she had nothing to lose by hearing Sergio out. That, and the fact that the nervous energy radiating from her could use a break.

"Sit," she invited him. He smiled in relief and sat, gazing at her with such longing she flinched.

"I miss you."

Her stomach hardened, and the grape she'd popped into her mouth went from sweet to sour in a second.

"I…"

"I know you don't." He laughed bitterly. "But I wanted to let you know. I also wanted to clarify to you that I was hurt when you ended things with me."

She gazed at him skeptically.

"Why, Sergio? You're a fuck boy, and I was your longest and steadiest booty call. That is the best, most honest way to describe our relationship. We just fudged the lines and introduced each other to our loved ones and dated. That's about it."

"You'd reduce our relationship of five years to that?"

She shrugged. "That's what it was."

"That's what you made it to be," he accused, exasperated.

She reared back as if hit.

"Not true."

"If I answer yes, true, then I'm the child, so I won't do that. But I will tell you that I was the only one that would ever initiate the talk about moving in together, or at least moving into the same city."

She scoffed. "Yeah, but when I called you on your bullshit about having other girls in your city, you would stop that story real quick."

"I did because it would hurt me. Because I wasn't ever cheating on you."

"There was no cheating involved. I never told you not to fuck other people."

"But I wish you would have. That's the whole thing, Aayala, I wish you'd staked a claim. Whenever I tried to do it, you'd deflect or ghost me for days, or you'd quote one of your dad's lines…"

Aayala flinched at the accusation. That what he described sounded like her aloof, rolling stone dad? That one hit too close to home…

"That's not the entire story, and you know it. When you and I started dating, I wanted something serious, and you weren't ready. And I was ok with it. But then…"

"Yeah, you expressed one time you might want things to get serious two months into our relationship, and I was, yes, still on the slow side. But then that was it, never again."

"I don't need to be told twice."

"Aayala," he said with exasperation. She suspected he would have loved to be able to hold her and shake her to reason. But she wasn't being unreasonable, was she?

A vignette of memories rolled through her mind as she kept eating her salad, letting the silence stretch between them. He knew her well enough to let her stew for a moment, and as she pulled out each memory and turned it around from all angles, his words sounded truer and truer. She felt her stomach cramp at the realization.

"You decided you knew my mind, and since that moment, there was never space for us to have any other conversation that wasn't colored by your thoughts of me. Which I think were more what you think of your father, but I don't want to be punched in the face for blaming this on daddy issues. What I want you to know is that I wanted you. I still do. It doesn't seem like I have any chance with you, but I just wouldn't be at peace if I didn't tell you."

"I…" She paused, overwhelmed by what Sergio told her. To realize her image of their relationship had been skewed by her thoughts of him…

"So you never slept around?"

"I did, once I realized you didn't want anything more from me than a content, serious fuck buddy. But it took years for it to happen. And call me a punk ass bitch, but I cried the night it happened. I did feel like I cheated on you, but you… I don't know, Aayala. You're the smartest, most emotionally intelligent person I know, but you are stubborn and a bit judgmental, and that combination can be a mindfuck."

An icy chill ran through her to think about how she'd contributed to the demise of their partnership.

"Sergio…"

"I know, preciosa, you didn't mean any ill, it's what you knew. It's what you think relationships should look like deep down."

Was that true, though? She thought Sergio was partially right, but looking at things deeply, she also understood she was like that with Sergio because she wasn't ready to commit to him. She didn't need to be with him all the time. She could live in separate cities because their connection had been superficial at best, no matter how he wanted to see it now. She probably had a part in it, but it was her instinct to protect herself.

But when she thought of the man waiting for her at home… She knew it was different with him. With Malik, she wanted it all. She wanted him close, and she wanted to see his face every day. There was nothing superficial about her feelings for him. It was all seamless and easy.

"I'm sorry, Sergio, for any hurt I inflicted. I do think we are better off apart. And I thank you for your sincerity, but I think we work better as friends." She smiled gently, and Sergio gave her his rueful, youthful grin that used to make her melt.

"Can't blame a man for trying."

IN HER ROOM, AAYALA TOSSED AND TURNED, THINKING ABOUT today's exchange with Sergio. There was enough truth threaded with his one-sided view of their relationship to have her considering Malik and their situation in a slightly different light.

What did she need from Malik? Her stomach did a lazy somersault at the thought of him staying in South Florida. For him to truly live at home. Her heart beat faster when she pushed things further in her mind, arranging their imaginary future, living under the same roof, sharing their lives together.

She put name and last name to her wants and needs.

Malik Johnson.

But not a part-time Malik, she realized. That would devastate her, carry her back to her old ways. Make her regress to her thoughts on what relationships should or shouldn't be because of what she saw at home.

She texted him, asking how he and Andre were doing.

Malik: We miss you. Hey, why don't you come to my parents when you drive down? We'll have Sunday dinner with them.

The thrill of doing something so easy with him, Andre, and his family confirmed to her what she really wanted from him. She knew what to ask now.

Tomorrow couldn't arrive faster.

CHAPTER TWENTY-EIGHT

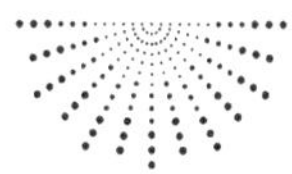

"I can't believe I'mma tell you this, and if you tell the rest, don't call me no more. But I have to tell someone," Malik said while painting the outside of his parents' house.

"What happened?" Daniel asked, perched on a ladder next to his while they both worked the top parts of the front of the house. Gabo, Mason, and Damian were doing the laterals while his mom and pops chilled inside with the baby after Malik had threatened them both with no visitations from Andre because they both were trying to boss them around and tell them what to do.

"Yesterday, Aayala asked me what my plan was in February, and I choked."

"What the fu— Why would you do that?"

"Bruh, I really don't know. I was ready to tell her about my conversation with Cap and how I was planning to take his spot with that family, but something in her eyes… I just want to have the plan all laid out, you know? I wanted to buy a house, but now I want to buy it with her. There are so many details that she and I just don't even discuss because we still assumed we're just Andre's parents."

"I hear you, but Malik, don't let time pass by and not tell her how you really feel."

"How do you know how I really feel?" Malik asked Daniel with a raised eyebrow.

"Come now, are you really going to play this game with me? Like I don't see how you've been breaking your head figuring out how to be the man she needs you to be? By the way, I do think all of that shit is in your head. Because Aayala has been independent her entire life. I don't think she's looking for a provider."

"I disagree. She has goals, goals that would be achievable if she had me to hold down the fort financially so she could do what she needed to do."

"Bruh…"

"Daniel, you mean well, but you gotta let it go. This is the right choice for me. Being the captain of a yacht will give me less extended times away, and I would be based here for all trips. It would work."

"With the exception of Gabo, I'm uncertain how we all ended up being friends and holding onto that friendship. Man, are we all stubborn as hell," Daniel pondered.

"You're not lying," Malik agreed as he continued to paint. He was unbothered by the fact Daniel considered him stubborn. He knew he was. His stubbornness had sustained him for those first years as a merchant marine when he wanted to throw in the towel, and it would sustain him now.

He knew without a doubt that the right thing for him was to stay here and take this lateral move that would allow him to be close to Aayala and Andre but still be able to provide and keep his financial plan in place.

The painting of the house couldn't happen without his pops making an event out of it, with his grill outside and his mama's gospel music blaring through the windows. Soon, they were all congregated around the grill, shooting the shit and trading jokes with beers in hand, the first coat on the house finished.

Cap made an appearance right when the ribs were ready.

"Old man, you have perfect timing," Malik joked when Cap ambled his way toward them.

"You know me. I have a perfect sense of smell, and when you told me Darius here was doing his BBQ ribs, well, son, I couldn't miss that, could I?"

Malik noticed Cap seemed uncharacteristically subdued as he greeted everyone.

"What's up, Cap, you want a brew?" Mason asked, probably noticing the same.

"What the fuck? *A brew?*" Gabo mocked. "Who calls it a brew? You're so extra, bruh."

"Whatever, just because you're a simp don't mean the rest of us can't use elevated language." Mason sniffed his nose in the air, holding back laughter.

In the hilarity that ensued, Cap maneuvered himself next to Malik.

"You gotta minute?"

"Yeah, inside?" Malik replied.

"Yeah, best if we do."

Once inside, Malik's usual calmness deserted him. Cap's face was grim, and Malik knew whatever was coming next would be bad.

"The family wanna go in a different direction. The son, he's twenty-two, he got a friend that fancies himself a captain. Has the credentials, and they fudged the hours to get him the permit. Long story short, my boss, the father, called me yesterday apologetic, explaining even though you are far better qualified than this chump, his son had wanted his parents to give his friend the job instead." Words kept coming out of Cap's mouth, but Malik's ears malfunctioned, his chest tightening with a pressure that built there and traveled up to his head until everything seemed to come through a fog.

"And they want to 'empower' him, so they agreed. They've withdrawn their offer. I quit on the spot. It was shady business what they've done, son, but we can get something else."

Malik shook his head. He should have known.

He loosened his jaw, which he must have locked while Cap said his news. Cap's grimness had transformed into regret, and he knew the old man was blaming himself for bringing Malik's hopes up.

"You good, Cap, you were just looking out for me. Nothing less, nothing more. What they did, it's not on you, old man. Know that."

Cap shook his head, concern written all over his face. "But we can get something else. It's time for you to stop these long tours. When you aren't a hundred percent in it, mind and heart, it's not good for your sanity or your safety to be out there."

"Nah. It's a'ight, Cap. It's all good. Look, why don't you go and get that beer that Mason offered? I'll be right out."

The fog cleared and left nothing behind. He felt numb and empty. The hopes and plans he'd made in his head all disappeared as he pictured himself going back to the ship in two weeks.

He needed to. This was his skill set. This was what he knew. He couldn't take a step back and have nothing to show for the years of sacrifice he'd put in the sea. Fuck that.

He should have fucking known not to trust his future with anyone but his damn self. But he let himself be lured by the perfect way his life had aligned, beginning with that fateful night in October when Aayala let him in her body to create a gift he never thought to receive from her. And having a shot with her…fuck. Having a shot with her was everything.

He had to believe this was just a setback. With everything they'd been through, they should be able to overcome something as insignificant as distance. A few years of this wouldn't break them. Would it?

The front door swung open, and Damian swaggered in. Compared to everyone else, who had specks of paint over their shirts and pants, Damian was pristine. The latest Jordans adorned his feet, and he wore a t-shirt and jeans that seemed to be freshly pressed. Malik's temple throbbed at the implication.

"What's up, bruh? Listen, I know we have another coat of paint to do, but I'mma need to bounce."

"Where you gotta be that's not here? We planned to get the house painted a week ago. You chose the date."

"Well, I met this girl…"

"Check me out, Damian. I'm not your keeper, but I'm your older brother, and I have to tell you, you are fucking up your life with your lack of ambition and direction. You fucking have everything set for you and—"

"Nah, bruh, you can't just throw that in my face. I never asked you to do nothing for me. You decided to be this big brother protector. No one asked you to be."

"No one asked, but that's what real men do. They take care of their close ones."

"So fucking take care of your baby and your baby mama! Take the money you saved for me and just use it on them. Then you can get off my fucking ass about everything."

"That would be the straightforward route to take, ain't it? Then you can pretend you have no avenues and rail at life. Well, that's not happening. I prepaid your tuition. I've been doing that since you were a kid in school, so I don't have access to that money. That money is yours."

"You what? Why no one told me this?" Damian stood, struck by Malik's words. He was tired, so fucking tired of Damian and his brand of bullshit. The ungratefulness of his behavior, of his words…

"Mama wanted you to focus on your own merits and not because you knew I was paying for it. She didn't want you pressured. But then you graduated with good grades, and it was time for you to look at colleges, and fucking nothing. And now there's your money doing nothing for you."

"Babies, what's mothertucking taking so…" his mom asked then paused in the entrance when she saw her two sons squaring off.

"What's happening here?" Her eyebrow rose, and she placed one hand over the other on her lower belly, the stance so reminiscent of their younger years, he felt pulled to the past and yanked back again to the present.

"Nothing," they both said at the same time.

"This don't look like nothing. Y'all think I was born yesterday?"

"Ma, why didn't you tell me Malik prepaid my college account? That's fucked up. I should have known."

"What difference would it have made? You don't want to go to college," his mom said, and Malik's stomach felt sour at the confirmation. She knew. And he was certain his pops knew too. And they'd allowed him to make the wrong choice.

"So you weren't gonna tell me you decided not to enroll at all?"

"Bruh, I've been told you. That university can give your money back, they have to. I don't need it."

"So you just don't care, huh? You're just gonna give up."

"Fuck you, Malik, you don't know anything. You don't fucking know!" Damian stared back with cold eyes, and his indignation sparked a match inside of Malik. He pushed past his mom and out of the house, with Malik hot in pursuit.

All the helplessness of his situation threatened to overcome him. To see his brother, that actually had it made, just toss it all aside. He grabbed Damian's shoulder and spun him back to face him.

"We're not done talking. You don't get to leave, not until we finish," Malik said with preternatural calm.

"Listen, you two, calm down," his mother urged.

"What's going on?" his pops asked from the grill, the guys all turning toward them, realizing something was wrong.

"Fuck you, Malik, with your self-righteousness! You think you are such a dutiful son because you took one for the team, going to sea. But you know what? I'm the one here. I'm the one who takes Pop to his medical visits and sits with Moms at night when she is sad because she feels they failed you and you had to leave and goes to all the church events with her. I!" Damian poked his chest with a conviction Malik had never seen. "I'm the one, so when you come into this house all handyman-fixing and shit and demanding for me to stop my life to accommodate your sense of responsibility, fuck off, bruh. I'm not here to assuage you of your poor decision-making. No one told you you needed to pick up and leave. You did that on your own. So don't make me the poster child of your sacrifice. Own your shit."

Malik saw red. The words coming from Damian's mouth had enough ring of truth that they slew all his sense of equanimity. He swung his fist, mind filled with visceral emotions, and connected with Damian's surprisingly hard jaw. Damian stumbled back, then charged forward, using all his strength to tackle him to the ground. Malik, being the taller and larger of the two, squared his feet, side-stepping Damian at the last minute.

Shouts of "Stop!" and "Don't do it!" went around them, but he couldn't listen to any of them right now. He was too far gone. Damian course-corrected and turned back, catching him by surprise and punching him in the stomach. The air whooshed out of him. Damn. His little brother could actually swing.

Damian's error was celebrating the hit. He didn't see Malik's hook coming until it was too late. Malik swung again, but his fist never connected with air. Two arms held him back, and he could see Mason restraining Damian, who was tearing up in pain.

"Malik. You need to calm down now." Daniel's stern tones penetrated through the rage that was consuming him.

All the words Damian had said were colliding in his brain, dredging up all the insecurities of the years. Had he made the right choice? The right path in life? And the worst one of all, what did he have to show for it? His pops had gotten his settlement, and now Damian was telling him he didn't want to go to college. What was it all for, then?

Gabo moved away from Malik, making sure Daniel had him, to go hold his mom, who was hysterically crying. Somehow, she had found one of her church purses and started taking turns whacking him and Damian with it. His pops and Cap tried to hold her back, and it wasn't enough.

"You better cut this shit, Malik! Why the fuck are you trying to still swing, Damian, calm your ass down!"

Whack! Whack! Whack!

"See, now you got your mom started. Serves you right," Daniel said, pushing him back, not that Malik needed it. His sense had returned.

"What's happening here? Where's Andre?" That soft question from behind him made all the hairs on his arms stand at attention. In all this mess, he'd forgotten he'd texted Aayala, asking her to come here instead of home so they could have dinner at his parents' house.

He turned around, and all the rage from the day dissolved when he saw her concerned face.

"Nothing, just a little brotherly squabble," he said, and Daniel snorted.

"Mama, alright, alright! Fuck, I'm leaving." Damian breezed past them all, now all wrinkled but still determined to leave. Malik had zero intentions of stopping him again. The words he'd told him had left him raw to the touch, and he knew his brother and him might never be the same after this.

"What happened?" Aayala held his hand and squeezed, and he felt it all the way inside his chest. This woman had his heart in her arms.

"We got into a fight because…shit, I don't even know anymore. I guess it was about him not going to school and me using the money I had set aside for y'all instead of him."

"Nah, Andre and I are good. He needs to go to school or a vocational institute or something, get some skills, and then figure out the rest. But why would he say that about using the money for me?" Her outrage soothed him. At least she got it. His chest contracted, realizing he needed to tell her. They had less than two weeks together, and keeping things in the dark made no sense.

"Because…because I had news today I was supposed to give to you. Good news."

He saw her eyes light up, and it sparked hopefulness in him. Maybe she'd be ok with being long-distance. Maybe he could still salvage this day.

"Come."

They walked back inside the house. Cap and his pops had pulled his mom to sit on the bench on their front porch, and Daniel, Mason, and Gabo had gone back to the grill to make sure the food didn't burn.

He stood in front of her in the living room.

"I was supposed to take over Cap's job. But he found out today they are giving it to someone else."

Her face went through several expressions: hope, anticipation, excitement, pride, disappointment, resignation. It all went so fast he thought he might have imagined some.

"So you are leaving, of course."

"So I'm leaving."

"I get it. I mean, this is what you know. Stopping now…"

This woman. She got him. She understood. It might not be perfect, and he might not make sense to others, but it made sense to her.

"So…"

"I know what you are going to ask, but I want to stop you, Malik. I… I… I love you so much." Tears started falling down her face, each lonely drop sliding down with no one to hold her.

"We both have our reasons to be how we are…and I realized with you," she whispered between tears, "that I need you. Not just the you that stimulates my mind and loves me and fucks me until I can orgasm, but the you that holds me accountable to take care of myself and notices if I haven't drunk enough water and holds me until I'm comfortable loving myself again. The you that whistles while going through his morning routine and refolds all the baby clothes I've folded while I'm not watching. The you that knows more deep cuts than I do, and the you that sings under his breath and has a beautiful voice. The you that stares at me with bedroom eyes that make my legs shiver and my panties melt.

"I have family and friends, but I've held myself apart, protected for a long time. But with you…" Her tears flowed freely now, and he pulled her to him. Her soft body yielded to his as if it was his right, his hope disintegrating under the weight of her sorrow.

"With you, I don't feel like I need to protect myself no more. I'm always the one there for people, but I thought I didn't need it when it was the other way around. But what I had failed to notice is that I don't need most, but I do need you. And I don't think it would be healthy for me and my state of mind to have you halfway there. I need closeness, that closeness that was so effortless between us…"

"I get it, baby girl. Today was the day for both of us to break each other's hearts. I get it."

And Aayala broke down in his arms while he held her. Like he always would. He'd figure out how to put himself together again later. Right now, he needed to make sure she'd come through this. He knew he wouldn't. He was irrevocably hers.

CHAPTER TWENTY-NINE

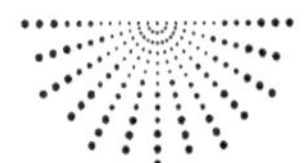

A cup of hot tea steamed in front of her. Tea cured all ailments. Or so she thought. This ailment she had hurt from the inside of her body. It wasn't going away, not with all the ginger tea in the world.

"Drink your tea, Aayala. It's late."

"Thanks for staying over, Licy."

Alicia stood by the stove in Aayala's kitchen, her eyes full of concern.

"Ras, Licy, me no need no pity right now, ya hear?" she said through a stuffed nose.

She'd gotten used to the looks from her family and friends these past two months. They all used the same gentle voice around her as if she was made of crystal and would break into a million pieces if they spoke louder.

A cold had emerged a few days ago and taken over her, tackling her down until she'd succumbed and asked for help. Keeping up with a crawling speed demon meant she needed help. Andre was an active ten-month-old, and he demanded her full attention. One minute he sat playing with his teething toys, the next he was gone, playing underneath the table while trying to insert anything he found into his mouth.

"Why not just do the long-distance thing with Malik?" Alicia asked.

"Well, I guess you're going straight to the point."

"I am because it's been two months, and you've been cagey, not opening up to Mari and me. I mean, you're usually a vault any given day, but you were getting a little better with sharing…"

She sighed, taking a careful sip of the hot tea and putting it down. The sweet, pungent warmth traveled all the way down, soothing everything in its path.

"I realized what I need, and he can't give me that. At least not now."

Licy slowly sat down across from her, her own cup of tea between her hands.

"Aayala, you seemed so happy with him. Shit, you were smiling and giggling, even. My tough cookie of a cousin! How did you go from there to him not giving you what you need?"

Aayala glided her fingers from the bottom to the top of her cup, absorbing the warmth into her body. The congestion was ever-present, but it wasn't such a distraction as she sipped her tea.

"I need his presence. I realized I need him here. And anything in between is not enough. I don't want to be my mom and dad. I don't want to repeat that cycle. I understand myself enough and what I need from him, and he can't give it to me right now. Doesn't mean it can't happen in the future…because Licy, he has my whole heart. So, yeah, it's a not right now…" Tears prickled in her eyes, something that was becoming a habit she wasn't too thrilled about.

Since she had started therapy, her emotions were all so readily available to burst out of her as if they'd been under a lid, and now she had finally given them permission to come out.

"Oh, honey…" Alicia reached out to her, palm up, and she placed her hand in Licy's. She was glad for the comfort. Honestly, she craved it.

"It's ok. Not everyone gets a fairy tale ending… I'm certainly not surprised I didn't get one."

"But you do realize the ending is in your hands, though? Once that person, the one you want and need, the one you can't live without is in front of you, it's up to you to get that ending you deserve. So sorry for holding onto hope that both of you still have a chance."

Aayala smiled, her instinct to reassure Licy overriding her complete certainty that this wasn't in the cards for her. Malik had a clear-cut plan, and nothing would deter him from it. Not even love.

EMAIL FROM YARDIE4EVA@MAIL.COM TO HOOPSNGLORY@ iol.com 22:59

Andre misses you. He stares at the door of the office when we walk by the hallway and listens out for your singing and whistles in the morning. When I watch the videos you left him, his face instantly gets brighter. I actually sympathize with him. I also turn around corners expecting to see your face. I haven't been going to the crew hangouts because before it was fine being the non-coupled one, but now…

Sorry, I shouldn't be laying alla dis on you.
You're doing what you need to do for yourself. I would never tell you not to focus on your family, but you've been doing that since before eighteen. So focus on your needs now. On

your dream house, and being able to not depend on any job once you are done.

I got your package in the mail… I tried it out and it works… too well. I came three times after my bath last night. At first, it was hard because I was in my feelings, but then I played that video you left me behind, and…whew. That's all I have to say about that.

I have your schedule printed here, and your next stop should be in Shanghai. We will both be ready for your call.

PS: I'm still drinking my eight glasses of water and eating my three meals, but there is no one to ask me if I'm being a good girl.

Aayala

DURBAN LOOMED ON THE HORIZON, BARELY VISIBLE IN THE night sky as the tanker glided over the water. The deck remained quiet, him and the second mate basking in the silence while they worked in tandem because once they docked, things would become hectic with all the deck work that needed to be done once approaching shore.

He used to thrive in moments like this, following the step-by-step of his tasks, getting ready with the methodical discipline that centered him. But all of the calm had deserted him this time. Nothing had that effect on him; the dissatisfaction and discontent that had hidden behind corners in his mind had come out to play boogeyman to his peace.

This wasn't doing it for him anymore.

On his last stop, he'd connected with his parents via video chat, a call that still resonated with him days later.

"How are you, son? I'm glad you called. We haven't heard from you a lot these past days," his dad said. They both were sitting at the dining room table, their faces clouded with concern.

"Yeah, why the fuck you haven't called? You usually call more often than this!" his mom berated him, and he couldn't help chuckling at her.

"Momma, language," he chastised.

"Don't momma me, have you called your brother?" she asked, cutting right to the chase. He'd left without truly hashing things out with Damian. The things Damian had said still sat sour in his stomach, and he hadn't known how to bring himself back to center regarding his brother. Was it so wrong for him to want the very best for Damian?

He asked that same question to his parents, who'd always seemed to side with Damian in this college talk.

His parents gazed at him, then at each other, and his father cleared his throat.

"I know you feel we don't want the very best for Damian, but there's something you don't understand. We do want the best. It's just we know he's exhausted of trying and needs a break," his dad confided.

"Oh, for fuck's sakes, just tell the boy what he needs to know! I knew shit would hit the fan one day with all this secrecy, and I was right!"

For once, he agreed with his mom's impatience.

"What is it I don't know?"

"Well, see, we realized after middle grade why Damian struggled with reading and studying so much. His teacher called us to the school and explained that they had tested him and he had severe dyslexia," his father said, delivering the news with a nonchalance that told him how tense his father truly was. He absorbed this information and let it clarify so much for him. And as things became clear, he felt more and more horrible about the way he'd treated Damian.

"Why?" he asked.

"Why we didn't tell you? Oh, my boy, because you'd fucking do what you always did. You'd go into provider mode. Overprotective Malik to the rescue. And excuse us if we wanted to keep our oldest son as our son and not our parents," his mom said, uncharacteristically quiet, her voice trembling even through the video. His heart constricted at the pain in his mother's voice and the cautious concern on his pop's face.

"A'ight, I hear you both. Look, I can't promise that I can completely turn it off because it's how I am wired. When I was young, I understood that after Dad, I was the one meant to step up and help. I mean, Pops, you told me that. Every time you went to sea, you told me I was in charge…and I might have taken that shit to heart."

"Language, son!" his mom said, trying to cut the tension, making him smile again.

Days later and the conversation with his parents had become one of the main thoughts in his mind. During his deck hours, during his free time, during his time in the control room, his parents' words resonated through him. His brother had a learning disability, and Malik had been the asshole of the story.

And things with his folks were still tentative, his Pops blaming himself for it all when Malik had repeatedly assured him that regardless of anything, being a provider was part of who Malik was, with or without encouragement.

He knew he was wired this way, but he also knew he needed to figure out better ways to lean into it in the future. He had amends to make with his brother once he'd worked his way through all his own shit.

Even with all the baggage he carried with his family, his

main constant was Aayala. All of these thoughts had been an eye-opener to his situation with her.

He wanted Aayala with an intensity that made his palms itch every time he read her emails and she confessed to transgressions that deserved punishment, made his heart trip on itself every opportunity he heard her everyday stories during their port calls, made him brick up when she shared her adventures with her toys as she rediscovered what worked for her.

After three months away, Malik knew another trip away from her would ruin him. But his deep-rooted baggage floated over his decision-making process, clouding what should be a straightforward decision.

***

EMAIL FROM HOOPSNGLORY@IOL.COM TO YARDIE4EVA@ **mail.com 08:14**

I've started writing you poetry. It's awful as fuck so I don't know if I'll ever share it with you, but that's what you have reduced me to, creating spoken word a la Pablo Neruda. Last week, in Durban, you seemed sad. I don't want you to second-guess your decision. It was the right one. You deserve a man that can give you everything. You don't need to compromise for me. I need to be all you need. I'm not asking you what you bring to the fucking table. You're the house, the table, the roof. You are everything, and I need to ensure I'm ready to provide everything for you, body, mind, and soul. Provider. That word almost became a dirty slur for me. The other day, I video-called with my parents and I realized the reason why Damian doesn't want to go to college is because he is severely dyslexic. He had the hardest time in school and somehow still managed to get good grades. I missed knowing that, being a provider. I didn't know my own brother had a learning disability. Fuck. I didn't mean to drop all my problems on your lap here in this email. I just wanted to say goodnight. I just came back from my 4-8 night watch, and now I'm gonna lay down my head. I want to dream of you and all the nights you gifted me, baby girl.

P.S: After you read this, go to your room, drop those black panties you're wearing and grab that last dildo I got you. The one that's almost my size. Fuck yourself with it while you play with your clit like a champion. And yes, I know you save these emails for the nighttime so that you can go and do your thing after you read them.

CHAPTER THIRTY

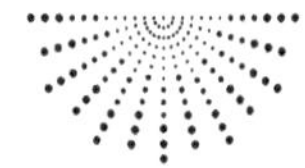

The house was crowded. Again.

She didn't understand when she'd dropped her defenses—maybe that night two months ago when she spilled her guts to Alicia in uncharacteristic vulnerability —but now, there was always someone around.

Licy and Gabo were always puttering around her house and keeping Andre entertained, who was standing on his own and showing signs of wanting to take his first steps. Aayala was always encouraging him to do new things, but this one particular milestone she hoped he delayed, if at least for another month. She knew it would break Malik's heart to miss it.

If not Licy and Gabo, then it was *the Three Hornyteers,* as she'd taken to calling Daniel, Mason, and Mari, who were always squabbling and making up in corners around her house. It almost felt like their current home was too small for all the feelings they were feeling with Mari pregnant.

"Good boy! Look at you standing, yes! That's your toy? You're giving it to me?" Licy chirped, making Andre do his cute baby squat bounce.

"Aayala, do you have some BBQ chips? I need some BBQ chips." Mari's belly made an appearance around the corner, then Mari, then her two men.

"Sweetheart, but you complained about heartburn—"

They all stared at Mason, the brave soul who dared tell his eight-month pregnant girlfriend what not to eat.

"Babe…" Daniel warned.

"Oh no, Daniel, let him finish and tell me what I can and cannot do." Mari attempted to whip around but ended up waddling instead until she was face-to-face with a contrite Mason.

"Mari, those chips give you heartburn. And you know what, you didn't get with me because I'm a punk, so I'mma tell you right now, I don't think you should eat them. We can get you regular chips, or salt and vinegar, or those nice Mexican ones we saw at the store the other day…"

"Good save." Daniel chuckled, going across the room to wait for Mari, who needed assistance every time she dropped herself into a chair.

"So y'all have nothing to do?" Aayala asked the room at large, not understanding how every weekend the entire crew found themselves here. If it wasn't them, it was Malik's parents, sometimes even Damian.

"What do you mean?" Gabo asked with complete sincerity. The asshole. He knew exactly what she meant.

"I'm fine."

"Sure, and I look like a swan about to dive into the lake," Mariana said, irritated, while Mason rubbed her back. "Look, Aayala, you've been there for all of us, especially Licy and me. Let us be here for you. It's your turn. Let us do this for you, that's all. No need to hash it all out. We know how uncomfortable you get, and yeah, it sucks to be on the other side of it. But once Malik is back and y'all fix your shit and he's dicking you up and down and all around, then we will make ourselves scarce."

Mari then turned around to Mason. "Love, my prince, my boyfriend, mi bello, how about those chips?" she said in a syrupy voice that fooled no one.

Well, it seemed it fooled Mason and even Daniel because they both stood up immediately and promised to be back in a jiffy. *A jiffy*. Pregnancy was messing with their three brains.

"Well, if y'all need to know, I've decided to go see Malik."

Three faces all turned to her, and she hid a smile.

"What you mean, you're going to go see him?" Mari asked suspiciously.

"I have the website for flights open on my computer upstairs and was planning to leave tomorrow, maybe even tonight."

Gabo and Licy's heads whipped up, and Gabo's eyes widened in surprise. They exchanged a long look, then he stood up from the floor and walked toward Aayala.

"But can you do that? I mean, sometimes Malik doesn't even get to get off the tanker," Gabo asked curiously.

"Yeah, but in Singapore, they always get two days because that's where the tanker is originally from. So..." She shrugged.

"So you are going to Singapore...to see Malik...who you could've talked to here before he left and laid all your cards on the table?" Mari wondered.

"Yes, don't give me that attitude, I know. But I guess life is too short. I want to be with him, and even though this long-distance sucks, I guess we'll have to make it work. I don't want anyone else."

Mari stared up at the ceiling and mumbled something that Aayala missed, but she wasn't really paying her too much mind. Her heart had felt light since last night when she'd decided this was the right thing to do for herself.

"So, when do you need to leave?"

"I'm probably buying the 8:46 p.m. that leaves today with Qatar Airlines." She shrugged and sat next to Licy, who looked thunderstruck while Andre sat again, playing with his toys. Tenderness filled her as she ran her hand over his coils while he kept playing, taking the gesture as his due. A pang resonated within her to think of being apart from him for days. With the number of hours it took her to get to Singapore and back, it would be close to a week before she saw him again.

"I spoke with Malik's mom last night before even thinking of all of this, and she will take time off to take care of Andre, but I figured I'd ask if he can stay with you for a couple of days? That way, Mrs. Johnson keeps him during the day while you are at work, and he hangs out at night with you and Gabo while she's at the home?" she asked Licy, who still seemed to be poleaxed.

"Uh... Uh, of course, but, I mean…do you think it's a good idea?" She stared at Gabo, who stood behind Aayala, out of her line of sight.

"Girl, of course, it's a great idea! It tells us where Aayala's heart is, which is in the right place!" Mari exclaimed. "But I think probably what Licy's concern is like, is it too soon? Is there a stop after Singapore that we can plan in more detail? To make sure you have everything you need, you know."

Aayala stared at her cousins, noticing finally how odd they were behaving.

"What do I need? I need myself, the vibrators Malik bought me, and the clothes to get there and return. I don't plan on doing much more than that."

"What about sightseeing?" Mari asked.

"Sightseeing? Girl, are you alright? You? The one who constantly talks about having sex all the time?" Aayala stared at Mari as if she had transformed into a nun.

"Yeah… You got me there…" Mari shrugged and rubbed her belly.

Aayala's Spidey senses were tingling, but she didn't have much time for their usual intrigue.

"Gabo! Gabo!" Mari growled, and Gabo jumped to attention. "Help me up. I need to call the boys."

She shifted her head back and forth between Licy and Mari but couldn't detect what was off. Something was, though, but she had no time for them. She had a few hours to get everything squared away to leave.

"I'm gonna go upstairs to buy the ticket and find a hotel. I'm actually gonna call Michelle to see if she has any connections."

"Oh, so you're buying it right now? Like now?" Licy asked, getting up and picking up Andre with her.

"Yes. And when you both decide to tell me what's going on, I'll be all ears, but I want to see Malik, and I am tired of holding back."

Michelle wasn't available, so she left her a voicemail and threw a few clothes into her carry-on, enough to get her through the travel and to Malik. She packed up her toys and all her toiletries and tried Michelle again.

She made arrangements with Michelle to book her a room in a popular hotel in town, thanking her for all her help.

She took a quick shower, looked at the time, and calculated she had two hours before she needed to be at the airport. Her insides were vibrating, so attuned to the seconds ticking by, getting her closer and closer to seeing Malik.

She breezed into her office and stopped in her tracks.

Air left her first, lungs emptying without her permission. Her stomach did a deep dive, then jumped back, soaring in the air. A cold chill ran through her, then turned hot, her skin tingling and her ears buzzing.

She smelled sweet milk, diaper cream, and the woodsy scent that had held onto the walls of this room that she sneaked in to smell at least once a day for the past four months.

Lightheadedness hit her, and she realized she hadn't eaten anything and flushed red. Because how could she tell him that? He was there, sitting in the office chair, holding a smiling Andre, who seemed convinced he'd conjured his dad all on his own.

"You're here." She said the obvious, the whole day, her cousins and friends' oddness all clicking into place. The potato chips, the drama, the shock. It all made sense.

"I'm here."

"But the tanker should be back here in a month."

"And it will be, but we were ahead of schedule, so I left them in Singapore. I got another colleague of mine to cover the last month, and I owe him big, but I have the means to repay him."

"But how?"

"I can't be away from you and Andre. That's the why. The how, when, and logistics can all wait. Can I hold you, baby girl?"

Her feet never felt lighter as she walked into his arms and hugged him with Andre between them. That's when the tears started to fall, and at the same time, she laughed and laughed as Malik held her tight, and she felt loved and safe again.

CHAPTER THIRTY-ONE

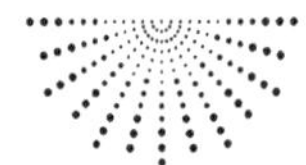

The hotel was just as she had described. Lush greenery grew seemingly unrestrained, even though it was pruned daily, around the valet area with a welcoming staff waiting at the entrance. Without giving her too much explanation, he'd gotten Aayala to go with him on this mini-getaway he'd planned in less than four days with the help of Daniel, Gabo, and Mason. Their ladies had ensured they contacted Michelle, Aayala's friend, to book the suite here in the hotel, the one she'd loved the most during the photo shoot.

"You remembered." She stared at him with a grin, shock still written all over her face even though they'd played with Andre for a couple of hours before heading out.

"I remember everything you tell me."

He heard her sigh in contentment and let the valet attendant open her door. He dropped the keys off with the attendant at his side, eager to get settled into their suite and have this conversation. He'd been anxious all the way until he arrived on land, wondering if she would be amenable to what he had to say.

Their suite was exactly as Aayala had described it, a modern beach affair, but he had no bandwidth to admire the architecture or the decor.

"We're here," she said, studying his face.

"You keep making obvious statements, baby girl. Are you nervous?" He approached her, moving closer.

Her breath hitched, then she bridged the gap between them, throwing her body at him. Malik welcomed the impact and held her tight, her curls soft against his beard. He pressed kisses to the top of her head, letting the soft warmth of her body cradle his weary heart.

"You're here, and I was about to buy a ticket to go and see you. Did you know that? Did Gabo and Mason tell you?" she asked, her voice muffled by his chest.

"They did. And I knew I needed to get my ass to your home as quick as possible."

"Ours, if you accept."

His chest expanded at the simple invitation, the sentence that told him everything he needed to know. But he wanted to make sure.

"Are you telling me I can live with you, Aayala?"

"Well, if you are planning to stay, then yes, please, let's live together. We can figure out the logistics after, and then when we are ready, we can buy."

"We can buy now if you want," he murmured in her hair.

"But you are leaving the merchant marines, aren't you?" She flexed back, looking at his face.

"I am, but that doesn't mean I am giving up on my financial plan. I'm just taking a different path."

"Why don't you tell me more?" she said, gesturing at the sofa in the suite's living area.

He plopped down on the chair, not letting his arms disconnect from her. After four months, every part of him wanted to be fused to her. She came along gladly, settling on his lap with another sigh of pure joy.

"Daniel and I are going into business together. We've invested in three luxury yachts, and we are starting luxury rentals for extended trips to the islands and other tropical locations. It's catered to the Black bougies that got the money but not the time to buy and maintain a yacht. Daniel, with his business mind, had done a market study and had been pressuring me to look at it with him. But I was…"

"You were afraid to trust you could do it," she whispered, settling herself more comfortably in his lap, making some areas of him harden and others soften in relaxation. Her scent of jasmine and chamomile greeted him, soothing him.

"See, I don't even have to bear my guts to you, you already know." He chuckled.

"Of course, I know. I know how hard that must have been for you to take that leap of faith."

"Nah, it wasn't hard at all. Once I realized I couldn't be away from you, every decision after that was easy. Which I knew all along, but I'm nothing if not stubborn. Daniel had been trying to hit me up with information since that night I came home and you were in the tub, but I wasn't ready to hear it then. After all my talks with my parents and the emails we exchanged, there are things I understand better about myself that allowed me to get over my shit and come home to you."

"Oh, Malik." She hugged him, shifting position so she could straddle his lap.

"And you?" he asked, feeling vulnerable and exposed.

"I realized I could compromise for you. I knew you had a plan and that it wouldn't take long for you to settle back on land. So I just said fuck it, I want him, he wants me. My love was too big to ignore anymore. And I also realized I'm not my mom nor my dad. They had their own way, and I don't begrudge them that anymore, but I know no matter what, I will ensure I not only prioritize you but that Andre is always top of the list."

He couldn't help himself. He captured her lips, drinking the joy she felt at their reunion, giving all the relief back to her in each swipe of his tongue with hers.

He left her gasping, disoriented by the force of his passion.

"You hadn't eaten lunch when I arrived."

"What…what?" she asked, hair escaping out of her pony-tail wild around her face, eyes wide and dilated. Her ass squirmed on his lap, and he held that ass still, knowing if she kept moving like that, he'd have to fuck her hard and fast.

And he wanted to take his time.

"You need to be punished," he crooned, and she whim-pered at his words. His chest grew in size, knowing he could do this for her, to her. Taking care of Aayala was all he needed in life—her and his son.

"I… Well, I was going to go see you. Doesn't that count?" she asked petulantly, but the spark in her eyes told him she was on board for whatever he had planned for her.

"You know better than that. Stand up, baby girl."

She immediately did as commanded, her face filled with love and excitement. He was so hard he had to adjust his dick inside his pants, lest he ended their play too early.

"Let your hair down, and unbutton that shirt."

She took her time with these orders. He could tell she was savoring the groans and growls coming from him as she revealed inch by inch of her body to him.

Again, she was different. Again, he loved each inch of her.

She dropped the shirt on the floor, waiting for instructions.

"Take everything else off."

She did cooperate this time, her hands gliding faster over

her buttons and zippers. She was wearing jeans again. He suspected they were new because those hips of hers hadn't listened to one bit of Aayala's complaints and attempts to exercise. And thank God for them and her lovely fat ass, which he couldn't wait to eat tonight.

Her body had slimmed down on the top, her arms back to their toned lines, her breasts still full and beautiful, sagging more than before. She must have weaned Andre because she immediately touched her nipples, moaning and creating moisture between her legs.

"Are you done breastfeeding?"

"I am."

"So all dried up? Back to normal?" he asked tentatively.

"Well, not all dried up, but definitely completely weaned…"

The news made him brick up in a way that had him pausing, but he'd study the reaction later. Right now, his baby girl was standing so pretty and naked, and she was begging to be punished.

"I didn't tell you to touch yourself."

She whined.

"But I want you, daddy."

"Bend over there on that couch," he instructed her, and she complied like the good girl she was.

He pulled his belt out of his pants and opened his jeans so he could make more space for his dick to breathe.

The clack of his belt buckle against the coffee table made Aayala jump, and he loved that anticipation had her so on edge.

He ran his hand across her lower back where she bowed, awaiting him. Her ass was so fucking beautiful, full of pretty dimples that showed what a good life she led. He knelt behind her, lured by the scents of earth and light musk, and took a dive into her soaking pussy.

"Aahh, Malik!"

He slurped, licked, and gorged himself on her, dragging his tongue from her entrance all the way to the top of her ass, then dove into her pretty hole, and she started keening.

"Shhh, you're going to get them to call security on us."

"Sorry! Sorry, but—ahh…" She sighed when he circled the tip of his tongue over her puckered hole, then all around.

He made sure Aayala was all gone, pushing back against his mouth, moans filling the room, then…

SLAP!

He hit the side of her thigh while still dining on her ass. The force of his slap against her was measured but unexpected, and she jumped, removing his tongue from her ass as she moved away from his impact play.

"Oh, fuck," Aayala said.

"Baby girl, don't make me grab that belt I just took off."

She bent over again, offering herself to him, and he went back to pleasuring her. It was what he was born to do. With one hand he kept up a steady pace of spanks against her thighs as the other hand pinched and tapped her clit.

In no time he had her screaming, her punishment becoming her reward, her ecstasy, the gift he'd never take for granted.

After bringing her back from subspace and providing aftercare by getting her into the bathtub and cleansing her, he carried her to the bed, in which she lay boneless with a goofy smile on her face.

"Baby girl, are you good?"

"I would ask you that same question, daddy, because that dick looks ready to drill a wall."

He sputtered a laugh and plunked himself next to her in bed.

"Are we good, Aayala? I know you were gonna go look for

me, but you already knew my heart was yours. So I want to make sure I'm understanding this correctly."

Even though his dick was hard as a rock, the fact he'd been able to make her come had allowed him the clarity he'd been missing when they walked through the suite door earlier on.

"We are more than good. I want you to move in. And I want us to be us. Marriage, all that shit… Well, you know how I feel about weddings and bells and whistles. And I know how you feel with your soft ass corny self, wanting a big wedding. So we can compromise as we've always done," she said.

"How do you know I want to marry you?"

"Because you ate my ass," she said matter-of-factly.

He stared at her, then remembered and shook the bed with his laughter.

"Right! I told you when we were younger that if a woman would inspire me to eat her ass, I would marry her. Fuck, I was oblivious back then."

"Nah, you were twenty and sure of yourself. So now that you ate my ass, where is my ring?" she added, laughing.

He stared at her, shocked at the way she'd hit the mark, and stood from the bed in search of his jeans. He sauntered back to the room, enjoying how she stared at his hard dick. He was a chill guy, but he still had an ego to maintain.

"What is that?" she asked, voice trembling.

"You asked for the ring, so I went to get it," he replied, his hands growing damp.

Her hands flew to her mouth, hair all curly and alive around her. Her eyes were wide pools of astonishment, and her soft curves invited him to feast. He'd never forget how lovely she was in this moment, lying naked and crisscrossed on this suite's bed.

He opened the box and went down on one knee next to the bed.

"Aayala Powell, would you do me the honor of becoming my wife, mother of my child and baby girl?"

"Oh… Fuck, I can't believe I'm being this soft," she sobbed. "Of course, yes. What else but yes!"

Thug tears escaped his eyes without his permission as Aayala jumped into his arms, kissing him all over.

With his arms full of her, and his heart brimming with joy, he finally felt he'd accomplished what he'd set out to do that day when he was eighteen years old. *Be a man*—because he was Aayala's man.

CHAPTER THIRTY-TWO

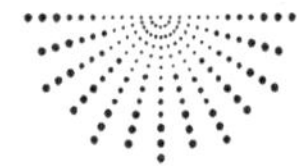

The cacophony of music, hilarity, and conversation filled the summer afternoon at Gabo and Mason's student center. Their friends and family had gathered to celebrate their little family—to celebrate Andre, who had no flipping idea what was happening and was alternately squealing or deeply upset.

It was their baby boy's born day.

A sense of accomplishment and awe ran through Aayala as Andre toddled toward her, followed by Malik.

"I was hoping he wouldn't walk until you arrived. And won't He do it? He waited, and a day after you got home..."

"Little man was ready to go, right, Andre?" He scooped Andre up, who promptly started squirming to be let down.

"We are in trouble, aren't we?" Malik asked as he squatted next to Andre, who again asked to be held.

"Oh, yeah. Now he's fully mobile, so we are essentially fucked."

"Shiiit."

"Who is getting fucked?" Mason approached them, voice booming.

"Do you not have another volume setting? Is it always just loud?" Aayala laughed as Malik deposited their son in her arms.

"I came over because Mariana and Daniel say I should be gracious and accept you were right."

She turned to look at Malik, who had his calm and collected mask on.

"What's up, bruh? I'm always right, so you're gonna have to narrow it down for me."

Aayala could feel the extreme effort it took Mason not to roll his eyes and say something in return.

"Thanks, man, the mutual aid plan is working. More than working. We're probably going to be able to help more kids in the community regardless of their sports skills come next school year. We have sixty patrons, all donating monthly from eight hundred dollars per month to fifty bucks. It's…"

"I know, man, you don't gotta say thanks, I know. It's gonna be good. Look at this place. It's because of your vision, don't ever forget that."

Aayala refused to get teary-eyed watching these two big men embrace each other, but it was a close call. She buried her face in Andre's curls just in case one threatened to escape.

"So y'all getting married, huh?" Mason pulled back from the hug and gazed at her with mischief in his eyes.

"Yeah, but we're in no rush. First, my man and your man need to work on their business, then we'll figure out the rest."

"I heard that, well— Oh, Mariana is summoning me, but we gotta talk about this wedding a little more in detail, a'ight?" Mason ran toward Mariana, who was indeed crooking her finger at him.

"I promise never to do that to you." She laughed at her cousin and her men.

"What? Oh, please, summon me whenever you want. I'm yours, after all."

"Oh, for real?"

"Yeah, and claiming me as your man like that… Just know that every time you do that, you'll get a reward," he whispered in her ear.

"Oh, really? I'll make sure to do that…daddy."

And she sped away with Andre in hand before her fiancé tackled her in front of all these people and showed her how much he loved her.

EPILOGUE

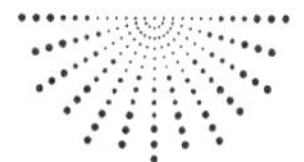

Their hips swayed together to the fast rhythm of soca. Two years since that fateful night, and they were back in the field where it all began.

Their crew was all around them, and for a moment, she saw them all in slow motion, capturing details with her eye: Mariana's hand gripping Daniel's upper thigh as she whined against him. Licy's lips stained red from the rum punch they were drinking as she kissed Gabo. Mason wukking up toward Mariana with a wicked smile on his face.

And Malik.

He stared down at her while she held onto his extended arm and whined a sweet, dirty whine that made her think of sweaty sheets and last night when he came inside of her, then made sure she came too with his wicked mouth.

She righted herself, still keeping the gyrations as her back met his chest, then she stood on tippy toes, the scents of teakwood, sweat, and smoke intoxicating her, and whispered in his ear:

"You want to make another baby?"

Her hand in his, she followed his long strides, giddy with all that would come next for them.

ACKNOWLEDGMENTS

Hasta Luego, Alicia, Mariana and Aayala. The ladies are the first characters to give me the courage to publish.

Thank you, Wordmakers, Inclusive Romance Project, and the BRAG Chat ladies, for the support even when I am buried under the "day job."

Thank you to the Mr. because you get me, and you celebrated all the little wins that came with this series.

Thank you to my kids for giving me space to write…after bedtime :)

Thank you to Kaitesi, Gabrielle, Katrina, KaSandra, Whitney for your feedback and words of encouragement. Thank you for caring about these characters same as I do!!

Thanks to **you** for falling in love with these characters!

ABOUT THE AUTHOR

A.H Cunningham is an introvert that weaves lovey-dovey contemporary romance and erotica. Her characters are Black and Multicultural adults, trying to navigate their grown folk lives while contending with all the horny feelings and falling hopelessly in love in their journey. In her writing, you will find a deep love for the entire Black Diaspora and all the ways we connect through our heritage. When she's not writing, you can find her reading, snacking at odd hours, dancing some Panamanian song, and playing the metaphorical Tamborine as her family navigates a new move.

Join A.H's newsletter to get all the latest updates!
http://www.ahcunninghamauthor.com

9 781737 859758